~ Beyond the Veil ~

By Jessica Majzner

Printed in the United States of America

First Printing, 2016

ISBN 978-0692720905

Night Wolf Publishing

www.beyondvalwood.com

Acknowledgements

To Phillip and Chris,
I truly could not have made this book without either of you.

To Nick,
Thank you for bringing Natalya to life.

To Dennis, my love
Thank you for helping to turn my ideas into a story.

To Nissa,
For your wonderful editing skills.

And to all of my friends and family who supported me

~ Prologue ~
Destiny Unfolding

Anesa had never before been mistaken about anyone's identity and so it would be with the girl that now entered her shop. Numerous chimes sounded as Natalya walked in, trailing morosely behind her father. Anesa laid a weathered hand onto the book she had been skimming through to mark her page and peered over the desk at her customers.

The man was handsome with pleasantly arranged features, but Anesa only gave him a cursory glance before studying his daughter.

She could not have been older than twelve years for her face had not yet lost the gaiety of youth. Her eyes though were too wise and too lined, and they seemed to hint at some tragic event that seemed to have already aged her. She walked without intent or purpose, merely following her father, though he too seemed to have drifted in nearly by accident.

1

The two of them wandered through the store, her father stopping every once in a while to leaf through a book or remark on a handmade dream catcher, but the girl only nodded blankly. She passed by armored dress forms, bows, spears, healing crystals and other oddities, but nothing seemed to garner her attention until she drifted to the front counter. Here, the girl's eyes finally lit up with interest, and Anesa smiled down at her kindly.

Like a moth, helplessly drawn to light, she had become entranced with the crystal ball that decorated Anesa's counter. The old woman nodded approvingly as the girl studied the swirling depths, though she could discern nothing from them.

"Would you like your fortune read, dear?" Anesa asked kindly, though the girl jumped slightly. Her father had heard and he too approached the counter after returning the crystal he had been holding to its proper place. He nodded encouragingly at his daughter and answered for her.

"Natalya would be honored, Anesa," he said with feeling, and the old fortune teller knew that he meant it. In her many years she had gained much respect from her people and most considered it a great blessing for her to predict their futures. Even the foreigners of which she had seen many of in the last few weeks had known of her, and those that had allowed her to read their fortunes would later find her talents to be unfailing in their accuracy. She did not know what brought these two to her unassuming antique shop during this trading season, but she had a feeling that fate itself had something to do with it.

"Thank you," she said. "It has been many years, but the stars have foretold our meeting again. Not many still seek out my shop, not since the vampires and werewolves have been banished from Valwood."

At these words the girl's eyes widened in fear, and Anesa felt a strange compassion stirring within her. She led her away from her father to an unmarked back room where yet another crystal ball lay waiting in its center, and Anesa settled herself behind it. The silver glow from the ball cast shadows on Anesa's face, deepening her wrinkles and making her appear even older.

"Don't be afraid," she whispered and the girl nodded. The cloudy contents of the ball began to swirl even faster and darkened in color. For a few moments, they sat in awed silence, though the girl could not see what Anesa could. A scene was forming in the indistinct mist, and Anesa narrowed her eyes, struggling to take it all in.

"I see much in your future, child," she said after a short while. "A future with much power and strength in it," and the girl smiled, though her expression knew no understanding.

"Though not all of it is good," Anesa continued, and the girl's face fell. "I see much sadness and much loss as well, for you are marked."

"What do you mean?"

"You are the next vampire huntress, and so destined to bring their kind to an end from this place. Your destiny has already cost you your mother at a young age, but I know you are meant to avenge her death."

The blank and unknowing façade that the girl seemed to be fronting had finally shattered. "How are you sure that it's me?" she asked and Anesa smiled. It was the smile that a magician gives a prying child when asked his secret.

"Wait here," she murmured and disappeared through the door.

A moment later Anesa returned with a small box that was wider than it was tall and held it out to her.

"Open it," the fortune teller encouraged.

The girl did so and gasped in wonder. Inside was a pendant unlike anything she had ever seen; a precious onyx gemstone in the shape of a perfect teardrop that hung from a delicate chain. When she inspected it more closely she realized that the black stone did not seem to be solid-it shifted and writhed within its casing almost like the crystal ball before her.

"It's beautiful," the girl managed to whisper. Anesa delicately lifted it from its box and as the girl held her hair, she clasped it around her neck. Almost instantly the color changed to a pure amethyst, and her face was caught in its purple glow.

"Only the next Huntress could make it turn that color," Anesa explained, and the girl went to take it off. Anesa motioned for her to stop.

"It's yours."

"I-I can't, Anesa."

"It will help aid you. Your family's blood is especially potent, and this is reflected in the present color of the necklace. This amulet will allow you some protection, as any vampire that tries to touch you will find that he cannot. The power of your blood will be amplified through the stone. It will change colors subtly with your mood and it will also burn warmly against your skin, warning you of impending danger. It is the one thing I can give," she said.

"Thank you," said the girl simply, taking the amulet carefully in her fingers. Her face showed no doubt now.

"It suits you beautifully," Anesa said. "Now listen to me child. You have a great path before you. But it cannot be done alone. You shall succeed only if you are willing to trust those who have not been trusted."

"What do you mean?"

The woman smiled, almost sadly. "This you must learn on your own, dear. There are many paths to victory. You must walk the finest line between our two worlds and not be corrupted yourself. And there is more, child, about your mother."

4

The girl lowered her head, her hands resting in her lap. She hadn't known much about her, only that she had been killed when she was very young.

"It is your destiny to defeat the Vampire that killed her, Arkadith. But you must be careful. He is ancient and Vampires have long memories, almost as long as their immortal lives. They do not forget easily, and forgive even less easily. Your identity will have to remain a secret in order to protect your loved ones. He will not be easily defeated, and he will use anyone near you in order to get at you."

Natalya's eyes flicked towards the door where her father waited in the other room, and she shivered.

"Even he cannot know about you," Anesa said sternly. "Arkadith will target him if he can and we cannot take any chances. If he knows too much I fear for us all."

"But I have faith in you. I believe you have the power within you to succeed where others have not. Avenge her," Anesa whispered, and the girl nodded gravely. Natalya slid the amulet beneath her blouse where it lay hidden from view and it dimmed in response. She returned to her father and he placed a hand on her shoulder, guiding her out of the shop. Anesa watched them go, the girl who was ready to confront her destiny and the old woman knew that fate had chosen well.

~ Part I ~

~ Chapter One ~
The Death of a Legend

Five years later

The fabled castle was near. Anesa could see where it stood, silhouetted high upon a mountain crag on a winding staircase of crumbling stone. It lay in the heart of the great forests of Valwood, shrouded in mystery and a long lost symbol of man's journey into the peaks.

She was still miles away from it, but all of the surrounding trees stood in the mountain's shadow. She knew that the foreboding citadel was adorned with gargoyles and turrets that seemed to disappear into the rising mist and reappear with the patterns of the weather. A fence, black wrought iron, encircled the castle, rising and falling with the contours of the land and hidden in places by looming pines. She was not near enough to see these details, but she could envision them clearly even though she had never once traversed the great steps into its stony walls. She knew because it was her destiny to know and to pass all she knew to the next vampire huntress.

Anesa thrust her walking stick into the ground and leaned heavily against it. She rested a moment, her breathing slightly ragged in the late summer breeze. With the onset of old age, her strength and stamina had been diminished, but her mind, it seemed, only grew sharper in defiance. The woods were beautiful, and she could not help but notice the way the sun cast brightly colored rays through the gaps in the trees, outlining the green foliage in glowing amber.

She pressed onwards. She did not need to rely on the walking stick as heavily as she had before her brief respite, and gradually her breathing slowed to a normal rate. The sun began to die, and dusk fell. She was making good time.

Anesa felt a gradual warming at her neck. The dark forest was saturated in topaz as the amulet she wore brightened, illuminating the trees with its yellowish light. She slowed again, this time not out of weariness but out of instinct, borne of the deer that knows a wolf pack is trailing her scent. The vampire she had been tracking was near.

Her ears strained in their quest to dissect every call of the bird or drone of an instinct for some more sinister source. Her icy blue eyes shifted to each side, scanning each rock, tree, and bush for movement. She did not feel fear, but her heart beat quicker in anticipation.

Anesa heard him before she saw him. But as the snapping of twigs grew louder and a subtle hissing like a many-headed viper seemed to fill the air, she realized she had walked into an ambush. The vampires were closing in, and by the sounds of it, there were at least four of them.

The elderly woman withdrew the stake that had been strapped to her thigh beneath her clothing, abandoning the walking stick. Five vampires approached at every angle. She could not possibly face them all, but she circled anyway, not wishing to show any of the creatures her back.

Their mental nudges to drop her stake or forfeit the amulet were easily pushed aside, and she used almost no energy in defying their efforts to seduce her mind.

At the signal of whom Anesa presumed to be the leader, a sibilation that was strangled with thirst, the vampires attacked simultaneously. Anesa responded with reflexes honed by years of training and enhanced by the magic of her amulet, wielding her stake like a sword and plunging it into the unfortunate heart of the first fledging that had raised his fangs to her. Fledglings they must have been, for they lacked respect for the huntress and fear of her pendant and weapons.

She had dispatched two already when the third made a desperate reach for her throat. With his canines extended, the newly turned vampire's hand closed over her amulet in a bid to clear his way towards the vein in her neck. The chain snapped under his grasp, and a moment later he hurled it into the trees where its light was lost in shadow.

Anesa heard his gut wrenching scream as contact with the amulet had scorched his hand black. As he watched in horror, the blackness traveled up his arm where it came to rest as the poison settled. Not even his regenerative abilities could heal this terrible wound, and he held his useless arm to his breast, doubled up and reduced to gasps that wracked his stricken body. Prolonged contact with the amulet would have killed him, but Anesa's stake found his heart instead. After the third vampire lay dead, Anesa turned to the other two but with less confidence as she had before.

She seemed to age before them; the lines etched in her face deepened, and her eyes sank into recesses beneath her brows. Her hair thinned, her movements slowed, and she stooped slightly as the power of her amulet left her body. The vampires quickened in their pursuit, knowing that she was vulnerable now. With no time to search the woods for her amulet, she raised her stake.

She was not at a complete disadvantage. Many years of experience with the stake had hardened her muscles under loosening skin, and her extensive knowledge of the vampire's weakness, their ravenous thirst, made her quite the dangerous prey even without her amulet. But even she could not take on two vampires without the protection of the poisonous magic. For several moments she managed to hold them off, and they loathed to get too near of her deadly stake. But as one of them closed his hold around her slender neck, and the other had sunk his fangs into her arm, the strength left her dominant hand. Her grip relaxed on the stake, and it fell to the ground, never again to bury itself in a vampire's chest.

But Anesa never carried just one stake. She ripped another that was concealed at her left thigh from its holdings, and forced it into the neck of the vampire at her throat. Her attack gave her just enough time to rip it from his spurting wound and gain the leverage needed to thrust it into his heart. With an agonizing howl, the fourth vampire died.

Her own neck was bleeding; a trickle fell from where the vampire's teeth had made contact with her skin. Likewise her mangled right arm was crimson with a gushing torrent.

Her spilled blood was a catalyst to the fifth vampire's thirst, and he tore at Anesa's flesh in his quest to soothe the burning in his throat. Her worn skin broke easily, and he wasted no time in plunging his own fangs into her neck once again. Incensed, his desperate feeding had become a frenzy, and Anesa felt herself falling, in slow motion it seemed, to the dirt and fallen leaves.

She felt her blood, her very life force, cascading from her body, and as her head collided painfully against the ground, she closed her eyes. The feeding of the vampires seemed like a distant dream, and she felt her consciousness separating from her ravaged body.

She could remember it so vividly, the memory she now found herself within the throes of— the ending of spring long after the snows had melted away. She and Natalya were cresting a hill, far within the limits of their own border though secluded enough to not be disturbed. The uphill climb had been strenuous, and she pretended not to notice Natalya's concerned frown as she paused again to catch her breath.

They had reached the top of the hill, and Natalya flopped down onto the grass, savoring one of the last pleasantly cool days before the summer heat would set in.

Something was bothering the girl; she was absentmindedly plucking the blades and gathering them into her hands. She lifted the green fronds to the skies and scattered them to the winds, watching as they were gently carried to the earth again. After a while Natalya broke the silence with the question Anesa knew had burned in her for too long.

"Anesa, why me? Why am I the next vampire huntress?"

The old woman chuckled slightly and thought for a while before speaking.

"Irena asked me the very same question many years ago," Anesa murmured thoughtfully. "You are both so much the same," she continued. "Always learning and questioning. And neither of you willing to simply accept things as they come."

The girl was waiting patiently for her to continue, though her fingers betrayed her eagerness by continuing to ceaselessly pull at the grass. Anesa smiled warmly, and she drew a long breath as she thought of the easiest way to explain.

"I knew from the moment I met you that you were destined to hunt vampires just like your mother, though you possess neither special abilities nor unique prowess over any other of humankind. And when your father was christened an elder of Valwood, it became even more evident to me that you were fated for something great. Our destinies are not laid out before us when we are born, for we are all given the power to choose what life we lead for ourselves."

"I didn't choose this," Natalya muttered. She looked away and a tiny part of Anesa's heart broke.

"But you have, dear. From the time Irena was killed, you chose to avenge her. It is that which has brought you to this end. Our people have always opposed the vampires, but very few have what it takes to drive them from Valwood for good."

Natalya gazed up at her mentor, and Anesa felt almost a motherly concern for the fourteen-year-old girl before her. The feeling was mutual, though neither could bring themselves to say it, and they merely sat in the grass, enjoying each other's company.

Slowly Anesa's eyes opened as the memory dissolved. She was faint and confused, but Natalya would be along soon and she knew that everything would be alright then. *She was not too far behind her after all…* She smiled fondly.

She did not have much time left. But as she tried to bring the mountain where she knew Arkadith's castle lay into view, she could only see the tree tops looming into the starry sky. She was lost in her delirium; unsure of which reality she resided in: this distant memory or the stifling blackness.

And as her vision swam and the last of her blood had finally escaped her flagging body, she died with the knowledge that she would be succeeded by a girl whose power would someday come to surpass even her own.

Natalya knew that the vampire could still sense her. He heard every beat of her horse's hooves and every nicker that sounded from her mare's mouth. Each breath that she took and every command she uttered to the mare, acted as a beacon to her location with his superior hearing. He could smell them too-the earthy scent that unfurled from her skin, and the sweat that was beginning to gather on her brow. All allowed him to pinpoint the position she held in her perch. She was like a spider lying in wait for its prey, and so they were both aware of the other. But he could not see her. Not yet.

High above the ground Natalya was leaning into the crook of a tree, her handsome gray mare, Methea, grazing contentedly below her. She scanned the landscape around her, keenly searching for any sign of the vampire. The view was breathtaking but hindered by its unfamiliarity. In her seventeen years, Natalya had never before ventured this far into the forest. The woods, rich and lush with green life, laid before her in every direction, nestled under the distant peaks that marked the border of Valwood. Despite the nearly endless sea of trees, she trusted her instincts to guide her and would not easily become lost.

Nimbly, Natalya climbed down to the lowest branch and jumped the remaining way to the ground. Her hunt was coming to an end, and she smiled in satisfaction.

She untied her horse and mounted her, kicking her into a run. The mare was beautiful and lean, with a finely shaped head and ringlets of differently shaded grays that faded into black at her knees.

Above her an owl soared above the treetops. Its white face glowed in the darkness as it flew almost in slow motion, though still keeping up with her easily in flight and not allowing a somber note to escape its beak. Its penetrating glare picked through the brush with ease; mice scurried through the dirt, and rabbits chewed absentmindedly at the grass with their ears perked for any noise, but still the owl flew on. Its coal black eyes were only interested in the girl, and it followed her with intense purpose as she and the horse swerved between the trees and sailed easily over boulders and fallen logs.

The two continued on at their pace for a quarter of an hour before they began to slow and the owl pulled up, hovering in the air. It watched as Natalya pulled the horse to a stop, and it swooped, deadly quiet now in its pursuit.

It splayed its talons outwards and perched in the low hanging branch of a nearby tree. The owl turned deliberately in its roost to face Natalya, cocking its head slightly as she dismounted from Methea. The bird waited, diligent in its vigil, keenly attentive to her every move. Occasionally it turned to preen its feathers or listen to the far off movements of a distant squirrel, but it did not abandon its post. Its gaze was compellingly eerie, the eyes like twin pools of unfathomable depth and impossible understanding, but Natalya never saw. The bird blended with the landscape, as unremarkable to her as the bark of one of the many deciduous trees.

She knew the vampire had not lost track of her movements. He paused, and Natalya froze. All of her senses flared to keep him within reach. They were in perfect balance with each other. The predator moved as the prey moved, and he was hunting her just as much as she was hunting him. She

14

weighed her chances. He had sizable fangs and unnaturally sharp nails that lengthened into claws. He also had superior strength and speed. She had her horse, reckless daring with matching cunning, the stake, and the mysterious amulet that hung from her neck. She also had the bow, but with its silver tipped arrows, it was of more use against Werewolves than vampires. Made of finely polished wood that curved into a graceful arc, it was a beautiful weapon, though Natalya found its deadliness most attractive. The two were evenly matched. The seconds slipped into minutes as they each waited for the other to make a move.

The vampire acted first. Without warning he began to run. He was smoothly cutting a path through the woods, so fast it was only a mere moment before Natalya lost sight of him. She returned to her horse and pulled herself into the saddle again as the gap between them began to close. She urged the mare into a frenzied gallop, inwardly relishing the challenge of the hunt.

Back at the tree, the owl took flight again after her. Swiftly they ran, froth running from her horse's lips at the bit, and still Natalya pushed her to run faster. Fallen leaves and dust flew into the air after her pounding hooves as the trees flew by, but the vampire continued to elude her.

It was another hour before they had caught up to their quarry. He had finally stopped running and was kneeling on the ground, his back to Natalya. She pulled sharply on the reins and her horse began to slow, sweat glistening on the mare's chest and legs. Her nostrils flared and she was breathing heavily.

As quietly as she could, Natalya followed the vampire, anxious to know why he had suddenly stopped. She snapped on the horse's reins, but Methea did not move.

The mare had stopped, snorting anxiously and refusing to go any further. Natalya tried coaxing the horse into a trot, but she knew the smell of blood was in the mare's nostrils, and it was only

15

by leading the horse on foot that Natalya was able to make any more progress.

When she had neared the vampire, Natalya secured Methea to a nearby tree and unsheathed her stake. She could hear gut wrenching noises from the hunched over vampire, and she crept closer. It was clear the vampire was feeding, though it was impossible to tell how long the victim had been dead.

Natalya swallowed the bile that rose in her throat, silently willing herself to not be sick. The smell of blood was also heavy in the air, concealing Natalya's scent. She knew his thoughts were consumed with quenching his insatiable thirst and of nothing else, and so she was able to get quite close behind him.

She raised her stake above her head, prepared to drive it through his heart. Instead she gasped, nearly dropping the weapon in shock as she saw the weathered face of the dead victim.

"No!" she moaned aloud before she could stop herself, and the vampire, alerted to her presence, whirled around with inhuman speed.

The victim was Anesa. Her age and slowing reflexes had finally failed her after all of these years. Blinded with grief, Natalya lunged with her stake, but the vampire had already fled with blood still dripping from his fangs. Natalya merely watched him go with tears coursing down her cheeks, unable to summon the will to follow him. *No. Not her.* The mantra repeated in her head until the words had lost all meaning.

The body was already showing signs of decay and had been partially drained of blood, but Natalya couldn't be mistaken. She studied the woman's face, from the innumerable lines that weathered it to her wispy white hair. Her neck was absent of her amulet, and it was clear that she had fought without its protection. What had befallen the woman that she had been forced to remove it?

16

Anesa's lips were parted slightly as if she had still been speaking, longing still to impart her knowledge to Natalya even after her death. Natalya tried to imagine her final moments, but she couldn't reconcile the raw, uninhibited strength her former mentor had so easily demonstrated with the frail, defeated woman beside her.

One of her triumphs lay next to her though, the bloodied and broken body of one of the vampires. Anesa's stake was protruding from his chest, and Natalya wrenched it from the body, ignoring the sickening crunch of his collapsed chest as she slid it from between his broken ribs. How many others had she faced, and how many others had this stake felled? In her prime the woman had been a formidable force, though Natalya knew bitterly that all life must someday yield to the failings of age.

She circled her mentor, searching for clues to her demise. It was clear she had been dead for at least a few hours, and it was likely the vampire had returned to this place many times in the night to replenish the fading strength that the chase had taken. Her rounds in the surrounding woods revealed three more dead vampires in varying degree of injury and decomposition.

One thing had struck Natalya as strange though; Anesa's body did not exhibit the classic two pronged bite to the neck as most vampire attacks did. Instead her body had been unnecessarily mangled and precious blood allowed to flow into the earth from multiple wounds. Natalya looked to the surrounding scene, though her suspicion that this had been a newly created vampire had begun to grow.

Many footprints that pointed in erratic directions filled the scene, hinting at a struggle. And as Natalya counted the sets of prints, she realized she and Anesa had walked straight into a trap.

She returned to Anesa's body and began rummaging through her pack, searching for the thing she had picked up a few days earlier on a whim. At last her fingers closed on what she had been looking for, careful to avoid the thorns. She pulled out a single red rose that had been perfectly preserved by one of Valwood's shopkeepers and arranged it carefully, closing Anesa's hand over it. The woman instantly seemed more serene, though the ruse still could not hide the old woman's blood.

It was the closest thing to a decent burial Natalya could provide now, though she knew it wouldn't be long until someone else discovered her and a proper funeral would be held. The vampire she left to the coming sunlight that would render his and the other bodies to dust.

"I'm sorry I couldn't do more for you," Natalya murmured aloud. As she had leaned over the woman, her amulet swung downwards, nearly touching Anesa's body. The fog shifted and began to swirl very fast until it faded into a cloudy gray. Natalya clasped the pendant in her hand, for it seemed as if it too were mourning the woman's death. She entwined her hand with the dead woman's in parting before standing up once more.

She began to shake as pure rage began flowing through her veins. The adrenaline lent strength to her body, fueling her desire to avenge the woman. She knew the time for grief would come, but now was not that time. Her only thought was to avenge Anesa's death. With cold blooded focus she untied Methea and studied the prints the fleeing vampire had left behind. Her eyes widened in surprise as she connected his footprints to his destination in her mind.

It couldn't be. Confusion forced itself through her sadness. He seemed to be heading straight towards the *Ruins*—the territory of the Werewolves. It made no sense for the vampire to seek out his bitterest enemies, though the footprints were clearly travelling in that direction. Natalya shook her head and looked at the woman sadly for the last time. Now that Anesa was gone she remained the only person in Valwood capable of defending her people from the ever present threats of the Vampires. Their numbers were thriving with the abundance of human blood her city provided them, and Natalya was determined to break the cycle.

"I promise I won't sleep soundly until the last vampire dies," she vowed to her fallen mentor with a shaking voice. She sheathed her weapon, mounted her horse and continued towards Claw Haven. No matter how many vampires her mentor had faced, Natalya would kill them all and avenge Anesa.

As the night deepened and Natalya followed the fleeing prints of the vampire, she allowed the rhythmic gait of the cantering horse to soothe her terrible thoughts. She rode, numb and nearly unfeeling to the trail's end, until she could see a looming gray wall before her-- the fabled wall that had divided the citizens of Valwood from the territory of the werewolves for over one hundred years.

~ Chapter Two ~
Into the Ruins

She could turn back. Natalya pulled Methea into a stop and looked up at the great stone wall, hesitant to enter. A tentative truce had existed between her people and the werewolves, and crossing into their territory now could endanger every citizen of Valwood.

The wall was starkly unfitting amidst the green forest, though beautiful in its own constructed way. Numerous vines clawed their ways up the sides, taking root within the many cracks and gaps as nature reclaimed her own.

Natalya thought back to the stories her father used to tell her about the long war that had raged here. When she closed her eyes, she could almost hear the screams that had rent the air, from both human and werewolf. Each side had fought bitterly, the humans with silver, the werewolves with only their claws and teeth.

With the help of their sister cities, the people of Valwood had mustered an army that nearly wiped out the werewolves completely. But the horrors of those terrifying creatures those men had faced had prevented them from offering more men to Valwood's cause. Now they were vulnerable, and the werewolves were only growing stronger.

The wall's entrance needed no guards or gate; her people rarely strayed from their well-lit buildings unless to hunt in the edges of their own forest and never to these woods. The werewolves too kept to themselves. The hanging skull of Sakarr, darkened with decay that was staring at Natalya sadly from its entrance, made sure of that. Every one of her people knew his legend, and they slept more soundly at night knowing his savage reign of terror had been put to an end. His severed and fleshless head was unnerving, its mouth stretched widely open as if to swallow her after death, and its unnaturally large teeth seemed poised to attack her from beyond the grave.

The wall was silent testament to the werewolves' violent natures and a reminder of the war that threatened to be unleashed at their slightest offense. Their fear of the humans had kept them within their own borders, but Natalya knew they would not hesitate to kill her if she trespassed into Claw Haven.

Natalya paused at the edge, indecision stilling her tread. It would be so easy to abandon her quarry, to let the werewolves take care of the intruding vampire and return to the safety of her own people.

She wavered, uncertain on the spot. She even allowed herself to play out the scenario in her head. But it had never been in her to run away when danger beckoned. As Natalya deliberated, she realized that it wasn't only the danger calling to her. She was curious as to why the vampire would seek refuge in werewolf territory, though the evidence lay before her. Could he possibly be unaware that he lay cornered by enemies on all sides? Alliances between werewolves and vampires were unheard of…but she would have to be sure.

The full weight of what she was about to do lay heavily upon her. Her eyes wandered over the contours and cracks of the skull, and she nervously brought a hand to her brow. She felt a thrill of fear that she be caught here, in this most forbidden place. The werewolf city darkened her thoughts and saturated her mind with a burning sense of dread. But it held a fine wonder for her as well. With her decision made, Natalya dismounted from her horse and walked boldly through the inner walls, the reins in her hand.

She passed through the gate, and it was as if she had been transported back in time. This place was so different from her own home that Natalya had almost forgotten about her quarry.

Her faithful horse trotted dutifully into the Ruins even though the scent of wolves permeated the gate's entrance. Many of the buildings' windows had been shattered and hastily boarded up, and little light shone through the gaps. The many stenches of this part of the city had long ago melded together to form one highly distinguishable scent that was almost unbearable to her nose.

The Ruins had once been the werewolves' greatest pride, but it had mostly been burned to the ground during the war. The buildings that still stood were blackened with rotting wood and in varying states of deterioration. Natalya had heard that all of the different packs had found peace here monthly under the full moon and traded their beers and kills, but that was long ago. Now they were largely disbanded into small groups of rogues or one greater pack that was still rumored to live near here. There her knowledge of the city ended, but her people still referred to the Ruins as their great victory and as a great insult to the attempts of werewolf civilization.

A fine layer of dirt and soot had settled over the streets, so unlike the immaculate cobblestones that she had grown used to. Everything about the Ruins was a direct contradiction to the neat, orderly buildings that filled her own city. Natalya imagined that even the trees here seemed darker, somehow more ominous. Despite the unnerving stillness of the Ruins, Natalya could not bring herself to surrender to her fears.

The buildings she passed now grew more shady and decrepit. She was thankful now for the dirty streets as they effectively muffled the echoing clatters of Methea's hooves. Then she saw him.

Methea started, nickering uneasily as the creature's scent came to her nostrils, though she did not throw her rider. He was leaning casually against one of the buildings, his dirty blond hair hanging loosely past his shoulders and swept over one eye. His face was almost completely obscured by the shadows of the building. To Natalya, he did not seem much older than herself, but his tired, haggard appearance made him seem so. He was lean, but hard muscle rounded his form.

A scowl marred her soft features at the sight of him. She knew instinctively what he must be. He did not need to be in wolf form for her to know for she had heard the stories of his kind. She was proven right when he raised his head to look at her, shaking his hair carelessly to the side. His eyes flashed hungrily in her direction. They were beautiful— a startling shade of gold, the irises rimmed with the purest of blacks. They held the intelligent complexity of human eyes, but also the secrets of the wilderness. His eyes belonged to that of a wolf.

Natalya raised her bow, but he made no move to approach her. He only eyed her weapon at a distance. He seemed more curious than hostile, and they both allowed their eyes to wander over each other unbidden, taking in each other's strange appearances. Crudely inked black tattoos ran down the man's arms and legs and disappeared under his loose, torn clothing, suggesting that they did not end there. Still more were etched in his hand and snaked out of the ends of his fingerless gloves. Although the lines were irregular and without an obvious pattern, they had a wild beauty to them.

She noticed he was studying her too, running his eyes over her olive skin and her almond shaped dark eyes. Every movement was caught with a predator's eye, from the tossing of her dark hair to the black layers of her clothing that flowed gently in the wind. Her clothes concealed her stake, although she knew he could sense the presence of the silver. She saw his nostrils contract, and she knew he was pulling her scent closer to him, gaining still more information about her. She wondered what unspoken secrets his nose could detect.

Although her people lived on the border of the Ruins, Natalya had never seen a werewolf in person before. She was among very few in Valwood that had now and her fearful emotions were tinged with awe.

But the werewolf made no move to attack, and they passed each other without incident. She thought of putting an arrow in his heart to ensure his silence, but if he chose not to attack, she would do the same.

She forced herself to put him out of her mind and focused once more on her prey. The vampire was nowhere to be seen. Silently cursing herself for getting distracted, Natalya pushed Methea onwards. It wasn't long before she was able to find his tracks once again, cutting a wide path around the forest on the outskirts of the werewolves' shelters. Eagerly, she began to follow them, nearly forgetting that she was in enemy territory. All of her senses were strained to their limits, but they revealed nothing of her prey. Vaguely, she wondered if the werewolves had gotten to him first. Her thoughts strayed to the lone werewolf. She had made sure to stay well hidden, but still he had seen her, and he must have scented her. Doubt began to seep through her consciousness, and she did not know if it was bravery or foolishness that spurred her forward.

A low growl sounded behind her, interrupting her thoughts. She resolved on the spot, the hair on the back of her neck beginning to rise. She fingered the stake on her leg and scanned her surroundings, but they were deceptively quiet. She knew that at least one werewolf was hovering just at the edge of her senses, but she did not delude herself into thinking she would only face one. She knew all wolves traveled in packs, and her eyes shifted through the darkness, refusing to be taken unaware.

If she were lucky, she could probably take out one, maybe two of the werewolves with the stake, but she would need the advantage of the bow if there were others. There was a large tree she could shoot from if she could just get to it in time. Carefully she unsheathed the stake and slid it in front of her. She moved slowly, not daring to make a break towards the tree. She had almost reached it when a subtle flash of movement caught her eye.

"I know you're there, werewolf!" she called into the night, failing to hide the disdain from her voice. Her eyes darted in every direction, but the trees behind her were still, not ruffled by even the tiniest breeze. She looked towards the shabby buildings, but nothing stirred among them. Her eyes narrowed. The eerie quietness of this place was foreboding.

She acted quickly. Dropping the reins, she slapped Methea hard on her rump, and the horse fled, neighing loudly in the distance. She did not worry for her mare; she was confident it was herself they were after. In the midst of the confusion, Natalya broke into a run in the opposite direction. Sprinting towards the tree, she shoved the stake back into its sheath and pulled herself onto the lowest branch with practiced ease. She continued to climb, not stopping until she had nearly reached the topmost branch. Breathing heavily from the effort, she secured herself into the tree with her legs and knocked an arrow into the bow. Motionless she waited, still searching for the slightest bit of movement.

It wasn't long before she could see three strange figures in the distance. They walked with purpose towards her, not speaking to one another. They wore identical black cloaks with hoods that hid their faces. At a nod from the one in the center, the other two fanned out around her, drawing even closer, and Natalya figured him to be their leader. She trained her bow on him, but curiosity stopped her from trying to kill him just then. She wanted to know more about the creatures she had been forbidden to approach. She lowered her aim and released the tension on the bow. It sent an arrow whistling through the branches to land in the dirt in front of his feet. The man didn't flinch, but he stopped and look up at her— his features hidden in a veil of shadow.

"What are you doing here, miss?" he asked, inclining his head politely. He glanced at his companions, and Natalya didn't miss the look that was exchanged between them. *They knew she was concealing the only substance that could destroy them.* The metallic scent of the silver that was already irritating their noses betrayed her intentions.

"I am tracking a vampire," she answered.

The werewolf's eyes widened in surprise but he quickly recovered. "I see," he said smoothly, coming closer still. Natalya raised the bow so it was now pointed at his forehead. The silver tip flashed dangerously in the moonlight.

"Not a step closer," she warned. He merely smiled in return, not speaking. A moment later he threw himself at Natalya.

~ Chapter Three ~
Savior

She had nowhere to go, and the fall from a jump at that height could break any of her bones.

In mid leap, the werewolf passed through the moons light and began to shift into wolf form. His fingernails extended into wickedly sharp claws, and his face stretched into a muzzle of glistening teeth. Gray fur shot from his spine as he leapt. The cloak lay in a heap, forgotten, on the ground. He pawed at the trunk of her tree, scoring large lines down its sides. He growled furiously, his eyes glinting. *Could he climb trees?* Natalya didn't know.

She let another arrow fly, but her hand shook with fear, and she sent it into his foreleg and not his heart as she had intended.

The werewolf yelped and shrank away. Natalya cheered inwardly, but her joy was short lived. Some kind of message passed between him and his companions, and they too changed forms. After a moment, their leader leapt back into the fray. He was limping, favoring his front paw, and the wound could not completely close over the arrow. It did not stop him as Natalya hoped though, and they prowled around her tree, barring her escape.

Natalya's haven had become a trap. She felt the beginnings of despair and she fought it, determined not to allow it to overwhelm her. She thought of the risk she had taken by following the vampire here. If she didn't make it…if the werewolves killed her, surely her people would try to find her. Would they risk another war by searching here when they couldn't find her remains within their city limits? Would they declare war themselves against the werewolves when they found out they had killed her? The morbid possibilities that ran through her mind grew more and more bleak. She shook her head. She was a vampire huntress, and she would not allow these things to come to pass. She would fight to whatever end she found herself in. Invigorated, she turned to her present problem. She would have to come down at some point, and she couldn't afford to lose any more of her arrows if she missed.

She didn't risk hurling her stake into one of their chests; if she failed to penetrate one of their hearts, she could lose her precious weapon. She would have to keep both weapons on her in case they attacked her at close range.

An angry growl snapped her back to the present. The leader of the werewolves charged swiftly back into a human, reaching for the cloak again. He threw it around himself and stalked towards the tree, measuring the distance between himself and Natalya. His features were twisted in anger as he grabbed one of the lower branches of her perch, intending to climb after her himself. He was almost upon her, having climbed the tree faster

29

even than she had. His gnarled hand reached for her, the rapidly shrinking nails at the ends poised to claw at her flesh.

Natalya froze for a mere second before her instincts took over. She reached for one of her arrows and raised it above her, not bothering with the bow. She thrust it into his hand, half expecting the brittle wood to snap in two with the impact. Instead, it had buried itself into the werewolf's flesh, and the strangled gasp of pain that came from him was agonizing to hear. He had let go with his injured hand. Natalya was sickened by the stench of burning flesh. The silver was already spreading, dissolving his skin as it moved swiftly through his bloodstream, seeking his heart.

He reappeared, but the pain had been enough to stop him from trying to climb after her again. With an enraged snarl he abandoned his human form in favor of the wolf again, ready for a second attack, but the arrow held stubbornly in his paw.

The werewolves were growing impatient. They could not reach her though they tried bitterly, snapping their fangs at her, and she remained safe high above them. Natalya grew more and more worried. How long could they go without food? She figured longer than her. She was growing weary. The cold of the night seeped into her exposed skin and she shivered with nothing to draw warmth from. Resigned to a long night, she leaned into the tree, the stake resting across her lap. She closed her eyes, but her body remained tense, ready, and unwilling yet to surrender to sleep with danger so close. It wasn't long before she heard another approaching. Instantly alert, her eyes snapped open. She counted the footfalls as he neared them. He was still in human form. The werewolves had turned to face him and he advanced, his human face snarling. Natalya leaned forward, anxious to know how this newcomer's presence would affect her predicament.

"She's mine," he growled in a voice that was more wolf like than it was human. The moonlight illuminated his face, and Natalya gasped. It was the werewolf she had seen earlier! The curious expression he had worn earlier was replaced by rage, and now he truly looked inhuman. He showed no fear against the three.

The leader didn't reply, and the next moment their visitor had transformed. *Fight,* Natalya willed them in her head, hoping she could escape in the confusion.

Slightly larger than true wolves, with gaunt but muscular forms, they circled one another, sizing each other up. Their bodies were sleek, defined and the same shade of gray. One of the beasts had raised a paw and raked it across another's side, and Natalya was lost in the chaos that had ensued. Still gripping her stake, she used it to steady herself as she descended from the tree. The werewolves were still fighting, biting and snarling in a writhing mass. She broke into a run and instantly heard snarling behind her. She chanced a look over her shoulder and saw that one of the werewolves had detached itself from the others and followed her at a run. He was gaining fast, and Natalya had only seconds to decide her next move. She moved to the side and waited. He was nearly upon her. The werewolf opened his jaws and leaped at her, trying to sink his fangs into her flesh.

But she was ready for him. For a split second, she could see his exposed chest. His paws were spread out on either side of her, prepared to knock her to the ground, but he didn't make it that far. Natalya thrust her stake into his chest. This time her aim was true, and his body struggled to close the wound around the stake that had penetrated his heart.

The werewolf fell to the ground, twitching uncontrollably as he whined. He rapidly changed forms without intention, from wolf to human and back to wolf. There he lay weakening, and

Natalya was surprised to also see a strange look of peace descend upon his features for the briefest of seconds before he took his last shuddering breath. He was strangely beautiful in death.

She had paused a second too long. She didn't have time to react as the second werewolf attacked. Coming at her from behind, he clawed at her back. Natalya screamed, waiting for his jaws to close around her neck. Instead, she heard a high pitched yelp.

Whirling around she saw him locked in battle with the other werewolf. He drove her attacker deeper into the woods, and Natalya took this time to withdraw her stake from the dead werewolf's body. She tore into the woods towards the fray, relying on the sounds of their fighting to guide her. She was done running, and adrenaline fueled her desire to kill.

All at once, the snapping and writhing of the werewolves ceased and Natalya felt the woods plunge into silence.

Breathing in short ragged gasps, she groped her way through the darkness, feeling vulnerable as any human girl when confronted with the unknown in the dark.

She nearly tripped over his tail before she had seen him. She silenced herself, even quieting her own breathing as she approached the unnaturally still body. She was tense, ready for the brute to suddenly awaken and attack, but as the seconds ticked on, he didn't move. She peered closer and was immediately overcome with the stench of freshly spilled blood.

The werewolf's throat had been torn out— his eyes staring ahead sightlessly, cloudy and full of sorrow. She swallowed the bile in her throat and looked up to see another werewolf approaching. He rose slowly and transformed into the gold eyed human before her.

Natalya stood up slowly as he neared her. He stood across from her, watching her intently. She did not know if she was relieved or not. The tension in the air was palpable. Neither one moved. Natalya spoke first.

"Two of them are dead. What became of the other werewolf?"

"He will move no more" he said simply.

"You saved me," she said, not quite believing it herself. "So you mean to take me now and kill me too then, I suppose." She raised her stake, ready to run it straight through his heart. She could think of no other reason for the savage to have done it, if not for the satisfaction of killing her himself.

"I could," he growled softly, taking a step towards her. She prepared to defend herself.

"You wouldn't make it another step," she warned, and he stopped. He laughed bitterly, then abruptly stopped his face almost mocking.

"You wouldn't kill your rescuer…would you?"

"My…rescuer?" His words confused her, catching her off guard more swiftly than a quick strike would have.

"Why else do you think I turned against my own kind?" He motioned at the dead werewolf.

Her voice was still hard. "You said I was yours. What did you mean? I am not a prize to be won, nor meat to be defended."

"I had to tell them something. They-I mean to say *we*, do not usually challenge another's claimed territory. It was possible they may have allowed you to escape if they thought I had already claimed you as my own. Unfortunately, it didn't turn out that way." He smiled coldly, and the sight of it enraged Natalya.

"One of your own lies dead, and you smile before me! You truly are a barbaric species."

"I saved your life human, and you should be thanking me! Without me, he would have killed you and the birds would already be gathering here to feed from your bones." He glared at

33

the dead werewolf, his lips curling with disgust. The confusion in her eyes must have been obvious as he spoke with obvious indifference to his fate.

"We are not the same, him and me," he explained without prompting. "I shall have nothing to do with *his* kind." With that, he spat on the werewolf's body.

Natalya paused, unsure. She didn't understand his motivations for saving her, nor his open hostility towards the fallen werewolf. She allowed her mind to wander over the possibilities, avoiding his gaze. Finally, she could stand it no more. She looked up, allowing her eyes to take in his body. She took in his rugged appearance, his muscles that rippled easily under his tattered clothing, the tribal like tattoos that ran down his arms and legs and his unshaven face. He must have retrieved his clothing shortly after he had transformed. Their eyes finally locked and she was pulled into their gold depths.

"You are both werewolves though."

"He enjoys his affliction, his *curse*. I do not," he growled.

"His…curse? But I thought you all enjoyed being werewolves," Natalya said stupidly. She had never thought of being a werewolf as a *curse*.

He barked out a dry laugh again. When he turned to look at her his expression was one of shocked incredulity.

"Is that what your people believe?" he snarled at her, and the hostility in his voice nearly made her flinch. "Do you think that we are merely powerful beasts that run under the moon as wolves? You think we are blessed with our immortal lives, stuck here until whatever end may or may not await us? You might have your romantic ideas about us, but the reality is far darker than that, *human*."

There it was again, the venom behind the word. What could she say to that?

34

"I'm sorry," she said. He looked away, and his expression seemed to deflate as his anger left him.

"Don't be." he said, not looking at her.

"What is your name?" she finally asked. He turned once more towards her and seemed to be deciding if he should answer or not.

"Please at least let me know the name of my rescuer."

Finally he spoke.

"My name is Voren."

"Thank you, Voren. I am Natalya. I wish to thank you for what you have done for me."

Voren winced at her words, and his face looked oddly pained, but he did not explain. There was a strangeness between them that she felt as palpably as anything else. Although Natalya found herself comforted by his presence and did not want to return to her quarry just yet, she felt torn. She thought of her people, especially Anesa. She wanted to know so much about this strange werewolf that defied her peoples' every attempt to vilify them, but he was so closed off that she wondered about his true motives. She looked up at him, and he too seemed uncertain, caught between wanting to say something or simply melt into the trees and disappear again like the wild wolf.

A few minutes had passed before he finally broke the silence.

"You shouldn't be here alone. Come with me." He was stiff, but his face was protective. Without hesitation Natalya followed, but the slight hint that she couldn't handle herself needled her.

"I can find my own way back," she muttered. "I have something that needs finishing here anyway."

"Natalya...you don't know what you are saying," he said. "Others of my kind will not be so permitting of a human trespasser. They do not look favorably upon humans and will not hesitate to attack like the others did."

"I am not a weak human *girl*, Voren. I am a vampire huntress, and I have proven I can defend myself against even werewolves. The three that surrounded me in the Ruins had me outnumbered. I would have defeated any of them in a fair fight."

"Celestial Hold," he interrupted, so quietly she could barely hear.

"What?"

"The name of our city was *Celestial Hold*," he growled. "At least that is how it is said in *your tongue*. The *Ruins*? *That* is what our burned city is known to your people? Is there no limit to the pride and arrogance of your kind?"

"I'm sorry! I didn't mean to offend you. It's what we call…your part of the city. I've never known it by any other name." she said quickly.

"I never knew." His voice was bitter.

"I'm sorry. I shouldn't have said that. Please forgive me."

He simply nodded and the moment felt strange. Just like their peoples, Natalya felt as if they were on a scale of their own, dipping towards enmity and peace constantly. There was a faint noise in the distance, and he stopped, motioning for her to stay silent. He sniffed the air suspiciously, all traces of his prior hostility gone.

"Someone approaches."

"I know," she said for her amulet had already burned warmly on her skin.

"He smells like ash, one that has touched death. A vampire! And he is within werewolf territory."

"Yes. I intend to kill him. He is the reason I am here," she said, and then she knew the Vampire had fled the deadliness of her stake.

"You would be destroyed! If not by him, by others of my kind! The others will have scented the vampire already and will be moving in."

"I am not to be underestimated."

"I didn't save you only to see you killed. But it does not matter; one makes their own decisions. My deed is complete; what is done is done," he said in a clipped tone.

He turned to leave, and Natalya watched him go with a mixture of resentment and near veneration. She blinked once, and he had gone, quicker than she could have imagined. She scanned the woods where he had been a moment before, but he was at home within them as any true wolf.

Good luck, Natalya. The words sounded in her head, and Natalya gasped for the thought had not been hers. Even though the werewolf had faded from her sight, she knew he had spoken to her telepathically.

"Thank you," she whispered to the empty forest. She shook her head, quelling a strange desire to follow the werewolf.

Instead, she turned back toward the vampire.

~ Chapter Four ~
Huntress

Four werewolves were perched atop the roof of a tall building, overlooking the streets of Claw Haven. Their silhouettes stood powerfully against the light of the half moon, sweeping the gray hairs along their backs silver. Droplets of saliva glistened from the tips of their slavering fangs, and their glowing white eyes cut cruelly into the darkness, nearly turning it into day with their efficiency.

A pungent odor had reached them, and their muzzles curled into distasteful snarls. The scent was an unpleasant irritant to their sensitive noses; the rotting of death and ash mixed with fresh blood that failed to bring forth the lust of hunger. The scent heralded the arrival of their bitterest enemy and with it ramifications that hadn't been invoked in over a century. The werewolves exchanged glances, their communication seamless and invisible to human eyes. As stealthily as they could, they leaped from one rooftop to the other, hoping to disguise their own scents and not rouse the vampire's acute senses. They followed with caution, unwilling to throw themselves blindly into danger while they wondered about this strange proceeding.

It was not long before they scented Natalya. Her scent was a strange combination of the arrogance of the hunter, impeded by a slight tendril of fear that wafted deliciously towards their nostrils. She could not move quickly, crouched as she was against the buildings, her stake held out in front of her like a sword.

The smallest of the four werewolves strained forward, his tendons quivering with nervous energy. He was longing to leap at her, to take her throat. He remained where he was though, rooted to the spot by a glare from his elder. His ears were still pricked eagerly as his teachings competed with his instincts.

The oldest among them watched Natalya, not with hunger, as did his fellows, but with calculating intensity.

What shall we do? The question was projected from the smallest to the other three, and they looked now to the oldest for his answer, each quelling their own desire to kill the trespassing girl. Below them, Natalya rounded the corner. She was not yet alerted to their presence, and instinctively they followed her and her weapon's movements with wary eyes. The metallic tang of the silver she carried in her arrows gave them respectful pause, and she passed below them unharmed.

Do? The elder asked sharply inside their heads. *We shall do nothing without the Alpha. This is the beginning of strange times. A human and a vampire stand within the walls of Claw Haven for the first time in over a hundred years. Now we shall warn him.*

The others growled in assent and with that the werewolves withdrew from the roof. As quietly as shadows, they melded back into the night as subtly as any true wolf pack.

Natalya was being watched. The fine hairs rose along the back of her neck, and her spine tingled as if she could feel the piercing gaze of this unseen entity. No unusual noises came to her ears, nor did her eyes catch anything unusual, but she knew it all the same. Her hand closed around the necklace Anesa had given her. It was warm to the touch, and the emerald had been replaced with a deep scarlet. She raised her head, listening, but no new sounds revealed themselves. Her eyes sliced through the night for any movement, but only an owl could be seen watching her intently from a low tree branch. They locked eyes, the owl's white face hanging in the air like a lantern, the rest of its sooty body obscured in the darkness. Natalya ignored the bird until it lit from its perch and disappeared.

The darkness of the strange place suffocated to Natalya's senses, and she half wondered if she was mistaken.

The amulet has never been wrong before. Though she took no comfort in the thought, Natalya felt reassured slightly by the pendant's power. She had never felt so alone or foreign as she did now within the Ruins… *Celestial Hold's border*, she reminded herself. She felt isolated and completely cut off from her people. The buildings were shabby and imposing as the broken windows leered down at her from either side. She seemed to see eyes that would disappear as soon as she focused on them or hear the muffled growling of wolves. Nearly identical already in their uniform infirmness, the mist that had rolled down from the distant peaks now bathed the buildings in a dense fog that served to further obscure her vision.

There was light in the wreckage that fought feebly against the pressing darkness; and streetlamps that weakly illuminated the roads through a layer of encrusted dirt that clung to their outer glass.

Fatigue too lapped at Natalya's heels. She pressed on, her gait stilled by her lack of horse, and she slowed further. Besides speed, Methea had lent her strength and height, and she felt especially vulnerable without the added protection the mare had provided. And although the beginnings of sleep pulled at her eyelids, she could not surrender to the urge, close as she now was to catching her quarry. Nervously, she shot furtive glances behind her at each rustled movement, though caused by innocent vermin or armed enemy, she knew not the difference. She grasped her stake in her hand and slung her bow over her shoulder.

The vampire's footprints were followed easily enough, having been set deeply into the layers of dust and dirt that littered the street. The monotony of the task allowed Natalya's thoughts to wander as she followed the meandering curve of the vampire's path.

As she walked, she thought of the werewolves. The three had been terrifying in their newness; she had never seen one before; let alone defeated one.

Though the secret of her trespassing had died with them, she had never enjoyed killing, even the vampires.

The leader of the three had been frightening enough in stature, but it had been his stubborn resolution to destroy her that had shaken her the most. She felt justified in her feelings towards the werewolves until her thoughts drifted to Voren. *How different he had been from the other three.* He had unnerved her with his raw honesty, and she had not been prepared for it. His presence stood in such stark contrast to the savage image she had stored in her mind, and it made her question everything she had thought she knew about them. He had seemed nearly *human,* and though Natalya's mind rebelled at the thought, she could almost pity him in his worn clothing and destroyed city.

He killed one of his own. A voice that had been listening at the back of her mind interrupted her thoughts, and Voren was relegated back to savage status.

That werewolf had tried to kill me, she reminded it, and the voice raised no more objections. He was dangerous she knew, but he had protected her when he could have easily killed her.

Natalya had come to no conclusions when the foot prints ended. The last two were clearly imprinted into the dust, and she circled the ground around them, searching for another pair. The earth was settled, giving no signs of displacement or a struggle. The path the vampire had been following continued to meander into a wide bend, but there was no sign that he had continued on this route.

Natalya raised her head to the buildings that surrounded her. Any one of them seemed a fitting lair for a hiding vampire, and her feelings of foreboding increased. Her eyes struggled to penetrate the thick layer of grime that shielded the insides of the buildings, and she was all too aware of the shortcomings of her own senses. The amulet had deepened in color to almost black, and Natalya's heart began to pound in anticipation. She knew she was close now.

It was not long before she found herself in a secluded alley way. Surrounded by grungy brick on three sides, she stood facing the night as the vampire dropped to the ground from his perch above her. He was in front of her now, blocking her escape, having appeared much swifter than any human could have. At first glance, he appeared somewhat handsome, having retained much of his human features. Natalya looked closer, and she could see that exhaustion and thirst had slowed his tread until he could barely stand upright. And when she grew closer still, he had become a frightful foe.

His pallid skin had reached a lightness that no ordinary human could. His veins were swelled and forged a ridged path through weathered skin that was stretched tightly over bony limbs. His pupils had dilated until they seemed to engulf his irises in black. Natalya looked away, avoiding eye contact. She knew all too well the power that seductive gaze could hold over her if she allowed it. Instead, she studied his arms and legs, waiting for a signal from them as to his next move. The hunt had finally ended and it was unclear who the predator was and who the prey was now. Either could walk away victorious, and both were determined to claim that title.

Time seemed to slow to a standstill. They met in the middle of the alley, two predators bent on killing one another. Natalya hardly noticed her surroundings as she fought desperately for her own life, and to avenge Anesa. Although his movements were jerky and ambling, the vampire's superior strength and agility proved to be a worthy match against her stake and amulet.

Many times the vampire's exposed skin flashed before her, and Natalya was able to plunge her stake into his body until fine rivulets flowed from the many flesh wounds. He healed as many times as she stabbed through him, as each lunge had missed his heart. It seemed as if the vampire could have continued fighting in this manner until the end of time; he did not falter or tire, despite the damage her stake continued to inflict.

With a powerful lunge, he made to sink his fangs into Natalya's throat, and she cried out in pain as her blood rose from the twin puncture wounds in her neck. His hand curled over her throat as he lowered his mouth to feed, and Natalya gasped, unable to breathe. She felt herself sinking as her sight faded to black. The next moment she heard a sharp intake of breath as her vision began to clear. The hand had jerked away and the pressure had lessened on her chest from where the vampire had pinned her to the ground. She could see again, though dark spots still flashed in her vision. The vampire hissed in pain, with smoke curling from ruined fingers. Her amulet was glowing, yellow citrine as it burned his flesh, and prevented him from touching her further.

His pause allowed Natalya to momentarily recover her strength while his own faded. The poison of her amulet coupled with his lack of blood had weakened the vampire. Despite the nearly endless strength he had displayed as they begun, he could not replenish the blood that had been denied him when Natalya had interrupted his feeding. His heart pumped frantically, but he had lost too much of his stolen blood to keep it beating. As he staggered slightly, Natalya found her opening and thrust her stake into his chest. The vampire hissed in agony, the last of the blood he had taken already falling to redden the earth. His skin tried in vain to close over the stake that protruded from his heart. But her weapon defied his efforts, and he lay weakening under the dawns coming light.

Natalya gave the fallen vampire one last measured look. He was writhing under the stake, though as she watched his spasms seemed to weaken until he lay merely twitching, and she left him to his fate.

Beyond the shadow of the castle the night waned. The sunlight that had been clawing its way over the horizon had finally burst over them in brilliant orange and red hues. Natalya watched almost grimly as the vampire fearfully began crawling towards the shadows of the alley, but the pure light had caught him in its grip. He began to scream as the light, so gentle to human skin, began to burn him instead. Smoke began to curl from the raised sores that lined his exposed arms and face. He was too weak to resist, and in an explosion of dust, the vampire vanished, his scream fading slowly into silence. Even the blood that stained the ground had disappeared. It was as if he had never been.

The stake had remained though, intact and bloody, and Natalya retrieved it from the ground. She wiped its point on the grass to clean it before sheathing her weapon and reentering the woods towards home.

"May your kind never darken our doorsteps again," she muttered under her breath as she started back towards Valwood. High above her the owl circled and abandoned its vigil, sailing dutifully towards the castle.

Arkadith had seen enough. With a pained effort, he pulled himself out of the owl's mind, and the room materialized around him once more. The terrible scream of one of his own still rung in his ears after his vision of the vampire's slaughter had faded. He shook quietly as his body boiled with rage, but it did not spill over. He was not given to destroying his possessions on an angry whim, nor was he pacing in the room, tearing at his hair. Only his black eyes betrayed him, the pupils so dilated, they completely engulfed his irises, as pitiless as the owl's themselves.

Beyond the soulless gaze of the vampire lay a calculating mind, and Arkadith thought furiously now. Hot blind anger was not conducive to planning, and he allowed himself to relax slightly. Grief would come later; the Vampire slayer would atone for what she had done to his kin, but rash moves could jeopardize his own safety. Slowly his anger simmered until it no longer ran hot through his veins but bubbled coolly in his belly.

He knew this vampire huntress was dangerous to him now. Through the owl's eyes he had seen the destruction she had brought to his kind and the life that faded from their eyes. She had known nothing of her victim's past, his story or his destiny, and she had destroyed them all with disturbing ease.

And her amulet...it's duplicate he had never seen. Apparently she could not be touched by one such as him. It did not matter. She would be killed as all others that had threatened him had been killed.

He raised a glass of thick crimson to his lips and drank deeply. As a plan began to form, his ancient heart awakened and began to beat. A slow thud at first then it began to quicken as blood flowed through his body, a catalyst to fuel his slight trepidation.

~ Chapter Five ~
A Storm Rising

"Is that all of it?" she asked, lightly shaking the bag and listening to its contents.

"Yes it's all there," the town elder replied in the darkness, and Natalya was satisfied. Keeping her weapons honed and ready required upkeep; the money would not go to waste.

It was midnight, the next night. Flickering firelight from the distant watch towers could be seen in the distance, faintly illuminating the outlines of the town sentinels that guarded Valwood by night.

"Are you sure that he is dead?" he asked.

"Positive. I saw him turn to dust in the sunlight myself."

"Good," the man said roughly. "I wish you the joy of it."

"Elder Edrich…Anesa was killed last night."

The smile on the elder's face slowly faded away before he nodded. "She will be missed dearly. I'll make the necessary arrangements; you take care of yourself. I know this will not soothe your grief, but the citizens of Valwood are in your debt, Natalya. Though they may not know of your continued efforts to keep their borders safe, they are better for it."

"Thank you, Elder Edrich." Natalya answered, knowing that she would trade all of the money she had if she could only see Anesa again. To hide her face, she placed the money bag in a pouch that she hid out of sight beneath her clothing. When she raised her head again, her eyes were burning, but the darkness hid her tears.

The man did not respond, having already disappeared over the ridge of the hill that marked their meeting place. She knew he would keep her secrets, but still Natalya checked to see that he was truly gone before she hurriedly began stripping off her outer garments.

She took off her black top first, revealing the lighter colored blouse beneath. She tucked the amulet beneath it, out of sight. She took her pants off next, also black, and stowed her excess clothing in the bag as well. She pulled a simple brown shirt from her bag and began to dress in the darkness. She shed her identity as easily as she had shed the clothing, and with their removal, she turned from a huntress to ordinary girl.

She transferred the stake from her leg where it glinted dangerously in plain view if her skirt shifted, to a sheath that rested under her shirt against her ribs. One never knew when trouble would arise.

Natalya wasn't sure how she felt about her double life. On one hand it was better not to draw unwanted attention in her direction, and when you blended in that was hard to do. Aside from her father's elder duties, she led a relatively normal life inside Valwood. But it was a lonely existence as well, and many times she longed to confide in her people and to relieve herself of the nightly horrors she was forced to confront.

48

She shook her head; her wishes could never match up to reality and she didn't do well to dwell on the fact. As much as she longed for someone to tell all of her secrets to, she knew she never could. She also did not wish to endanger any of her friends or family. The vampires were watching and waiting along the fringes of her deceptively neat society, learning and observing their prey much like the natural predators of the forest did. It would only be a matter of time before the people closest to her were targeted, and she continued to delay that day as much as she could by blending in, and appearing as she was, a teen aged girl. Besides, secrets were hard to keep and people harder to trust.

She threw the last of her belongings into her bag, slinging it across her shoulder. Physically and mentally exhausted, she headed in the opposite direction as the man had. She headed down the steeply sloping hill to her waiting bed, ready to surrender to the calm of sleep.

An hour passed before Elder Tomas Edrich first heard the scream. It had the desperate quality of a death cry coupled with a note of surprise that one utters when he has not anticipated an assault on his life. The sound had been a stark disruption against the sereneness of twilight, and now an unsettled silence permeated the scene. The other watchtowers were visible only by their fires, and they remained still and passive, their men having not heard the cry of their own. The elder turned back towards the hill, but there was no sign of Natalya. He had not been surprised, and bitterly he turned once more towards the source of the shout.

He had already completed his rounds after meeting with Natalya; each of the watchtowers had been visited and he had received all of their reports. Everything was quiet; the gongs lay untouched, and the guards were unconcerned by strange noises or visual disturbances. Until now.

He himself had never been the fighting type, but the cry of a fellow man had roused his instincts. Time had taken most of the man's physical strength, but his senses remained largely untouched. His body was tired now but still robust— stout and rotund, but still muscular. Resigned to facing the threat without the vampire huntress, he turned to where he had heard the man cry out. He kept to the shadows and headed towards the nearest watchtower. The firelight danced in its torch above him, deceptively innocent. Sweat began to drip from his skin as fear began to take hold over him. He had brought no weapons to meet Natalya so he held his hands out protectively in front of him, acutely feeling the absence of a blade in his fist.

It seemed to take forever for him to reach the tower. It was built entirely of wood and encased a large staircase that lead to the gong and the torch above where the man would have stood guard. The elder imagined him passing the long hours fighting sleep and tending to the fire, perhaps entranced by its unending dance within its confinements. How slowly the night might have passed before this fateful moment!

The elder pulled himself onto the staircase and began to climb, all the while dreading his destination. He did not know what he would find when he finally reached the top; he only knew that he did not want to see what kind of condition the man may be in.

He ascended the last of the steps and nearly cried out at what he found. The watchman lay in a thick pool of blood as still more trickled slowly from the wounds in his neck. He remained unmoving and the elder knew without approaching that the man would move no more.

Fighting waves of nausea and knowing the man was beyond help, the elder turned to descend the staircase, but an odd swishing noise told him that the danger had not yet passed. He froze in his position and waited with bated breath for the threat to reveal itself.

He did not wait long. His uneasy stance had given way to cold self-assurance, and he stood proudly before incoming death. He knew before he fell that everything he had done in his life to become an elder had given way to this moment and had defined his very being. His rise to power had been marked by a strong and true compassion for Valwood and his fellow citizens.

His end was marked by a sharp pain in his back as he was thrown forward. His wrists took the impact, and he slammed hard into them, bending them outward with the force of his fall. He had not yet turned to stand when another pain assaulted his neck and he cried out just as the other man had. His body crumpled as his blood was released and the man sank lifelessly to the floor of the tower, dead before he had reached it. His empty eyes had never seen his assailant, the creature that had bestowed upon him a quick ruination before feeding from his wounds and disappearing into the woods.

Far beyond the shadow of the hill, inside the ivy covered house with peeling white paint, Natalya lay sleeping soundly under the waning moonlight. As the hours passed quietly she had dreamed peacefully while the elder had been slain in the tower. And as the night came and went, she was unaware of the changes that were unfolding in her city. She had no way of knowing that a storm of destruction was already brewing in Valwood. Nor did she know that it could have been stopped by the very elder who now stared sightlessly in the night from the northernmost watchtower, having crossed paths with a vampire.

It seemed as if the coming morning could never be fully enough to erase the pain and loss of a night before, no matter how much one could try, and so it was the case with Natalya. She awakened at her normal time, dressed into her usual clothing and purchased her breakfast rolls at her favorite bakery, but nothing about her day could be called normal. She had returned home, her basket bulging with food, and now she walked purposely towards the woods, her bow slung across her back.

At regular intervals she checked behind her to ensure she was not being followed or seen, though she had grown so used to relying on stealth it had become second nature.

She disappeared amongst the trees, and they enveloped her form in their depths, hiding her from view. Natalya felt relieved in her solitude, without the somber conversations of her people buzzing in her head. Here she could mourn privately to only the sounds of the birds and insects.

She walked a long ways without stopping; she did not wish to run into anyone now. It was not long before she came across a secluded clearing, and she sat cross legged on the grassy floor. She bit into the first of her chosen bread, trying hard to banish the grief that had been gnawing at her gut.

By now Anesa's body had been discovered, and her corpse removed from the forest. It had been moved to the church where it was being prepared for the burial ceremony.

Natalya was no stranger to death, given her profession, but she had taken the wise old woman's particularly hard. She hid her grief well, but the elderly fortune teller had much in common with her own dead mother. Anesa had always commanded such a strong presence, showing a remarkable lack of fear about her own aging and the ever present threat of death. Just like Irena had.

Natalya turned her thoughts away from her dead mother. She was used to pushing painful memories to the back of her mind.

She stood up. She scanned the trees that were aligned in a circle all around her, searching for any distinctive markings. One tree had a large weathered cavity that was sunk deeply into it. *That would do.*

Natalya knocked an arrow into her bow and took careful aim, shooting for the large hole. It was stretched open, almost like a grotesque mouth, and she had no difficulty in pretending it to have a vampire's face. She closed one eye, concentrating. The next moment she released the arrow. It sailed through the air and struck the center of the hole, while the vampire in her mind screamed and died. Natalya smiled in grim satisfaction and stalked towards the tree to retrieve her arrow.

Several more times she repeated the process, and each time she hit her target exactly where she intended. Many years of hard practice had refined and honed her reflexes, her aim and her strength, shaping her into the deadly huntress that she was now. With the added aid of her amulet, she had become a very capable adversary.

By now the sun was blazing high overhead, but she felt no desire to return to her people. She didn't want to see her own sadness reflected on their faces or hear their own versions of what must have happened that night. She sighed, undecided. She couldn't stay here forever, and it occurred to her as well that she hadn't seen Methea since she had fled from Celestial Hold. The mare should have instinctively come back to Valwood but the horse hadn't returned home. Her friend's barn had often offered the mare refuge; perhaps she had fled there. It was as likely a place as any and Natalya could talk to Kaima; her friend always understood how she felt. Her mind made, Natalya began to follow the path toward her friend's farm.

When she got there, a whirlwind of emerald dress and flaming red hair enveloped Natalya in its embrace. She had barely knocked on the door when it had flung open and Kaima had pulled her inside, waiting to be told of every detail of her latest adventure.

"Natalya! Oh I've been so worried!" Kaima whispered into her ear before releasing her and regarding her disheveled friend. Natalya smiled weakly, but her somber feelings still registered on her face. The night was a blur that lingered upon the deaths of Anesa and the vampire. Correctly interpreting her friend's expression, Kaima's face showed her concern.

"What's wrong?"

"Anesa is…dead," she managed to say while blinking back tears. Kaima's face saddened. Although her interactions with the old woman had been limited, they had given her a glimpse of the world that Natalya alone was a part of. Anesa's infinite wisdom and caring guidance had shown through her stories and in the way her eyes gently creased at the corners. Through Natalya and Anesa, Kaima had gleaned much knowledge of vampires and guarded their identities just as fiercely as they had, but Anesa never knew that Natalya had told her friend of their identities. And although Kaima had been absent at the hunts herself, she had grown to appreciate the safety she had her fellow citizens lived in at the cost of the huntresses.

"I'm so sorry," Kaima said after Natalya had described how she had found Anesa's body. Her words were choked and forced but at least here she could talk freely; Kaima's family farm was an ideal place for private conversation, well away from the prying eyes of the village citizens. Natalya's day had been filled with sorrow though and she longed for brighter conversation.

"I was wondering if you had Methea," she said as lightly as she could.

"Yes," Kaima answered as she took Natalya's hand. "Seth actually found her in the streets." She paused as if she didn't want to say anything further, then seemed to change her mind. "She seemed happy to come here so we fed her for you."

"Thank you," Natalya said as she followed her friend to the barn. They entered through the large wooden door to the stalls where Methea waited. Kaima's older brother Seth turned from the chestnut mare he was saddling to look at them.

"Your horse is in the last stall on the right," he said pointing the way. Natalya ran to the stall he had gestured to and was instantly greeted by the horse.

"Methea!" Natalya exclaimed. The mare's eyes rolled wildly in her head and she paced nervously in her stall but seemed to calm at the sight of her owner.

"She galloped here in quite a state," the groom said sternly, surveying Natalya suspiciously. "Spooked out of her mind, it seemed, still wearing her saddle and bit. I've never seen a horse so intent on escaping anything before. What was it you said that befell the two of you?"

Natalya wordlessly took the lead that Seth handed her. Her mare's flanks were still heaving slightly and vapor poured from the horse's nostrils as she exhaled, but she was otherwise unhurt. Natalya pretended to be undoing a knot in the rope as she thought furiously.

"We sighted a bear," she murmured finally, avoiding the groom's prying gaze. "It was a little ways off but it raised its head and Methea spooked. She threw me off of her and headed back here, but it was not a hard fall."

55

"I see," the groom said finally. He did not appear to be thoroughly convinced and seemed to be mulling her story over. Kaima and Natalya exchanged glances. Kaima cleared her throat and announced that it was time for Natalya to be getting along.

"Yes, I must," Natalya agreed, grateful for the excuse. Wordlessly, she led the mare out of the barn before Seth could raise any more objections.

It was mid evening when Natalya rode onto her street.

She unlatched the gate leading to her and her father's modest white house. Ever since the death of her mother it had sunk into slight disrepair, but to Natalya it would always feel like home, despite the faded and peeling paint, and the many weeds that clawed their way up its sides.

"Father!" she called once she had opened the front door. Only silence greeted her, which was unusual. Normally he would be preparing dinner around now, or working on his latest woodworking project. She checked each room but he was nowhere to be seen within the house. Natalya found Elder Greg in the back yard polishing a strange object.

A weapon of the likes that Natalya had never seen before was on his table. It was long and thin, but had no edge or blade in sight for striking. So unlike the swords and daggers she had grown used to, it was cylindrical in shape except for the base that was squarer while the other end was tipped with an ominous dark hole. It was an attractive mix of polished wood and unrelenting metal, and Natalya felt it held potential for terrible power within its casing.

"What is it?" she asked, fighting to keep her tone light.

"It's called a gun," he explained. "More specifically, a musket. This model is newly designed and just imported from foreign traders. We own one of the first ever made," he answered with a touch of pride.

Natalya examined the gun herself, careful not to touch it. She treated it as if it were a bomb that could explode at any moment, though she could not fathom how the weapon was to be used. Questioningly, she looked back up at her father.

"How does it work?"

"I will demonstrate. Stand back," he commanded, and Natalya instantly obeyed, crossing the yard to stand behind her father.

"And cover your ears," he added, grinning. He lifted the gun and supported its weight with his shoulder, while his other hand supported the barrel. He lined his head onto its side, and took aim into the sky. Natalya's gaze followed his movements, and she squinted against the sun's dazzling light. He held his finger on the trigger, not pulling it for dramatic effect. Natalya continued to watch in amazement, her hands clamped over her ears.

His finger squeezed the trigger and the resounding crack was earsplitting despite her hands to muffle the sound. Her father's body had been buffeted slightly with the force of the shot.

"What do you think of that?" he asked, chuckling.

"What happened?" Natalya asked

"This thing just blasted a silver ball powerful enough to blow a werewolf in half!" he answered, beginning to reload it. Natalya willed herself not to cringe. She could still feel the noise of the shot ringing in her ears, and she knew now that this weapon contained far more power than any mere blade, or even her bow. With the men of Valwood outfitted with muskets, multiple enemies could be felled from a much greater distance than ever before. What would have taken her multiple arrows, could now be done with a single musket ball. She imagined that ball piercing Voren's hide and she felt sick to her stomach. At least with her bow, her prey still stood a fighting chance against her. She had prided herself that she had bested them when their own weapons were undiminished. *But this…this seemed nothing more to her than slaughter.*

"What do you plan to do with it?" she asked. The lines on her father's face deepened until he was nearly unrecognizable from the benign figure she had grown so used to. He began to answer in a hard voice that chilled Natalya with the threat of vengeance it held.

"I will not continue to sit back and watch our people be killed by werewolves. We have maintained peace with them for too long and they have shattered it by attacking Anesa in the dark. I intend to strike back. With this weapon, we have the advantage. Silver can be fashioned into bullets to allow us to rid the earth of these demons."

He paused and smiled coldly.

"If it is a war they wish to start, I will give them one to remember." His last words were drawn out and thick with malice. For a moment Natalya could not speak, so taken aback by the abrupt change in her father.

"Do you know for sure that she was killed by a werewolf?" she finally asked in as casual a voice as she could manage. "I mean no one has seen the body except for the elders."

"Who else could have done this Natalya? This was not the work of petty thieves or criminals and there have been no confirmed sightings of vampires for the last several years. No, it must have been the werewolves."

Her father's tone softened and he brushed back a lock of her hair from her eyes.

"We have allowed them to live in close proximity to us for too many years, my daughter. I intend to change that. With these new weapons we stand a chance against them."

Natalya forced a smile but behind it fear was fluttering in her chest. Her father had returned the musket to its proper place and was striding back into the house. She hung back, worry creasing lines into her brow, as she wondered just how far her father was willing to go for his revenge.

~ Chapter Six ~
Sacrilege

She did not have long to find out. The very next day, they buried Anesa. Nearly every citizen turned up for the event, held right outside of the weathered church. Flowers blossomed in every field and adorned the mahogany coffins while the sun shone overhead. Natalya could not help but feel thankful that Anesa's passing would be marked by such a beautiful ceremony.

She approached the casket to give her own last farewells before her mentors body would be forever enfolded into pitiless earth. She stood stock still against the prodigious hole, and it was as if every other person had disappeared. For the moment Natalya was lost in her grief, as if she had been turned to a marble figure that could not be moved from her vigil.

She looked down at Anesa and was shocked at how peaceful the woman now looked. Her body had been cleaned of the blood that had blemished her, and it was as if it had only been age that had taken her. Her worn hand still clasped the red rose to her breast, and a smile still lingered on her lips.

The lips that would never again guide her with Anesa's soothing voice. *Who will watch over Valwood now that you are gone?* Natalya wanted to scream, but with so many watching she did not dare give voice to what she truly wanted to say. Instead, she contented herself with mentally thanking the woman for everything she had taught her.

"Good bye," she finally murmured as the men began to pour dirt into the grave. They slowly closed the lid until the woman disappeared from view and dust showered over the casket.

As Anesa's body was lowered into the ground, Natalya finally saw the sorrow she had been harboring reflected in her neighbor's faces. She saw their confusion as well, for it was clear that no one knew for sure how Anesa had died. Natalya knew that whispers and murmurings of her absence had traveled through the city like wildfire, flecked with fear and peppered with rumors until no one but Natalya was quite sure what was fact and what had been made up. Only one thing was clear, there was not one among them that would be unaffected by her passing.

The elders were giving their last good byes to Anesa when Natalya came out of her preoccupation. They stood over the grave with their heads bowed, murmuring amongst themselves.

Natalya took a seat towards the back next to Kaima and waited for the elder at the podium to speak. She could see he wanted to announce something, and she raised her head in interest. At her side, Kaima squeezed her hand reassuringly. Her father, Elder Greg Vrushko, approached the podium, and Natalya could only listen incredulously to the speech he now delivered.

"Citizens of Valwood!" Natalya's father cried from the podium, overlooking the crowd. "Anesa was a revered fortune teller and respected by all who knew her. Her wisdom guided Valwood through times of turmoil and peace. And now we assemble as one under Zulae, benign Wolf Goddess of the Moon, to pray that she take her gently in her arms. May she find peace in the afterlife, as she did not find peace in this life."

Her people nodded and bowed their heads in grace for the woman's soul. But Elder Greg's next words had once again commanded their rapt attention.

"It is now time you have all learned the truth about what has really befallen our beloved Fortune Teller! I tell you now that it was the werewolves who have killed her and it is them that will pay!"

A collective roaring erupted from the stands, and Natalya and Kaima exchanged horrified glances as they turned to their fellow citizens. They all stood now, all around them, as one embodiment of their unified rage. Disbelief was written on every face, and behind their tears, Natalya could see their mutual longing for revenge and justice. The same question seemed to be written in all of their expressions: *why her?*

It was the very question that Natalya had asked herself many times, but her anger was sated slightly by the justice she had already enacted on the fleeing vampire.

"Elder Greg!" a voice cried from the crowd, and every head turned to listen. "Last time we had help and armies from our sister cities. We no longer have that luxury and our men are only a few hundred strong. How do you intend to defeat these monsters?"

Natalya's father gestured to the crowd, and at once they fell silent, listening with eager ears for his solution.

"With the arrival of muskets that have been fitted with silver, we will drive them from Claw Haven and expand our city! The time for peace has ended!" he continued from the stage. "We

62

have generously allowed the werewolves to live alongside of us for all of these years and this is how they repay us! By flouting the peaceful nature of the she-wolf, and shedding the noble bravery of the alpha to steal among us in the dead of night! These slithering serpents stand against everything that Zulae stands for, and as we speak preparations are being made for our first strike against them! No longer will we stand back and allow ourselves to be picked off, one by one!" He finished his speech, and the citizens applauded from their seats. Her father bowed slightly and returned to the other elders.

The citizens of Valwood shouted their approval until the nearby trees seemed to quake with the force of their anger. Natalya was seated, a mere face in the crowd, although hers did not share the same enamored passion for vengeance that her fellows did. Her expression was of silent, resigned horror that her people were going to start a war they could not afford to lose. She chanced a look at the people around her, knowing that while they waved their hands and cried for blood, that it would be much of their own that would come to stain the ground. She studied their familiar faces and wondered just how many of them would come to be buried next to Anesa.

At the end of the funeral, Natalya approached the podium as the citizens of Valwood began to disperse from their seats. Her father was in the corner with the other elders, their heads bowed as they talked in low somber voices. She waited impatiently as they talked until Chief Elder Olek raised his head. He gestured to the others and their voices instantly died down.

"What can we do for you Natalya?" her father asked. His tone was light, but Natalya knew he objected to her interruption.

"I wish to speak to Elder Tomas," she said, but as they raised their heads to look at her she realized he wasn't among them. The remaining elders exchanged guarded glances and her father detached himself from them. He pulled her out of earshot of the other elders before sitting her down in an empty seat.

"Elder Tomas Edrich was killed last night. Along with a watchman." He stated it bluntly, without softening his words. It had always been her family's way to face cold reality with unflinching honesty.

Natalya's face instantly paled, and she bowed her head, but she allowed no other sign of grief to register onto her face.

"He was a great elder," was all she said and her father nodded. He sighed just then, and his face seemed to age ten years. He shook his head, and Natalya realized that he, her father and invulnerable elder, was every bit as lost as his face betrayed.

"Their bodies were every bit as mangled as Anesa's, but there was no sign of their attacker. No human could have done that," he said and his eyes went sightless with the memory of seeing the carnage.

"Not another attack," Natalya whispered and her father came out of his reverie.

"Their bodies were ripped and shredded. What else could have done that?" he asked and Natalya shook her head. How could she convince him to stop this war when Tomas lay dead? He had been the only elder that had known her secret and it lay hidden with him. There was so much to tell, so many gaps in the years to fill and without Tomas to back her, Natalya knew she could never hope to sway him.

She opened her mouth then immediately closed it again. For a moment, she had considered telling him everything, but she remembered her promise to Anesa. He could not know that vampires had not been sighted in recent years because of her and the fortune teller. If he found out how Anesa had really died and went after her killer himself Natalya knew it would end in her father's slaughter.

"I don't know," she finally murmured and her father had nothing more to say. She left him to the elders and returned to her seat.

She had to warn Voren. The thought had burst into her mind, unbidden. She dismissed it then paused. Perhaps he could help her if she could find him. If they talked to his Alpha, maybe they could stop the war before it happened. Natalya thought of her father, oblivious to her plan. He hadn't glanced her way since she had walked away. He was still deep in conversation with the other elders and guilt began to needle her side. She remembered the three werewolves that had tried to kill her already. He had already lost his wife. *If she did not return…*

She sat down where Kaima waited, still absorbed in her thoughts.

"What will you do now?" Kaima asked after the crowd had fully disseminated and the elders had retired.

"I don't know what I can do," Natalya said, pulling at her hair nervously. "Arkadith is the only vampire powerful enough to create these fledglings. I can't tell my father how Anesa really died and he wouldn't believe me if I did. The vampires will have turned to dust by now. Tomas could have convinced them all, and now he's dead…" her words trailed off and the two friends sat in silence.

"All these years, sneaking out at night to keep Valwood safe and it still isn't safe," Natalya said bitterly to herself.

"You have to do something."

"Father and I both intend to go to Claw Haven. Him to destroy the werewolves, and me to stop him. If I go there I will risk death, but his will be ensured if he goes. I must speak to Voren. Maybe we can stop this before it begins."

"You cannot trust him," Kaima whispered.

Natalya gazed into the distant woods where she knew the wall stood, dividing Valwood from Claw Haven. She could not explain her driving need to see him, not even to herself. It was true that he shattered every preconceived notion she had of his kind, but there was something else as well.

He stood, emblazed in her mind's eye, in direct contrast to the image she had conjured of a cruel, barbaric creature that didn't deserve to step within her city's boundaries. She had never questioned her people's opinions of the werewolves, never stopped to consider the possibility that maybe they could have been wrong, at least about some of them. Perhaps some of the werewolves chose to be different, to somehow break free of their natures, although this contradicted with everything she had been taught about them. It was that moment that she knew that she wanted more than to stop her father. If Voren was more than that which he appeared...*she had to find out.*

"I must go to him," Natalya said. Kaima shook her head.

"You will be betraying your own people to do it," her friend countered.

"I am trying to help my people. We cannot start a war with the werewolves," Natalya said.

"Natalya...this talk is forbidden. It is sacrilege to even be discovered past the wall. Please don't go..."

"I must," Natalya said, and with that she ran to the house to ready Methea.

~ Chapter Seven ~
Among Wolves

A single leaf detached itself from its tree and fell to the ground, spinning delicately like a snowflake. Far beneath it, Natalya nudged her mount deeper within the great forest.

There was no path to follow to the wall so instead she relied on memory, threading her horse in between the trees and carefully guiding her through hidden snake holes or over fallen logs. The overlapping buzzes of multiple insects were constant, though occasionally punctuated by the shrill call of a bird or chipmunk. Methea picked through the uneven terrain gracefully and confidently, never losing her footing or startling at unfamiliar noises.

In a few hours' time, Natalya came to the border that marked the end of her people's woods. The wall disappeared past the limits of her eyesight on either side of her, and instantly the woods felt darker and more sinister. The werewolf skull stared unceasingly at her, and Natalya found herself uncertain once more. She remembered Kaima's words and knew that passing through could lead her people down a path that they could not escape from.

She also knew that her father had already made his choice. The only way to stop the oncoming war lay just beyond this gate if she could only find Voren.

Natalya inhaled deeply and guided Methea past the skull. The two were swallowed up into impenetrable forest. The trees spread out their branches above her like a canopy, effectively blotting out the sunlight and she wondered if she would lose her way. She felt deaf and blind, for even the sounds of the animals had died away for it seemed as if none made their homes here.

As the darkness settled, Natalya's amulet began to glow a bright shade of amber. It lighted the way before them, and they trusted its beam to guide them through the woods. The steady gait of her horse and the monotone of shadowy trees gave way to Natalya's thoughts, and they raced through her head. She imagined her father following from behind on his own gelding, his gun loaded for the first kill. She remembered the shock of the blast and closed her eyes to the image of it piercing Voren's flesh and his eyes closing forever in death. Several minutes passed as more visions of the oncoming war danced before her eyes, each one more terrible than the last. She was so absorbed in her thoughts she barely noticed when a twig snapped behind her.

Methea had heard the noise though, and her rearing startled Natalya back into reality. She whipped her head from side to side, unable to locate its source while she patted the mare into calmness. All was silent now, and she gradually began to relax as no threat revealed itself. She prodded her horse forward, and the two headed away from the mysterious noise.

Her amulet had changed subtly to a dark ruby, and Natalya slowly turned to look behind her. She was on edge now, every one of her senses wholly stretched to the max. Her eyes raked through the trees, seeking movement, but not even a breadth of wind came to disturb the forest. Somewhere a bird screeched, but Natalya ignored the sound. She longed to call out, to face the potential danger, but her instinct urged her to stay quiet. Methea nickered nervously and pawed at the ground, and Natalya tried to soothe the frightened mare, but this time she was unsuccessful. She continued to scan the trees at eye level until *they* materialized before her.

Like wispy shadows, their paws hardly making indents in the ground, they stood in a neat line.

Their likeness to real wolves in stature was remarkable, but there was where the similarities ended. Some were taller than others, but none were as short as a true wolf. Clumps of dead fur clung to gaunt frames that held no muscle or fat. In color, they were all uniform, the gray that lines darkened storm clouds. But most different were the eyes. Cloudy, like twin crystal balls with no pupils; Natalya could believe she was staring at the most cursed of all creatures. She tried to pick out Voren, but could see no discernible differences between them. Any one of them could have been him, or he could be absent altogether. Slowly Natalya dismounted from Methea in one fluid motion, unable to take her eyes off of the two dozen odd werewolves before her.

As she watched, a single werewolf separated itself from its fellows. It was padding lightly, its nose quivering, and Natalya knew this one must be a female, as she was leaner and moved more gracefully than her brethren had. As she neared her, a thick swirling fog rose from the ground, obscuring her, and she rose taller and taller above it. Almost demurely, she turned to the side and her features began to twist, her muzzle thinning and shrinking back into her face. The milky whites of her eyes darkened and eyebrows emerged above them. Her fur began to rapidly fall to the ground in huge clumps until Natalya was looking at a naked woman, her supple breasts hidden behind her mane like hair. She had an untamed and wild beauty to her. But her body also held great strength in its muscles and limbs, all the way to her lean fingers, which ended in claws.

Like Voren, her body was covered in tattoos that wound up her arms and legs and covered her back that were in a language unknown to Natalya. The woman was not much taller than her and smelled strongly of earth, and Natalya rose to meet her, unsure of her next move. The other werewolves held their unmoving line, their milky eyes staring unceasingly. The woman finally spoke in a hoarse voice as if unused to using it. Her teeth ended in points.

"What business do you have here, human?" she asked roughly. "You know it is forbidden to cross the gate." With no time to argue, Natalya threw caution to the wind.

"All of you are in danger! My people are planning to mount an attack against you!"

Natalya scanned the assembled werewolves for the effect her words would have on them, but they were unwavering in their stillness. Only the female's face before her registered any surprise.

"You betray your own people to warn us of this? Or do I smell a trap lurking in the shadows? This is out of my hands *human*. I think it would be best if you saw our Alpha."

Natalya nodded while flurries of fear swirled in her chest. She was no nearer to finding Voren and could not be sure how she would be received by this mysterious Alpha.

Another werewolf had broken ranks to stand behind them and the female motioned to him.

"Tovu shall lead you to the Alpha." Again Natalya nodded. The werewolf dipped his head in an almost friendly way that did little to reassure Natalya.

Leading Methea on foot, she followed the werewolf deeper into the woods. Methea was uneasy, snickering at every sound and clearly distressed in the presence of so many predators, but the werewolf seemed completely relaxed. He was perfectly svelte, his hindquarters weaving back and forth in a slinking gait as they turned onto a hidden path. The path meandered in an out of view but his paws never once strayed from it. Here he seemed almost docile, and for a moment Natalya almost forgot he was one of her people's most feared enemies.

As they walked they could see large shapes through the gaps in the trees. It was only when they got closer that Natalya could see that they were makeshift homes. They were all cone shaped and held together with dyed animal skins that were stretched over long tree limbs. Some had elaborate drawings painted on them, and others were adorned with vines and leaves and whatever else the werewolves could find.

The trees had thinned, and she found herself in the midst of their village where werewolves in both human and wolf forms roamed. She could even see children dressed in animal skins, identical to their parents except for the many tattoos that embellished their parents' bodies.

What do you think? A strange voice questioned in her head. She remembered the sensation from when Voren had communicated to her in this way, though Voren's voice had been even deeper.

She looked up to see the werewolf staring at her intently, its head cocked questioningly, but his eyes were still blank and slightly sad.

"It's...different," she said aloud.

Indeed. Do not trouble yourself with Henovi; she will come around, was his reply and Natalya nodded. She thought of the angry she-wolf and worry continued to twist her insides into knots. The werewolf dipped its whitened muzzle cordially and returned to leading her along the path. Natalya could not help but notice as the werewolf walked still more clumps of fur fell from his hide, but he seemed unbothered.

"Is….is there something wrong with your fur?" she finally asked timidly. Tovu continued on as if he hadn't heard her, though his ears were pricked in her direction. But as a particularly large clump had caught in the branch of a giant pine, it was clear he could ignore the question no longer.

We are cursed creatures. She thought she could detect the faintest hint of a snarl in her head. Sorrow too.

She did not press the matter as they continued on their path. A quarter of an hour later, they came onto a large dwelling that was far grander than the rest they had passed. An elaborate hunting scene was drawn on it, a deer cornered by many werewolves hidden in the trees. It continued along in its conical fashion, and Natalya would have had to circle the entire teepee to discover the deer's fate.

The entrance was open, and Natalya could hear voices within. They paused at the opening until the werewolf nodded at Natalya.

We've been invited in, he growled in her head. He padded inside, and Natalya followed. More animal skins covered the grass inside and ringed a large fire that was contained in a circle of large stones.

Two wizened men dressed in furs conversed across from them, but their talk ceased at their arrival. The older of the two stood to greet them, his white beard nearly falling to the floor. Tovu went to stand next to him, and Natalya took this one to be the Alpha. She did not know whether to bow or attempt to shake his hand so she stood silently, waiting to be addressed. The instinct to flee tugged at her conscience, but she quieted it, knowing she would never make it to the wall. She doubted she could even find her way back to it now, and instead, she remembered the liquid silver she had reinforced her stake with for just this occasion. It lay resting in its place against her ribs, but she knew not to grow overconfident; she was still badly outnumbered.

Some conversation must have passed between the two werewolves for the Alpha motioned to Natalya, and she approached him apprehensively.

"Walk with me," was all he said and raw panic fluttered in Natalya's chest. She looked questioningly at Tovu. His cloudy eyes expressed nothing, but his tone in her head was somber.

I will not be accompanying you, he said. He turned his shaggy head away from her, and Natalya nearly protested aloud. She could not explain it to herself, but she had already taken to the kind werewolf. The Alpha beckoned to her, and she followed, unsure if she had just sealed her and her father's fate.

They exited the back of the teepee and onto another path that led even deeper into the forest. They walked in silence, and Natalya marveled at being in the presence of the most powerful and influential werewolf she had ever met. It was another fifteen minutes before the path they had chosen brought them to a secluded enough clearing. Natalya tensed, preparing to draw her stake if the Alpha attacked, but he remained still.

"What is your name, human?" the Alpha asked and the question took her off guard.

"Natalya."

"Natalya…" he repeated slowly. "My name is Anraq, Alpha of this clan. Why have you ventured into Claw Haven,

73

Natalya?" It was the first time she hadn't been addressed as *human*.

"I have come to warn you of an attack that my kind is planning against you," Natalya answered. She had decided to speak plainly, for although she knew he could kill her now in these deserted woods, she needed to trust in someone. Voren was unsettling in her mind for she hadn't seen or heard a sign of him since entering Claw Haven again.

"I see," the Alpha said without surprise. She guessed that Tovu had already relayed some of her intent beforehand. He turned to her and studied her face shrewdly before continuing.

"And what motive does a human have for telling me this?" he asked softly. The lines in his face had deepened and the Alpha suddenly seemed much older. His demeanor and stature were commanding but candid, and before Natalya knew it she found herself telling him of everything that had transpired during her hunt and how she had come to meet Voren. She left nothing out, and Anraq listened to her without interruption. She bowed her head slightly, waiting for his judgment, but for the moment he did not speak. They had looped through the forest and now they found themselves in the village once more.

They reached Tovu again, and Natalya listened again while some message passed between them. Finally Anraq addressed her again.

"For the time being, your survival has rested on Voren's testament to your trustworthiness and your cooperation. Tomorrow I will consult with the others to determine the truth in your claims. Tovu will arrange sleeping quarters for you tonight. I trust they will be to your satisfaction."

Without another word the Alpha bowed briefly to her, and Natalya watched him walk away, somehow more nervous than she had been before.

Follow me Natalya, Tovu growled in her head, and she obeyed, walking to an unadorned teepee that was set slightly apart from the others.

Gratefully, she entered to find another fire contained in its middle and a floor covered in more animal skins. After circling the inside of the teepee she poked her head out to thank Tovu, but the werewolf had already gone. Disappointed, she withdrew into the teepee again. She pulled some of the furs around herself in a makeshift blanket and pillow. She fell asleep that night to the firelight that danced before her closed eyelids, wondering what tomorrow would bring.

~ Chapter Eight ~
Curse of the New Moon

A hand closed over Natalya's mouth, and she awakened, struggling to breathe. Her fingers instinctively closed over the stake that lay against her ribs, and she raised it defensively, ready to strike against her attacker.

"It's me!" she heard a familiar voice whisper fiercely in the darkness, and her eyes flew open, though her fist remained closed over her weapon.

"Voren!" she gasped, lowering her weapon slightly, though she kept it poised to defend herself if needed. "What are you doing here?"

"I've come to see you," he answered, withdrawing his hand. "The others can't know; that's why I've come now." She clutched her chest, waiting for her heartbeats to slow. She stumbled out of the teepee and looked up to see the impassive sky, but without the moons light she could not know what time it was. She guessed that she only slept about three, maybe four hours.

"Anraq still doesn't know whether or not to trust your word," Voren explained. "It's odd that you've made it so far, they usually kill humans on sight for trespassing. Tensions have been growing between your people and mine. He is preparing to send scouts to the Valwood border to verify your claim. When they return everything will be decided."

"What if he doesn't believe me?" Natalya asked, feeling the now familiar pangs of fear flicker within her chest.

"I do not know," Voren answered, not quite hiding his own concern. He too glanced at the empty sky, and quickly changed the subject.

"Come with me," he whispered and his voice held an unexplained urgency.

"Voren, it's the middle of the night. Besides, what if we are caught?"

"We won't be. The others will not be out tonight," he said knowingly, and for some reason his words sent a cold chill down Natalya's spine. Still, she found herself rousing to follow him. Briskly he led the way, his hand clamped tight around hers, first along a path and then veering off of it to go deeper into the forest.

"*Where* are you taking me?" Natalya asked, but he merely shook his head. Breathlessly, she matched his pace, though her instincts to flee rose within her once more. She shook them off, reminding herself that he had had ample opportunities to destroy her before now and had not. She knew within that she still trusted him.

They reached a clearing that was dimly illuminated by starlight and it was here that Voren finally released his grip onto hers and stood in its center.

Natalya stared at him, transfixed, unable to figure out why he had brought them here. Almost in slow motion, he raised his hands to the sky, his arms stretched out above him as if he were trying to grab all the stars to bring them to earth. At first he stood stock still until he began to change. This was nothing like the graceful transformation she had observed earlier. Now his body mutated grotesquely and painfully it seemed, for he cried out in a torn howl that was carried away in the wind. His bones shifted and broke within his body with loud cracks as his skin rippled and sprouted fur along its length. His mouth elongated into a snout as fangs replaced his human teeth and his eyes clouded over into a blank gaze that shifted onto her. Natalya was rooted to her spot in fear, unable to even reach for her stake as she stared at the fully realized werewolf before her.

Natalya. Her own name sounded in her head and inexplicable relief flooded through her.

The fur that was hanging loosely from his hide had begun to gather into large clumps that fell to the forest floor, exposing the pink flesh underneath until a sparsely furred skeleton stood before her. Only small tufts of fur clung determinedly to the bone. The werewolf's skull itself was clean of fur or skin, and the cloudy orbs swirled without reason before dimming completely within their sockets. The blank, empty stare was nearly more than Natalya could handle, for at least the white eyes had been comforting in their familiarity. Instead these lightless holes implored her almost sadly. She found herself tentatively lifting a hand to the creature's cheekbone, running her finger over each crevice. The werewolf shuddered slightly under her touch.

Are you afraid? The voice in her head was heavy with threat, but still she did not remove her hand.

"No," she whispered, and the strength that was held in her voice surprised even her.

You understand now the depth of my curse.

Yes, she thought to herself. She now saw Voren for what he truly was. The skeletal werewolf gazed up at the sky, his expression unreadable. She followed the line of his sight to the cold unfeeling stars, as he reflected on his cruel fate. His bones quivered slightly, and what little fur remained on his body ruffled in the breeze.

The werewolf stiffened, his gaze locked onto something she could not see. He advanced, stiff-legged and menacingly onto Natalya. It seemed as if he had lost full control of his wolf form and for one tortuous moment she reached for her weapon. But the next second he shuddered strangely and began to transform once more.

He shrunk before her as the last of his fur was shed, and hard flesh and muscle formed over the sun-bleached bones. The foggy eyes closed. When they reopened, a brilliant gold iris reappeared and once again Natalya could see her own reflection in their depths. He had regained his naked human form, and he shivered uncontrollably as if he were in the throes of a mild seizure.

"Forgive me. I-I have not been myself tonight," Voren said strangely, his breathing still ragged and strained. With a pained effort he calmed his shuddering body and turned to look at her. Natalya could not summon the strength to move.

"What happened?" was all she could ask while she too shivered despite the heat of the summer night.

"I lost control. It took all of my resolve to stop and to force myself to change once again. It is…the hardest thing to deny the power of the new moon. I should not have allowed you to see me like that," and now his voice was full of bitterness.

"I didn't know before. You truly are cursed," she whispered.

"Yes," he said. "It's ok. I know what I must appear to you and your people. Everything about us is savage to your kind although we are not so different, you and I."

"Many of us believe that werewolves and vampires are basically the same thing."

"We are *nothing* alike! Vampires are soulless, mindlessly cruel in their search for fresh blood. They do not feel, and they do not pity. They cannot love. They know only their thirst. They are cursed even more than we. For at least we are not total slaves to it. And at least the horizon brings some promise of redemption for us."

His voice shook slightly with the effort of trying to explain to her.

"A vampire cannot rise above his nature or his thirst. We, on the other hand, can still remember our human natures and try to live by them, but we can never truly be free. I am a wolf now and dangerous."

"What did you do to...become a...?" her voice trailed off.

"A werewolf you mean?"

"Yes" she whispered. Voren thought long and hard before answering, and Natalya knew his mind was taking him back, far away to a distant memory.

"I was a foolhardy young man. The old myth is false; we cannot reproduce simply by biting someone. I could sink my fangs into your flesh right now and you would stay just as you are, pure, whole and human. I was different back then. I can't expect you to understand," he said almost angrily.

"Tell me," she whispered.

"Alright." He paused, thinking. He began slowly. "Arkadith was not always the ancient and powerful vampire he is now."

"Wait!" Natalya interrupted. "Arkadith?"

"So you too know of him, the ancient vampire." It was not a question.

"Yes."

"How?"

"He killed my mother," she said. Her voice turned hard. "I've been hunting him ever since, longing to avenge her."

"So her death too is on my conscience," he muttered darkly.

"What do you mean?"

"I am the reason that Arkadith has risen. It was my blood that allowed him to rise to power again."

"How?"

"Not too many years after he had been turned, he had been captured by a group of humans. I believe the elders of your city may be their descendants. The feud between immortals and humans has transcended many generations."

Natalya nodded, thinking of the great wall that had separated her people from the werewolves all these years.

"Anyways," Voren continued, "the humans had staked him through his chest, but they must have missed his heart for he still lived. He was much weakened, and although he was immortal, his chest could not close over the protruding wooden stake. They held him there, nearly dead in a dungeon below the earth. He had not fed in weeks. Perhaps if I had not come along he would have died there," Voren muttered.

"But come along I did and being young and rebellious, I discovered the castle that we were all forbidden to enter."

"The castle on the hill. No one has ventured there in years."

"Yes, that is the one. I climbed in through one of the windows and searched through room after room, filling my pockets with whatever valuables I could find. I reasoned that I would resell them later to help my hungry family, but I was just trying to quiet my guilt. It took me over a day to reach the dungeon below, and I wish I could have stifled my curiosity then, but unfortunately I did not.

"I found the vampire there, but he was just a corpse for he did not move. He spoke to me in my mind. He was not at the height of his hypnotic power and a stronger man might not have been coerced to do his bidding. I know now that he would have sunk his fangs into my neck and drained me if he had been in any condition to do so. But he could only rely on his mental power. He convinced me to get him blood at any cost, and I am ashamed to say that I did not tell him no. I was a weak man Natalya, and possessed of weaker honor than I am now.

"After that encounter, I went back into town with blackness in my heart. When I left the vampire the control he had over my mind also left, but my cruelty did not. I persuaded an elderly man to come with me, and we trekked to the castle. He did not know what I intended to do to him. When we reached the castle I took him into the dungeon by force, and once again felt the vampire's voice in my head.

"In the presence of the corpse, I lashed out and with a single strike to the head the old man was knocked unconscious. I brought him to the nearly dead vampire, and he lowered his fangs to the man's neck and drank deeply. When he was done the man lay on the floor dead and the blood gave him enough strength to escape his bonds and remove the stake from his chest. I was immediately consumed with regret at what I had done. I fled the castle, and Arkadith did not hunt me down. I do not know if it was out of weakness or for twisted gratitude for what I had done for him, but I escaped into the woods. The transformation was…horrible. The werewolves found me, starving and changed. I've been with the Greater Pack ever since."

"But that wasn't all your fault! Arkadith has immense hypnotic power and you couldn't help that."

Voren shrugged, the movement weighed down by resignation to his fate. "A curse is still a curse, unfortunately. Goddess Zulae must have believed that I could have overcome his voice in my head."

"But if that is how you became a werewolf…how did the all the others become them as well?"

"We are all cursed, in our own ways. Some of us have done something to become the creatures that we are. Whether it was a horrendous mistake as mine was, or betraying a family member in great need, we are all alike. Some of us have repented and seek to end our curse. Even our children are damned, for Zulae has cursed us to down to the last descendent for our father's sins. Others though, like the three back in Claw Haven, have succumbed to their evil natures and have no intentions of redemption. I will not mourn their deaths like I would of a member of my pack."

He finished speaking, and Natalya got the sense that he had been waiting a long time to explain this to someone. The revelation that they too, worshipped Zulae, had come as a shock, although she knew it probably should not have. After all, had not all of them started off as citizens of Valwood as well?

"I understand now," she said softly, and it was true. She saw Voren not just as a cursed werewolf, but almost a human who was as every bit flawed as she was. He began talking again, and Natalya leaned forward until she was nearly touching him. She looked up at his rugged and untamed countenance and no longer saw the feral nature of the werewolf. She leaned into him slightly, and he did not resist her embrace. For a while they sat in silence under the black night until the stars began to fade.

"Dawn approaches. I must get you back before anyone notices," Voren said at last, reluctantly relinquishing his hold. Natalya nodded and followed him back to the solitude that waited in her teepee and fell into a scant few hours of sleep.

The morning sun brought welcoming warmth onto Natalya's face, and her eyes fluttered under closed lids. Her dreams faded into nothingness as she lay peacefully. Then the memories of last night flooded in her mind. She jerked upright, her eyes flying open. Running barefoot in the moonlit forest, Voren ahead of her, his golden eyes, his brutal transformation and the murderous skeletal wolf— the images all flashed in front of her, and she knew she had not dreamed any of it. For a while, she lay under the rising sun, watching the clouds through the opening at the top of her teepee, thinking intently.

All of these years she had never known. Her lids closed into darkness and in her mind's eye she could envision the pack running in front of her. In essence, they were true wolves with flashing amber eyes and pink tongues that lolled from open mouths. Their fur shined in the sun, not uniformly grey, but every shade of white and silver. Their muscles gathered and released into bounding leaps that propelled them gracefully through the trees. They were beautiful to behold, and Natalya mentally savored the traditional image of the wolves she had held in her head.

In slow motion, the wolves ran, their paws outstretched as they leapt forward and as they landed they began to change horribly. Their jaws parted, revealing sun bleached fangs as the fur melted from their skulls, exposing the bone. Their hair rolled from their sleek bodies in clumps, leaving bare patches of stormy gray skin. Ribs jutted from their emaciated bodies as the fat shrank from their bones. Their eyes were the last to change though; foggy tendrils radiated from their pupils until the entire socket was clouded over in glowing white. The werewolves in Natalya's mind stopped their running and turned their unfeeling gazes onto her, and she gasped aloud. The image shattered, and she sat alone, shaking in her teepee.

The hours passed and still she did not venture outside of the dwelling. It was nearly dusk when she heard her name questioned in her head.

Natalya? The voice growled, and she recognized Tovu's voice. She parted the cloth to the teepee and stepped outside to see the werewolf waiting just outside. His cloudy eyes were spinning almost quizzically, and a dead rabbit was dangling from his mouth. She was so happy to see him with his white eyes and furry face that she nearly threw her arms around his neck. She resisted the urge though and hung back while the werewolf surveyed her curiously.

Is everything alright? he asked, and she shook her head. The werewolf narrowed his eyes at her, and she knew he was not convinced. He shook his shaggy head ruefully and glanced wistfully at the path leading into the woods, while the rabbit's ears were dragged through the dirt.

I brought you some meat. Why don't you start a fire and then tell me what is on your mind? Some of the others forget that you still must eat to live so you will have to excuse them, he growled with the slightest spark of humor in her head. He dropped the carcass and nudged it nearer to her.

"Thank you," Natalya said. "But you did not have to hunt for me."

You are our guest here, Natalya. It was an honor, he replied. She started a fire and began gathering kindling while the werewolf stood watch. She picked up the carcass and fished out a hunting knife from her teepee. She sat on a log bench outside and began skinning the rabbit, starting at its head. She finished the task quickly, and by the time she had finished, the roaring fire was ready. She offered the pelt to Tovu, and he accepted, dipping his head to her in thanks. Natalya smiled back, knowing one of the female werewolves would find a use for it.

The rabbit cooked on a wooden rack above the fire, and as the flesh began to cook, releasing delicious odors into the air, Tovu strained forward on his legs. He stretched as far toward it as he could without stepping closer, his nose quivering as he inhaled the scent.

"What is it Tovu?" Natalya asked and she swore the werewolf sighed.

It has been decades…and decades since I have tasted succulent meat, he growled longingly. When Natalya still looked confused he continued. *Alas it is part of our curse. That wonderful and nutritious food to you would start to dissolve to nothingness on my tongue. But for now I can smell it,* and he settled back to the earth, his tail swept over his paws. His eyes never left the rabbit, and Natalya was suddenly overcome with pity.

Tovu waited until the meat was ready and Natalya had begun eating to raise his question again.

Now what is bothering you Natalya? She looked at Tovu and then thought back to Voren. She could not merge the two werewolves; good natured, intuitive Tovu with the beast she had seen last night, and she could only shake her head again, at a loss for words.

Your expression betrays you. Something is amiss.

"It's nothing…," she started to say and Tovu had caught her eye again. His face was steady with need to understand her and she looked back at him, this creature that had shared so much of himself with her. She knew then she wanted to confide in him and so she began to speak.

"It's just that…I'm glad it is no longer a new moon." Tovu sighed and closed his eyes and Natalya could see him connecting the dots in his head. He padded to where she was sitting and settled on his haunches next to the bench and looked at her.

He showed you the true form, didn't he? Natalya nodded. *I would not have wished for you to see any of us like that. Least of all Voren. But what is done is done.*

"It was terrible, Tovu. He wasn't himself. It was as if he didn't even know who I was anymore."

No…I am sure that he did not. Under a new moon's influence we are closer to Death than we are to Life. Our bodies follow the cycles of the moon, waxing and waning with her. And when she is at her fullest power so too are we. And in her absence…we are terrible to behold. The moon rules us, and we all must answer to her light and our true natures. This is not the life any of us would have wanted if we had a choice.

"What do you mean?"

We werewolves hover on the verge between life and death. We are not truly dead, so we do not age or die of natural causes. Like vampires, we are unaffected by poisons, toxins or any of the number of gases that easily destroy your kind. We will heal from most traumas as long as our heads and hearts remain intact, but this is where the similarities end. We are so unlike vampires who must replenish their immortal bodies with sleep and blood. He looked again at the rabbit that Natalya was eating.

We do not consume plant or flesh of any kind. We lead a truer life then they, for we do not sleep when our minds cannot

87

rest, do not feed when it offers our dead bodies no nourishment. Although no method of strangulation could harm us, we do breathe as one if only to keep in tune with nature. No breath rises from a vampire's chest unless he has just fed. Their existence is an illusion, for they pretend to live when they are deader than we.

Natalya nodded as she listened, for she had been imbibed with much of this information regarding vampires already during her and Anesa's own studying. The werewolf continued.

And though we do not grow older, our bodies undergo transformations like that of the Mother Moon. When she is full, we are closest to Zulae, and we are also at our strongest. The faintest flickering of light and color awaken in our fur and eyes and we are often mistaken for true wolves. Our fur is at its most robust and never are we closer to life. It calls to us, and we can almost howl back to it.

Natalya remembered the running wolves from her vision.

"Beautiful," she murmured aloud, though Tovu continued as if she hadn't spoken.

And when she is new and unseen, our hold on the Earth fades. All of our color drains leaving a solid gray and our eyes cease to glow. Our fur falls off in clumps until we are very near skeletal and a terrible sight to behold. Here we are at our most vulnerable, for Death calls us now, and she holds a terrible sway upon us. It is truly a cursed existence, Natalya.

"Some of our people, they see your strength and your wolf forms, and they envy your kind for it."

Tovu turned his head sharply to look at her and there was anger in his eyes.

Foolish humans, he growled scornfully. *Always thinking they know what they want. But what do they really know of the world? Tell me, Natalya, do you think I would have chosen this fate for myself had I known what was to become of me? Would I have chosen to watch my family, friends and everyone I had ever known die one by one and cross into the next life without ever being able to follow them? No…that I cannot fathom. How anyone could envy this existence.*

I remember when the wolf was revered for her fierce loyalty and her songs. It was once said the mysteries of the world could be deciphered in a wolf's howl if you only listened hard enough. Now Valwood has turned from Zulae even as their prayers fall from their lying lips! But we are not so different, you and I.

"Tovu what happens when a werewolf dies?" Natalya asked.

That is a mystery that none know the answer to. Some of us long for death for only it holds some promise that our curse can be broken. Goddess Zulae is a vengeful god and many believe that because she has cursed every one of us and our descendants she will also shun us in the afterlife. For that reason alone, we fear our death for what comes after could very well be worse than what we endure here. And that is why some of us fear battle with the humans.

"But perhaps my father and the others could be persuaded to end the war before it starts. That is where we should place our hopes." Natalya questioned whether or not she believed her own words. She had been hesitant from trying to convince her father of the truth in Valwood, and his hatred for the werewolves seemed to be consuming him.

Let me tell you something, Natalya. She listened without speaking as Tovu continued. *No matter what may happen, treasure your time here on Earth, for you never know when it may be the end. For us, time passes slowly and still we age, waiting for a death that never comes and seeking answers to questions that can never be unraveled. It is tiring, the life of an immortal, and I am tired. To do something horrible, it has its price. And we are still*

89

paying for our mistakes. Do not let your people do the same.
Remember us, Natalya.

~ Part II ~

~ Chapter Nine ~
The Brink of War

Like ghosts, the two werewolves streaked through the trees. They headed towards the Valwood border, their lithe bodies seemingly floating above the ground. They slowed only after they had passed through the gate, fading into the forest as ethereally as any true wolves. Only their eyes exposed them for what they truly were, the cloudy whites casting twin flares of light that glowed slightly within the forest. Their ears rotated above them, straining to hear every noise while their noses pulled in every scent, sifting through them for signs of the humans.

The two scouts were formidable males, chosen for their imposing size and keen senses. They had waited for the full moon to disguise them as true wolves, and now they wandered along the tree line on opposite sides, staying just out of sight of the watchtowers that ringed the perimeter of the forest. The buildings stood dark and undisturbed in the distance while the majority of Valwood slept. Only the flickering firelight from the towers gave life to the night, and the muffled voices from them came easily to the werewolves' ears.

They listened intently to them speak, though the late night musings of the Watchmen held no interest to the werewolves. Their talk was unfettered by the fear or apprehension one would expect before a war, so the werewolves focused their attention elsewhere.

For several minutes, they continued along their chosen trails, noses to the ground sniffing intently. Finally one of them looked up. He stood rigid; only his nose quivered as an unfamiliar scent entwined itself around him.

What is it? The other werewolf asked, snorting in distaste at the intruding scent.

I'm not sure, he answered back. *Something powerful.*

The hairs along their backs involuntarily rose and their senses slashed through the night. They were instantly alert for any threat to reveal itself, but as the night lightened, their fears gradually began to abate. Only a man could be seen in the distance, wrapped in midnight fog, but the darkness concealed the werewolves as well. He had come alone; no other human scents intermingled with his. He walked with purpose towards them but without any sign that he had sighted them. The werewolves watched warily through the trees as he passed under the full moon's light, a man turned silver. He approached them, carrying what appeared to be a long metal staff, though he did not wield it as one.

The night was abruptly split by a deafening crack as fog and smoke integrated. A horrible keening cry could be heard through the din, and a mixture of sulfur and metal scents lingered in the air. One of the werewolves lay on his side, bleeding from a wound in his flank.

Two more shots sounded as the other werewolf rushed at the man, but the projectiles whizzed harmlessly past him. He flung himself at the human with such viciousness that the weapon had flown from his hands and landed in the grass beside them. The man fell to the forest floor, and the second werewolf buried his fangs into his throat as he hit the ground. He continued his bloody work, ripping and tearing with his fangs until he was sure the man would never rise again.

With that done, he was at the other werewolf's side, nudging him with his snout, urging him to stand. He could see the wound clearly now— a bloody trail that was laced with tendrils of liquid silver. The wound was not closing as it should have been, and the werewolf whined in pain as his flesh was slowly being eaten away before their eyes.

The werewolves began to flee, the injured one slowly and laboriously at first as the pain nearly overtook him, then faster as they neared the camp, fleeing from the first deadly strike the humans had mounted upon them.

The sun had not fully risen when Natalya found herself before Anraq once more. She had been roused from her tent by Tovu and herded towards the center of the forest along with the other werewolves. Palpable tension hung in the air as they all gathered around the main teepee. Anraq stood at its entrance talking somberly to what she assumed were other high ranking werewolves, although she could not make out the words. Occasionally one of them shot a glance at her, but for the time being she was ignored.

A pang of fresh anxiety shot through Natalya as she waited for to hear Anraq speak. She was not confined by chain or bonds though the ring of werewolves prevented her escape. She knew her future was completely dependent on Anraq's verdict, but she no longer entertained the notion of running. She had come this far, and no matter the outcome, she was determined to see her mission through.

She scoured the ring of werewolves for Voren, but without any discerning features, they were all identical to her. Much of the crowd was still in human form, but even these were absent of Voren. She could hear them talking quietly amongst themselves as she tried to locate him. She was not surprised that she could not find him. Ever since the night of the new moon she sensed he was avoiding her, and she could not help but feel a pang of sadness at his absence.

All at once the talking died down, and the circle of werewolves parted to allow for two others to join. They were strong men, both dragging something along the ground. Natalya moved as close to it as the crowd would allow, and she could see a third werewolf, still in wolf form and unconscious. He lay on a makeshift stretcher of animal skins and two parallel sticks that each of the men held. A hush fell over the werewolves as a fourth man joined them, carrying a bundle of herbs. He whispered urgently to Anraq before coming to rest in the center in the clearing. Anraq took his place in the center and he addressed them all.

"Werewolves of my clan! Today we face a danger greater than any we have ever faced before. The humans of Valwood bring a weapon of the likes that no one before has ever seen. Latuk, what is your word?"

The man that had followed with the herbs now stepped up to speak. He looked older even then Anraq, fully dressed in furs

95

of the purest whites. Feathers from every kind of bird it seemed and pale blue beads hung from around his neck and wrists. A white pack hung from his middle, and from it he pulled out more herbs that he brought to the fallen werewolf.

Natalya could see the wound now, a livid red hole that yawned from the werewolf's hind leg. Blood still soaked the leg around it, and the werewolf shivered in his sleep.

"This wound has defied all of my efforts to heal it. Not even his immortality has saved him yet. I fear this new weapon may be fatal to our kind."

No one in the circle made a sound now and all heads turned to look at Anraq for assurance. He in turn addressed one of the men that was carrying the stretcher.

"Hotah, what has become of the man that has done this to Kivah?"

The darker haired of the two let go of Kivah's stretcher to speak now to the crowd.

"We scouted the border of Valwood just as you asked. We neither scented nor heard anything unusual until we saw a human carrying the stick-like weapon. He did not strike with it like a sword, nor did he throw it at us like a spear. We saw nothing through the sulfur smoke but heard a deafening noise. Then Kivah was lying in the dirt, bleeding from this cursed wound. I attacked the man and heard the sound again but I did not bleed. The man however, will attack us no more. I made sure of that." Hotah's last words turned to an angry growl and he spit on the ground.

Cold dread flooded Natalya. *Could she have been too late? Had her father's rash actions already cost him his life?*

"What did this man look like?" she interrupted, fighting to keep her tone as light as possible. Hotah's hard eyes turned on her, and she returned the look as dispassionately as she could.

"He was a blonde haired, blue eyed man," Hotah said dismissively, his eyes snapping back to the Alpha. Natalya exhaled deeply in relief that was mingled with sorrow. *Not her father. But who? Had she known him, spoken to him, bought from him? Could he have been the carefree blonde that baked her favorite pastries? Or the kindly groom that tended to her father's gelding?* Her mind flew over the many possibilities and doubt began to take a hold of her. *Had she made the right decision in coming here?*

"What is done is done," Anraq said waving his hand. "The man has paid for our vengeance with his life, but I fear this act of retribution will fuel the humans' desire to hunt us from these woods. Natalya you must tell us everything you know. Hold nothing back."

Natalya bowed her head and began to speak, at first only to Anraq then with his encouragement to the rest of the werewolves. She found herself describing the gun and her own father's anticipation of ridding the world of werewolves. She too described the deafening noise that had exploded from it and how it had her covering her own ears.

"Silver," she murmured and at this she had the rapt attention of every werewolf. "The humans have fashioned this musket with projectile silver bullets. That is how Kivah has not healed. I do not wish to see us descend into war. My family's lives are at stake as much as yours are." She looked to Anraq when she said this, at his benevolent, almost fatherly expression. But lurking there too was the determination that hardened and lined it too; a steady willingness to do whatever it took to protect his clan. The werewolves muttered amongst themselves, but one voice rang clear above all others.

"We should kill this human girl now and every man that crosses that wall! We will not be forced from our home by mere humans!" Natalya looked to the source of the voice, and she locked eyes with one of the werewolves. He was in human form, a bronze skinned man with tousled brown hair and eyes that glinted with yellow eye shine. They were narrowed in Natalya's direction, and she met his glare with uncertainty. Some of the werewolves seemed to be nodding at his words. Natalya looked to Anraq to see how hard one voice could turn the tides against her favor. Anraq turned to address the discordant voice, his head held high.

"This girl comes to us in peace, Naktor."

"So she says! Would it not make our message clear to send her dear head on a stick back to her humans?" Naktor asked and the crowd seemed uncertain. Anraq cleared his throat and raised his voice so that each member of the pack could hear him clearly.

"Members of my Clan, hear me now! I understand the fear of death that this new weapon brings to us. To injure an immortal in this way has been unheard of until now. But we have no choice but to accept what Natalya has told us. We stand at the brink of war against the people of Valwood. Go from here now and begin making preparations to fight for our very survival. And may our fangs be sharp and our legs swift enough to defend ourselves from this threat."

For Natalya, time had lost its urgency as she spent more and more time with the werewolves. She felt more comfortable in their presence than she would have ever thought possible, although she made a point of avoiding Naktor. He had not raised any more objections after Anraq's speech, but Natalya stayed as close to Anraq and Tovu as possible. Under their steady protection she knew Naktor would not harm her, but he made his dislike of her clear with sneers and snarls whenever she passed by.

Being cut off from her own people made it seem as if her world had come to a standstill. Now, nothing seemed to exist outside of the great forest. Her longtime ignorance of Claw Haven had made it seem unreal in her mind, and it was now Valwood that held the faded quality of the unknown. Not once had she ever been taught of the rich culture, the shared religion or of the respect the werewolves afforded to all living things.

Still, worry for her people had grown to a clamoring within her, and she knew her time with the werewolves must come to an end. One man had already fallen. How many more would follow if she did not act? And so whilst she made her preparations to leave, the werewolves made theirs to fight.

All around her the camp was alight with change as they readied for battle. Adult males engaged in horrifying sparring matches in their wolf forms. It was these that Natalya could hardly stand to watch, for it seemed all of the savagery that her people had projected upon the werewolves seemed to be contained in these mock fights. With their claws they scored bloody lines down each other's flanks and with their fangs they ripped flesh from one another's bones, all healing as instantly as more blood was drawn. She could not help but imagine those same claws tearing through her father's body, and it made her shudder whenever she passed through the fighting ring.

The females too devoted themselves to testing their own muscles as well as burning incense sticks in the camp. They bowed their heads in prayer to Goddess Zulae whenever they did this, and Natalya watched them, fascinated. She wondered what fears, hopes or ambitions the immortals shared with the silent moon god.

The children in the camp played in large groups while their parents made preparations for the war. They fashioned toy spears and made up war games to go along with them. It was during one of these games that Natalya found herself talking with one of the werewolf children. He was a young boy, about nine, that could have passed for a human if not for the fine wolf hairs that trailed down his back. He grasped her blouse in one hand as she walked by and looked at her imploringly with eyes that held a slight tinge of yellow in the light.

"Natalya, will you fight against your people with us when the time comes?" he asked. Natalya smiled tenderly and shook her head.

"I cannot, for I care for both you and my father. And I've come to seek an end to the war, not fight in it. Your place is to protect your home here, mine is to continue what I've started. Vampires still slay our people in the night, and Valwood needs someone to protect it too."

"Indeed it does," she heard a voice behind her and she turned to see Anraq behind her, nodding approvingly. He was magnificently dressed in a long bearskin robe that stopped at his ankles. The deep browns and blacks of the fur complimented the blue feathers and beads that he wore around his neck perfectly. The boy bowed his head at the sight of the Alpha, and Natalya followed suit, blushing. Anraq looked down kindly at the child.

"Why don't you play with your sister?" he asked and the boy snapped his hand to his brow in a quick salute before dashing away to his teepee.

"I did not know you were there," Natalya said. The Alpha waved his hand and she knew it mattered not to him.

"Your time here is short now," he said wisely.

"Yes it is. I fear for Valwood, Anraq. So many things threaten our existence. I have to do what I can to avert the war before it happens and continue hunting the great vampire."

"It is a lot of responsibility for one person. And you feel more divided than any of us can even imagine. For you now owe your allegiance to both sides."

"Yes," she whispered.

"I know of whom you seek," Anraq said and he had her full attention now. "The Ancient One, Arkadith."

"Yes, his kind is the real cause of all this. If I can defeat him, my people will have no more reason to war with your clan."

"He is very powerful. He was turned very near the beginning and as he creates more vampires his power swells. You will need all of your strength and cunning when you face him."

Natalya nodded gravely and knocked an arrow into her bow. A distantly falling leaf spun towards them from the sky when she took aim. Without a moment's hesitation, she sent the arrow whistling through the air where it came to rest, quivering in the center of a nearby tree, the leaf pinned perfectly to its bark.

"I don't think you will have to worry about that," she said grimly as she went to retrieve her arrow.

~ Chapter Ten ~
Outrunning Fate

Onwards Natalya pushed the mare, her desperation lending speed to the horse's limbs. Although Methea's hooves barely brushed the earth as they flew above the ground, Natalya felt as if they were racing against the very bullets that shot from her father's gun. But as she neared Valwood, and her horse began to tire, she found herself reflecting on yesterday's events.

Her last night amongst the werewolves had been marked by a brilliant campfire that every member of the pack had attended. She could see all of their faces illuminated by the firelight, both wolf and human alike, young and old united in their curse. She had tearfully hugged Anraq, Tovu and Voren in turn and lamented that her time to get to know them had been so short. She realized that she had never even seen Tovu in his human form, nor Anraq in his wolf form. There was still so much about them and their ways that she did not know, but she had learned more of the truth than any human before her.

She had left immediately the next morning after speaking with the Alpha, and now the desperation of her mission urged her faster still towards home. She did not know how far her father had taken his plans in her absence, and she only hoped she would not be too late.

Methea had slowed to a loping canter, and Natalya allowed her to rest. The woods had lost their nighttime eeriness and now gleamed with every shade of gold and emerald under the daytime sun. They had made considerable time, and Natalya felt herself relax. They fell into a comfortable gait, and Natalya's mind began to wander. At this pace, they would be within the Valwood border by midnight.

An uneventful ride home was not to be though. As dusk fell, her skin began to tingle with unexpected warmth at her throat, and she saw that her amulet glowed bright red. Its glow was swallowed by the darkening forest, but her immediate surroundings were still cast in ruby light.

Natalya leaned upright in the saddle, scanning the trees for danger and listening intently. A doe was watching her warily from within the trees, her soulful eyes trained on Natalya's every move and her tail flicked upwards in warning. She stood frozen as Natalya and her horse passed; only her eyes followed horse and rider. Somewhere nearby an owl hooted, and the doe exploded away in a flurry of desperate motion from something unseen.

Natalya turned towards the source of the owl, but it was too late. Something collided painfully with her, and she was thrown from Methea with great force. She had struck the base of a large tree, and she could not muster the strength to rise. Vaguely, she heard her horse whinnying frantically though movement still escaped her. Slowly, she opened her eyes to see her horse rearing onto her hind legs and lashing out with her front hooves. She strained to see what had provoked her horse, and she could see a disturbance in the ground near her.

The fallen leaves that had littered the ground now began to shift and swirl upwards in a gust of wind that claimed no source. Before her eyes, the leaves drained of their color, the brilliant golds and reds receding into an unnatural black as a figure formed from the pillar of fronds. Her horse fled, and Natalya could not summon her voice to call out to her.

The vampire materialized before her, and Natalya knew his name even before he would ever utter it aloud to her. *Arkadith,* for no other immortal she had met before him had exuded such raw power. It emanated from his body in waves of touchable force, and Natalya reached for her stake, knowing she had never faced an enemy such as him.

He approached her with calm restraint, so unlike the others of his kind that attacked without thought and clawed at her throat with blind, thirsty abandon. Had he approached her mother in the same manner? Natalya was immediately disgusted, though she forced her face to stay neutral. His leisurely pace allowed Natalya time to study him as he approached her. He was at least a foot taller than her and dressed in a fitted black suit that was tailored perfectly to his form, over a white ruffled shirt that spilled out at his wrists and collar. His hair was jet black, but streaked and peppered with gray hairs that nearly dominated his head. He adorned himself with no pendants or staff, only a gold ring that lent a bit of color to his bland attire. She allowed her eyes to wander to his face, though she carefully avoided his eyes. She did not need to see them to know they were darkening; the pupils would be expanding over his irises any moment now as he prepared to feed. She knew too the hypnotic power of that black stare, and she did not wish to engage him in a mental struggle for survival.

His fangs glided over his lips, and he swept his tongue over them as if he could already taste her blood. His affliction hid his age well; he was devoid of wrinkles or flaws, and his wiry form still moved with the gracefulness of youth. Natalya did not know for sure how old he was, but she guessed around eight-hundred-years from his manner of dress.

He was almost upon her now, his face caught in the crimson glow of her amulet. She was close enough to feel his breath on her skin, and she struggled not to cough from the ashy scent of decaying flesh. From a distance, he had been handsome, seductive even. Only up close was he truly repulsive, and by the time any of his victims realized it, Natalya knew he was already feasting on their blood. Her amulet pulsed in warning, and he withdrew slightly, still smiling.

"So this is the great Natalya," he said, lacing each syllable with emphasis. His voice was deep and throbbed with ancient knowledge. "You have grown into a formidable threat. Though not formidable enough, I am afraid."

"Formidable enough to avenge my mother and kill you!" She did not care how he knew of her, nor why he was here now. Foolish confidence raged within her, and she lashed out with her stake, gouging it into his shoulder. She wrenched the stake from his flesh, knowing she had precious little time to recover her weapon. The attack had been seemingly unforeseen on his part, and he staggered backwards.

But he had recovered even faster than Natalya could have imagined. The wound rippled as it closed, and a moment later, it had sealed completely as he advanced on her again. They circled each other now, caught in a deadly dance of striking and retreating. She held her stake in front of her chest, protecting her center while she bitterly sought an opening to his.

Neither could gain power over the other; his agility and strength outmatched hers easily, and her amulet prevented him from delivering anything more than a glancing blow. Still, he managed to weaken her ever so slowly as smoke curled from his burning fingers. He hadn't made enough contact with her skin to damage him permanently, but she knew she would tire long before he would. She was panting now, her breath rolling from her mouth in ragged waves, while he deftly avoided her every move. She needed to kill him and *soon*.

He gained on her again, and this time she knew he meant to end this. She readied to strike him again, but instead she found her eyes drifting upwards toward his face without a mental command from her. She began walking towards him clumsily, as her legs slowly bent beneath her. She began to resist, at first only managing to slow his hypnotic power, then with all of her own mental fortitude, she wrenched her gaze from his. Her legs straightened, and at the same time, her arm buried her stake into his chest. For a moment his hold on her was released completely. She dropped to the ground, dizzy. The conflict of actions had left an unbearable pain in her head, and she struggled to bring him back into focus.

Arkadith was doubled over, the stake protruding from his torso. He appeared to be assessing the damage, and slowly the two enemies rose to face each other once more. A smile loomed dangerously on the vampire's lips, and Natalya knew the wound had not been fatal.

"It is funny," he murmured as the hole in his chest filled, forcing the stake from his flesh, and it fell to the ground, useless to Natalya now. There would be no way she could reach it before he did.

"What is funny?" she asked while drawing backwards. Her head was still cloudy, and now she relied solely on the power of her amulet to protect her.

"It is rather interesting that your mother once put a stake through my chest in almost that exact place. It is a shame that you both missed my beating heart! Now look into my eyes!" he commanded, and as Natalya's gaze shifted onto his and her vision blackened, she knew in that moment that he had been toying with her from the start.

He had let her strike him with her weapon, absorbed the damage her amulet and stake inflicted, even allowed her to spill some of his precious blood, and still she hadn't defeated him. Her heart pounded faster and faster until it thudded loudly in her ears, drowning out all other sounds. She touched upon the fear of the forever hunted, and felt the terror of a deer before the arrow. She did not have long to dwell on her predicament. Her thoughts emptied and placid indifference replaced the will to fight for her very survival.

Like a wilting flower, her body went pliant to his will; she was only vaguely aware of her hands unlatching her amulet. Force was no longer necessary; his thoughts directed her actions as easily as if the will had been her own. The necklace slipped from her fingers and seemed to fall in slow motion to the forest floor below. The owl swooped in, its legs outstretched to caught it before it fell. The bird disappeared into the horizon, her only protection from the vampire clasped in its talons.

Natalya's legs finally buckled beneath her, and Arkadith moved quickly to support her weight. With a grunt of effort, he lifted her into his arms, standing impressively against the light of the moon. Her head fell to the side, exposing the curves of her neck and Arkadith faltered slightly at the sight.

He could almost smell the blood running furiously just below her skin, and he resisted the urge to sate his never-ending thirst right then. His fangs slid involuntarily over his lips, and his power over her dimmed. Natalya groaned slightly and opened her eyes, but Arkadith had already mastered himself again. He sighed deeply, and his fangs receded while Natalya fell into the blissful unknowing of unconsciousness once more. He closed his black eyes and in a spiraling motion of shadow, he and the vampire huntress vanished.

~ Chapter Eleven ~
Imprisoned

The darkness was oppressive. The room that Natalya now found herself in was not lit; not even a sliver of yellow from the hallway could be seen under the oak door. She fumbled in the dark, rustling satin sheets that had been carefully tucked in around her the night before. Her fingers met with cool glass. It turned out to be an oil lamp that she lit with the matches she found underneath. The flame roared to life, chasing away the remnants of the dream that still hovered at the edges of her memory.

A window was latched tightly shut beside the bed, and when she tried to wrench it open, she found she could not. The door too was locked when Natalya tried it, and she climbed back onto the bed, resigned to remaining there until Arkadith would come. His unknown location in the house was an omnipresent cloud that lurked over her. She presumed he was sleeping in one of the other bedrooms, and it could be hours before he collected her. She shuddered at the thought.

He must have had a motive for keeping her here; death at his hand would have been swift last night had he wanted to deliver it. How long had she been in Claw Haven? Almost two weeks, it seemed. And how much time had passed since her capture? *One day, perhaps longer?* Her father would be frantic. She had never been away from home for this long. A peaceful resolution to the conflict between Claw Haven and Valwood had rested on her ability to reach her elders. With her capture, the war would be inevitable. She gathered the down blanket around herself. The black stitched detail was beautiful, as was the rest of the bedroom, but she was still a prisoner here. The thought banished any comfort she could gain from the comfortable bedding.

Her hands sought the stake she kept at her ribs, but of course that had been removed. Her neck too was absent of the soothing weight of the amulet. Not having her weapons made Natalya feel weak and powerless, and frustration welled at the surface of her mind. But frustration hindered movement and restricted thought, and Natalya needed to regain her composure.

She climbed out of the bed and crossed the room to the latched window and drew open the black curtains to look below. Her heart sank as she assessed the drop, much too great a height to jump. Breaking her way out of the window would not be an option.

She examined the door next, running her fingers along the wood. Experimentally, she threw her weight against its length but was unsurprised to find the barrier unyielding. Her eyes strayed to the iron hinges that held the door, and she eyed them for weaknesses. Finding nothing by sight, she turned to the rest of the room, now in search of something to pry open the door. Her gaze fell upon the pokers that leaned against the fireplace. They seemed narrow enough to fit. Natalya grabbed one and placed it between the stone wall and the door and pulled as hard as she could. Her muscles strained with the effort and she gritted her teeth but the door did not budge. She switched to pushing, hoping to gain more leverage, but still the hinges held true.

Sweat had begun to gather at her brow, and she wiped it away impatiently. She continued to try until her muscles gave out, and she threw the poker away from her, defeated. It clattered heavily onto the floor, and she froze, fearing she may have awakened Arkadith. A few minutes passed uneventfully, and she returned to the door, this time to study the lock. It was a simple mechanism, but she would have to find an object suitable for picking it. The vanity that had attracted none of her interest before now held a plethora of possibilities for her escape.

Its top was bare except for the mirror that curved elegantly towards the ceiling. The wood had been crafted beautifully. She rummaged through the drawers finding only a hairbrush and assorted makeup. Her hands closed around the last handle, and she opened it, gasping in elation. Inside were multiple hairpins of differing sizes and fashions, and she eagerly scooped them up. She carried them to the bedroom door and began inserting them one at a time into the lock. She twisted each one, listening for the tumblers. Finally, one of the pins shifted within, and she heard the satisfying click as the door swung ajar.

"Yes," she hissed quietly in the darkness. Her instant jubilation was now tempered by the harrowing journey through the castle that still awaited her. She did not know how much time her escape from the room had taken, and she hoped that Arkadith would still be sleeping. *If he slept in the day at all,* she thought sorely.

Her fingers dragged against the wall as she crept along the hallway. She passed many more lamps enclosed within sconces, but she dared not light any of them. She found the edge of a banister and began the slow descent into the belly of the castle.

The staircase curved grandly to her left, and she stood up slightly as the downstairs came into view. The lower floor was brightly illuminated by torchlight. Dread began pooling in Natalya's stomach. Something was wrong.

All of the years hunting down vampires had honed her natural instincts and sharpened her senses. But in the castle her role as huntress was reversed. She was a fly, enclosed inside a giant Venus fly trap, and she buzzed helplessly within its walls waiting to be devoured. Desperation to avert the war and protect her loved ones lent her body bravery when she could not summon it herself. She shook her head, her thoughts dissipating. She froze like a startled hare against the walls, angled on the stairs so she could watch without being seen.

She could hear no movement, not a rustle of cloth nor footsteps over carpeted stone. When her eyes caught nothing either, she resumed her venture downstairs. She approached a long splendid dining room table and gasped.

Arkadith sat at its head at the far end of the room, surveying her. He seemed almost bored.

"It took you a while to come out of your room, child. I am almost disappointed."

"Why are you keeping me here?" she demanded.

"Come now," he replied smoothly. "One does not talk to an honorable host in that manner, you should know that. Sit down, Natalya."

"How do you know my name?"

"Owls are *fascinating* creatures. They can see for miles and can hear across great distances. And when they swoop in for the kill, the air flows silently over their wings."

He took a long sip from the glass of red wine before him, peering at her over the rim.

"Stop speaking to me in cryptic riddles and explain yourself plainly."

He merely chuckled, and motioned towards one of the seats along the table. "Sit," he repeated.

"No."

"My patience wears thin, child. It will not go well for you to disobey me again."

Natalya settled herself into the crimson colored seat farthest from his, at the tables opposite. It was an armchair made of the finest velvet that rose gracefully above her. *Elegant,* she thought, like the rest of his castle. It was furnished in lush purples and reds and blacks but surprisingly *normal* with a somewhat gothic influence.

Arkadith gazed at her intently but curiously from the other side of the table, his fingers interlocked beneath his chin. In spite of everything, she was fascinated, drawn to the thing her heart most hated. His skin was flushed from having recently fed and she suppressed a shudder. Unconsciously, she reached a finger to her neck and traced it downwards but she could feel no wound. He must have fed while she slept. She lowered her trembling hand, cursing herself for allowing her fear to show. It had now given way to rage, but she directed it more towards herself and her own vulnerability than the soulless creature that sat before her. She glanced at Arkadith, disgusted by the way his eyes mocked her, savoring her helplessness. He picked up a small bell from the table and shook it, sending a pleasant tinkling throughout the room. Natalya looked up to see an old woman, her spine bent forward with age, bearing a tray with more wine. She was dressed in a gown that had once been a rich blue but was now faded and moth eaten. The chemise that spilled out underneath was similarly off-white.

She hurried to Natalya, not making eye contact, and began pouring the bottles' contents into a crystal glass. Her hands shook visibly, but she did not spill. The woman smiled toothlessly at Natalya, her eyes fixed at the young girl's chin, and Natalya was horrified to see her neck. The exposed skin was wrinkled and creased as expected, but was interlaid with bruises and fang marks. Dried blood had congealed over the many punctures that overlapped each other, giving her neck an unusual red sheen.

"Th-thank you," Natalya said shakily and the woman nodded, unconcerned with Natalya's staring. She bowed slightly in response and bustled from the room as quickly as her arthritic legs would allow.

"I thought I'd invite you to dine with me" he said, inclining his head politely.

"That was very *thoughtful* of you," Natalya replied, her voice dripping with undisguised sarcasm. A flicker of anger flashed in his eyes, but the next moment it had disappeared. He took a long sip of his red wine and motioned for her to do the same.

"Since we are on speaking terms, I thought you and I should get to know each other a bit better, especially since you will be here for quite a while. How do you like your new…*arrangements?*" he asked, watching for her reaction. She didn't flinch. She wanted answers, but she wasn't fooled. *He was merely playing with his food. So, she could play along.* She thought for a time before answering.

"I love my new room," she said sarcastically. She then started to laugh, almost hysterically, struggling to get her words out. "It almost feels as if I'm not a prisoner in your lovely home!"

The vampire laughed too, but it did not reach his cold eyes, and he stopped rather abruptly before turning serious again.

"Is there nothing you would ask of me? Anything you would desire to know about me or my kind?"

She stopped laughing and rearranged her features in a questioning manner. She did not miss the opportunity.

"Tell me then, how are you drinking that wine? Do you thirst for more than blood?"

He took his time in answering, and for some reason he seemed genuinely impressed by the question. "We gain nothing from your food; we cannot even taste it, but we do have a certain….fondness for some things. Besides being red, this wine reminds me of a time long past….before I was turned."

Natalya expected some sort of sadness, or even a sign of remembrance on his face, but he spoke in a flat monotone. His voice did not falter with even a trace of wistfulness or emotion. It made her at once angry, but Arkadith did not seem to notice.

"How is your food, Natalya?"

She looked down, almost in surprise, for she hadn't really tasted it herself. The choice cuts of steak she had so eagerly devoured had usually only been reserved for the elders of Valwood. Even being the daughter of one, she could only remember a few meals like this in her entire lifetime. The vegetables too were seasoned with garlic and salt, and even a few flavors she did not recognize. She raised her eyes to his, finally taking a drink of her wine. It also had exquisite taste.

"It is fine," she said, not wanting to give him satisfaction in the knowledge that it had been among the best meals she had ever had.

"I must know though….how does it feel drinking the blood of an innocent human? If the wine alone provides so many fond memories, that is." At this his face darkened, and Natalya knew she had crossed the line in her bid to play with fire. His face twisted in insulted rage.

"*Innocent*? Tell me human, who among you is *innocent*? *Who among you* has not destroyed without need or hurt without pity? Should a lion ponder his role in thinning the herds? Does he question whether or not he is doing the right thing as he tears into a zebra's flesh?" he snarled. His next words were slow and measured, and more to himself than to Natalya. "No….he knows only that he has teeth and claws….and an insatiable lust for blood." He hesitated, reminiscing before continuing.

"But it is most different. When you humans see your food, you can resist it and enjoy it at your leisure, and when it is gone your thoughts are free to wander. It is not so with us. Our thirst is an obsession that never leaves us. It is always there, just below the surface of our minds, tempting us. When we scent it, nothing else exists. And when we finally do drink it is…." he paused, searching for the right word. "*Euphoric.*"

She looked up to see him running his eyes up and down her neck, his expression hungry, and fear flooded through her.

"Ahh but I've already fed enough this night. You needn't worry about me just yet." He grinned, revealing his canines. Natalya's insides twisted uncomfortably as she remembered the old woman. She thought of Arkadith's latest bite on her neck, the blood mixing with the old and dried with no one to wash it away. Then she imagined Arkadith at her own back, his fangs brushing against her skin, and this time she could not restrain her shudder as it flowed down her revolted body. She closed her eyes at the phantom pain that his fangs would deliver when they pierced her

116

neck. She felt her hopeful blood welling at the surface of her skin, pooling feverishly at its attempt to break free of its vessel.

Her eyes snapped open. *This was not the way it was supposed to be.* She needed to understand him better, his weaknesses and his strengths, if she were to someday defeat him. One thing was clear: he was confident, and he readily divulged any information that she asked of him. He seemed so sure of his victory over her. But wasn't he right? She was no threat without her amulet or her stakes.

"If you intend on draining me why not just do it and end this? Why keep me here?" She demanded bitterly, unable to disguise her fear anymore, and the effect her words had on his mood was instantaneous. He was instantly upright, and advanced upon her.

"Do not trifle with me *human,*" he growled, his face twisted with malice. "You think you are better than me? You, who have killed many of my fledglings, and you dare ask me this? You shall pay!" He grabbed her wrists, wrenching them upwards and threw her away from him with such force that she was knocked to the ground. Winded, she gingerly pushed herself upright as he shook from the rage that threatened to consume him. The next moment, she gathered herself and ran to her room and he did not follow.

~ Chapter Twelve ~
In the Midst of Enemies

The light of the following dawn had brought all of the forces that Valwood could summon, and now two hundred and fifty odd men stood at Claw Haven's border.

The men marched warily through the gate, past the open-mouthed werewolf skull. One of the men tore it from its hangings and threw it unceremoniously to the ground where it was trampled, its sightless eyes staring blankly into their ranks.

A cold longing to avenge their dead unified them and drove them forward, combating the numbing loss that threatened to still their footsteps. They traveled deeper into Claw Haven, spreading out into a throng against the edges of the wall, keeping the walls at their vulnerable backs.

Only a quarter of the men carried muskets; the rest of the men wielded whatever weapons they could get a hold of. They each held their weapons with varying degrees of confidence, with most of the men gravely unused to the turmoil of war. The elders were the exception; they and their horses were at the head of the throng, leading with trained purpose, and eyes that narrowed into determined slits. The center most elder was Natalya's father.

Elder Greg surveyed the forest before him from atop his own bay gelding, his face set. His gun was primed and loaded, cocked to fire at the slightest whim, while his hands shook with uncertainty. It was clear to him now in speaking to those that had seen her leave and his following of her trail that Natalya had been taken by the werewolves. Her and her mare's disappearance fell in line with the taking of the two watchmen and Anesa, and the direction she had taken had been straight into these very woods. *Why*, he could not fathom, but he knew she would not have gone freely. She knew the oldest law, knew that crossing the wall willingly would mean her death, either by werewolf or by her own people.

Natalya's death. Even now he was unable to voice that terrible possibility. He cleared it from his thoughts, lest he succumb to the despair that clawed at the dark corners of his mind. He *would* find Natalya and bring her home.

Night began to fall. The first day in enemy territory had been spent making camp and planning their initial strikes. Scouting, gathering firewood and guarding duties had been delegated, and the elders on horseback had circled the men on foot, distributing water in canteens and murmuring words of encouragement.

Both men and horse were restless in the stillness before battle. The men told somber stories of past battles with other villages while the horses chewed on their bits and sent furls of steam into the air from their noses. Anxiously, the men watched as the sun died and the moon brightened overhead. Their eyes fought the blinding darkness and the sleep that pulled at the corners of their eyelids.

A fire had been lighted, and the men gathered around its warmth. Some of them were excited at the prospect of battle, but others dared not voice their reservations. The forest danced behind the firelight sending deceptive silhouettes through the camp. The glowing embers became the light that flickered from within the eyes of the werewolves, and the shadows took on their limber forms. As the fire began to die and the men struggled to stay alert, they knew the werewolves were somewhere just beyond the trees, about to awaken and meet them in war. All that remained now was to wait.

Hotah had never seen this many human men gathered in one area. His eyes glowed through the gaps of the trees as he watched them pass through the entrance of the wall one by one.

Their air of hatred was palpable in the wind; he could scent their anger as well as the slight tendrils of fear that wafted towards his hungry nostrils. He could not stop his hackles from rising defensively, and his muscles quavered with the urge to report back to Anraq. The werewolf ran back towards Claw Haven, kicking up a spray of dirt as he turned. The subtle movement had caught the eye of one of the men, and he fired a bullet at the fleeing beast. The crack exploded in his ears as the bullet, infused with silver, sliced through the air. The shot buried itself in the flesh of his front leg with devastating effect. A yelp tore from his throat, and the werewolf collapsed painfully to the ground. Steam hissed upwards from the ruined leg as the fallen werewolf turned to lick the wound. His blood, twined with coils of liquid silver, seeped heavily from the hole and already blended into the dirt.

Hotah struggled to rise, but the ravaged leg collapsed uselessly under his weight. He panted in torn breaths, exhausted from the effort. His immortal body struggled to close the wound, to push the silver from his body, but the bullet refused to yield to common flesh and bone.

A slight pounding of the earth came to Hotah's ears, and they rose to meet the sound. Four men on horseback were pursuing him, and the werewolf keened softly in his solitude. The riders swiftly approached him now. He did not have much time. He dragged himself into the cover of the trees as much as his injured hind leg would allow, but he could not flee far.

The wound was not fatal, but there was no time for him to rest and heal. The horses skidded to a stop as the stench of blood, sulfur and silver hung heavily in the air. They whinnied shrilly; rearing up on on their hind legs as their riders loudly urged them forward.

Hotah drew himself even more tightly within his hiding place, ears pressed against his skull, and his tail tucked into the curve of his body. He could see the men by the light of the lanterns they held, as they swept them into every nook and corner of the forest trying to pinpoint his location. They circled the area, one nearly trampling the werewolf in the bushes, before moving off again. For a moment Hotah exhaled in relief before he realized the two men were headed straight towards Claw Haven's center. His kind was strong, but they had never faced a weapon of this kind before. *How many bullets could the four men fire, and how many werewolves could their guns slay with no one to aid them?* Hotah watched the forest swallow his enemies, and he growled sadly to himself. Shakily, he stood again, his powerful form tempered by the pain in his leg. It shook uncontrollably, but he was up, drawing himself to his full height. His white eyes glowed majestically and unfaltering loyalty gave him courage.

He lifted his head towards the skies and began to howl. It was not a hunting cry, nor was it a deathly lament. It was a warning that his voice gave wings to, and it travelled to the heart of Claw Haven. The sound was like a wailing siren that warned every werewolf of the impending and inevitable danger. It contained all of Hotah's desperation and his last feverish attempt to rouse his kind into defensive action. The magnificent howl tapered off into a low moan as it finished, and Hotah listened intently. The men on horseback whirled into his direction as he had predicted, and he rose to meet them. He stood in the open, his position clear. They charged at him now and chased away any notion that the werewolf might have had about fleeing.

The horses slowed as they came upon him, and the lead man dismounted while his companions kept their muskets trained on the cornered werewolf. He growled defiantly as they circled him, his head swaying back and forth to keep them all in his sight. He backed into the surrounding bushes as far as they would allow, his tail swishing uneasily behind him.

"So this is the werewolf of legend," one of the men said. "He is nothing more than an abomination before Zulae."

"A filthy beast that could never survive in a civilized society," another agreed. He gathered all of the saliva his mouth could hold and hawked it onto Hotah's muzzle and settled himself haughtily into his saddle, his musket resting in his lap.

"He probably cannot even understand a word we are saying," one of the other men said. He began to laugh, and the other three joined in.

Hotah shook his great hide, spattering the saliva into the dirt. His eyes glowed with anger, and the men stopped laughing immediately at the shift in the werewolf's gaze.

It is your kind that is the beast, he snarled within each of their heads. Shock surged through the men's bodies as he addressed them so. They recovered quickly though, and tightened their grips on their weapons, preparing to fire.

"The *beast* who has taken Natalya and gorged himself on the bones of our men now dares to face our wrath," one of the men answered.

Neither I, nor any of my kind, have done any such thing, Hotah growled.

"Lies! All it tells are lies!" Before the werewolf could react the lead man had pulled the trigger of his musket, and it exploded into violent fury, propelling a second bullet into Hotah's chest. His heart shuddered and collapsed with the impact, and the werewolf fell once more.

His milky eyes closed, and his tail unfurled sadly as all of the blood in his body trained out into the earth below him.

The lead man, sobered by what he had just done, backed away from the scene and pulled himself back into the saddle.

"Let's go," he muttered, "For next we shall bring the hounds." He signaled for the men to follow, before digging his heel into the flank of his horse. The men began to ride back towards the camp. Their pounding hoof beats receded into the coming night, leaving Hotah's body to the wind and the falling leaves.

There would be no escaping this time. The heavy door to Natalya's room had been fitted with a crossbar and her window reinforced with a pad lock, even though its height from the ground had served as deterrent enough from jumping. She paced along the length of the room, planning furiously. She no longer rummaged through the dresser or the fireplace; her room had long since been thoroughly plundered of its secret holdings, and no item could lend itself to her escape.

The vampire left her alone, and this was perhaps more chilling than her encounter with him. In their battle, her blood had been laced with adrenaline that had blocked her fear and given strength to her attack. Here, in this empty dark room, the gravity of her situation settled all around her. The walls throbbed along with her own fears, at times seeming to draw in tighter, closing her in.

A resounding knocking that reverberated through her room's walls awoke Natalya from her contemplation. She stopped her pacing and crossed to the fireplace, keeping her eyes on the door as the sound grew more insistent. She looked for something to defend herself with as she heard the crossbar being lowered from the other side. She drew one of the fire pokers and brandished it outward like a sword. She called out to come in.

She had been expecting Arkadith himself, not the old woman that had poured her wine with the bloodied throat. She bustled in with a covered tray and a new bottle of Sherry. Natalya lowered the poker, feeling a bit foolish. She did not drop the weapon though; she mistrusted this stranger just as much as she did Arkadith.

The woman did not seem to know how close she had been to being run through with the poker. She hurried to serve the meal: an exotic looking meat with a generous portion of fresh vegetables that were laden in a sweet smelling sauce. Natalya was again surprised. She did not expect to be served such fares as a prisoner. This meal was completely foreign to her and would have probably cost her father a month's wages. Her stomach rumbled involuntarily, and Natalya suppressed her hunger. She viewed the dish with suspicion and instead climbed onto her bed.

"I won't eat what that vampire serves," she said stubbornly, looking resolutely away.

"Better the food, better the blood," the woman replied cheerfully. She poured the wine now in glass that was etched with excessive detail, and Natalya was once again taken aback by the richness of the entire castle. The woman, having done her job, headed towards the door now when the light of the lamp threw her ruined neck into sharp relief. Natalya could hide her disgust no longer.

"How do you endure it here? Him feeding on you like that?" she asked. The woman turned to face her, and Natalya was confronted with the whole horror of her visage. Frazzled white hair stuck out on either side of the woman's head, and her eyes were hard and devoid of compassion. They were a light shade of icy white infused with electric sapphire and blotted with cataracts that raked over Natalya from deep within the contours of her skull. Wispy eyebrows snaked over a fleshy nose and a rather square jaw. In a strange way, she vaguely resembled Anesa, but her face held none of Natalya's former mentor's gentleness.

From the front, the damage to her neck was even more pronounced. Tendrils of blood had dripped onto her clothing and remained there, stained red against the pallid blue.

"Endure it, dear? I *enjoy* it," she said with relish, her voice only slightly louder than a whisper.

Natalya gasped and withdrew to the furthest corner of the bed. She swallowed nervously, unable to comprehend the notion that any human would willingly sacrifice their lifeblood. The woman laughed, a hoarse sound hindered by scratched vocal cords. She approached the bed now but did not attempt to touch the girl.

"I don't know how you can," Natalya murmured. She looked at the woman, now with more curiosity than repugnance. "What is your name?"

"That dear, is a question I have not been asked in almost fifty years. Arkadith has certainly never used it!" she cackled again, and Natalya fancied she caught a note of bitterness in her laugh. The old woman paused, as if she had to conjure the name from memory. Natalya could not imagine living in this place for so long that her own identity could be so easily forgotten.

"Anna…" the woman said finally, drawing out the syllables as if unused to hearing them. "I was once called Anna." Her voice grew harsh. "But that was a long time ago."

"And you've stayed here all these years. Why don't you leave? Certainly death would be better than this!"

"Oh he'll kill me for sure, he will," Anna murmured, circling the bed. "Sure as the sun falls in the West. My blood, old and sluggish barely sustains him anymore. He will enjoy feasting on the blood of a supple youth! And he will keep you here as his servant, just as he did me. There will be no escaping it, so you may as well learn to love it, just as I have!" The woman turned to the door now and produced a key from within her dress. She opened the door, but before she left, she turned back towards her, smiling wildly.

"Enjoy your stay, Natalya!" she laughed wickedly before slamming the door behind her. The sound echoed throughout the room and Natalya, the fearless slayer of vampires, jumped at the sound. She sat on the bed, her hands hugging her knees.

The food lay uneaten on its tray, the wine too untouched. Natalya simply stared at it, caught between hunger and stubbornness. Her stomach rumbled unpleasantly, but she ignored it as the hours gradually passed.

She drew the satin covers up to her chin and remained there on the bed for the rest of the night. She wondered when the true Anna had been destroyed and this mad old woman had come to replace her in this desolate place.

~ Chapter Thirteen ~
Echoes of the Past

So this was to be her fate. To be fed on and worked until she grew too old and decrepit to carry a tray, then she too would be changed out for younger and sweeter blood.

The morning's beauty had never before been dampened by such thoughts. Natalya yawned widely and found the lamp match with ease and lit her room. Her stomach keened loudly in protest at its lack of dinner the night before, but she did not go to the tray. She did not really have a plan, and she knew that starving herself could not stave off the inevitable, but she drew some sort of gratification for having spoiled at least one little aspect of the vampire's plan.

She also did not change her clothes, having none on her person to change into when she had been captured. She visited the chamber pot and smiled despite herself as she filled it. She imagined Anna attending to it later and had much difficulty in pitying the old woman in that task. She knew also that it would not be long before the woman entered her room again to bring her breakfast, and she dreaded that moment until it came.

The familiar knocking came just an hour later, and this time Natalya forewent the fire poker. She knew Arkadith would come for her eventually, and the weapon would do her no good against him. Still, she could not help but wonder what she would do when it was the vampire that came for her instead.

Anna did not acknowledge Natalya as she brought in a new tray. She replaced the old one and uncovered a tray filled with assorted pastries paired with mead. Natalya's mouth watered at the sight of the moist rolls drizzled in frosting and fresh fruit, but she resisted tearing into the food. She turned to look at Anna who finally spoke.

"Master Arkadith has requested that I prepare a bath for you. I will boil the water for you while you eat and will come to collect you once it's hot."

Natalya nodded blankly but the old woman was already half way out the door. It swung shut, and Natalya listened closely as the padlock was secured and the crossbar refitted. She listened for careless forgetfulness, but Anna was steadfast in her duties; never neglecting to properly lock up her charge.

She turned now to the pastries and hungrily devoured them as well as the water that accompanied them. She justified her breach in the plan by telling herself she needed to maintain her strength for when she finally faced Arkadith. The mead she was slower to drink, but the fruity aroma masked the smooth alcohol that went down easier than anything she had ever drank in Valwood. She swayed slightly on her feet, dizzy and slightly queasy. She sat down, waiting for her head to clear. For now she just had to survive in this castle, and she turned her thoughts instead to the first time she would be let out of her room in three days.

Anna returned around midday to lead Natalya from her bedroom. She did not grab her wrists or otherwise restrain her in any way. Natalya did not try to run; she knew the vampire was near and did not wish to rouse his anger with another futile escape attempt. Instead, she followed the woman's ambling gait through a labyrinth of halls until they came to another carved oak door set into a stone archway. Anna turned the knob, and they entered into the largest bathroom that Natalya had ever seen.

A spacious claw footed tub that was partially obscured by a heavy curtain that hung from the ceiling served as the room's focal point. A mural painted onto stained glass depicting armed men on horseback riding to some unknown location, decorated the opposite wall above another small vanity.

The tub was already filled with hot water, and Natalya gratefully began to undress. Her feet and fingers were nearly black from encrusted earth, and her hair was tangled and dirty. She hadn't bathed properly in over a month, and she settled comfortably into the water. Anna dutifully added hot water and soap, and when Natalya was done, she found that the old woman had laid out a beautiful ball gown for her to wear. As she stepped out of the tub and ran her finger down the laced detail in the front, she could not help but hesitate. There was no doubt in her mind that Arkadith intended her to wear the dress tonight for dinner, and her body trembled involuntarily,

Anna sensed her uncertainty and offered to lace up the back for her. Natalya allowed the woman to help, fighting the urge to flinch when the cold weathered hands touched her skin. The dress was breathtaking— a rich sapphire in color with a black lace overlay that revealed more black detail beneath. The neckline draped loosely across her chest, revealing her collar bone and ending in sleeves that hung over her shoulders. Natalya could not help but circle in front of the mirror, having never worn a dress of this fashion in her life. She wondered vaguely at the cost of it, knowing it was much more than her family could have ever afforded, and she faltered before her own reflection. She looked like the high bred ladies that sometimes travelled through Valwood, though they never stayed for long, preferring their expensive manors and the delicacies that evaded her forest city.

Anna slowly ran a comb through Natalya's hair and attached a headpiece adorned with metal flowers that were studded with diamonds. A sapphire necklace completed her look.

"There, you are ready," Anna murmured with an almost motherly concern that gave Natalya pause.

"Like a sheep before the slaughter," Natalya muttered bitterly before she could stop herself, but if the old woman had heard, she paid it no mind. Instead, she began leading her out of the bathroom and back towards the grand stairwell.

Natalya's heart thudded loudly in her ears as they neared where Arkadith was lying in wait for her. As she slowly descended, the urge to flee beckoned however hard she fought it. Her hand closed over the precious necklace that was like cool stone on her neck, offering her neither warmth nor protection as her amulet did. The breeze that penetrated through the drafty walls of the castle seeped through her dress and Natalya felt more strongly the absence of her bow and stakes in the soft flowing of the loose fitting fabrics.

Arkadith sat in his usual spot, and the sight of him banished all thoughts of escape. Without waiting to be invited, Natalya settled herself into the spot opposite of his long table. The vampire did not acknowledge the contravention in protocol; in fact, he did not turn to look at her at all. He seemed to be gazing past her, his eyes a normal brown and almost wistful. His hair had been swept back, and a fine layer of stubble graced the skin along his chin and jaw line. It was the most human Natalya had ever seen him, and for the first time since she arrived at his castle, she was truly unnerved.

Anna served them their evening meal, this time a group of what Natalya could only describe as black bubbles over assorted breads and crackers. She waited for Arkadith to start as she was unsure of what strange delicacy this could be. He finally came out of his reverie and began taking delicate bites of the crackers. His expression remained unchanged as he ate, and Natalya remembered what he had said about not being able to taste the foods he served her.

Natalya mimicked him and took a tiny bite. It was a pleasant mixture of salt and crumbling sweet bread.

"It's caviar," Arkadith said, seeing her confusion. "Fish eggs. There are many more delicious foods to try and rooms to explore here. In time, you will learn to love the castle as much as I do."

"You are a vampire. Cold, pitiless and *incapable* of love," she said. The vampire merely chuckled dryly without humor.

"You think I cannot love? I have loved...once." He looked away, his expression nearly unreadable. It seemed as if she had hit a nerve.

"Tell me then," she said scornfully.

"It was years ago, about two hundred now. Her name was Elizabeth. She and I met at the annual masquerade ball. I attended many of these balls, for after I was turned, they served as the only place I could truly meld with the humans without arousing their suspicions. My pale and mottled skin could be hidden beneath layers of cloth, and my eyes and fangs were invisible beneath the elaborate masks. I was not hunting when I found her. She wore a glittering red and gold mask that was adorned with feathers and jewels over a stunning red dress.

"What struck me about her was that she did not evoke my thirst as others did. Oh I wanted her blood, do not mistake me. I longed for her blood more than I had ever wanted anyone's. But when I watched her, I was not thirsty. I wanted more with her. I wanted her touch, her embrace, and to dance with her. I wanted to hear her laugh, and I wanted to simply hear her voice. It was magic when she spoke. So I did, and for a time, I felt nearly *human* again.

After the first night, I began to watch her from afar. I listened to the gentleness of her beating heart from the roof of her home. I heard of her travels, and of her perils and adventures through the bits and pieces she provided to her visitors. And in time, I fell in love. She never even knew I was watching her always, protecting her you could even say."

"Protecting her from what?" and at the question, Arkadith's face darkened. Natalya found herself leaning towards the vampire, genuinely interested now, her food long finished.

"There was a man…and I knew from watching him that he had evil intentions the night he followed her to her home. He made his plans carefully and waited until he was certain she was alone to execute them. Needless to say, he did not make it far." He smiled that horrible smile again, and Natalya did not need to ask what had become of him. She chanced another question instead.

"What did she look like?"

"She was beautiful. Her hair was lush and dark with pale skin. And her eyes, they were mesmerizing. Oh she wasn't without her flaws," and at this Arkadith laughed and Natalya smiled with him. "She had a mole, just outside her lips. She was stubborn and short tempered at times. But she had a spirit about her…a wildness that couldn't be tamed, and I felt myself instantly drawn to her. In short, I was fascinated with her."

"But that cannot be," Natalya cut in sharply. "Vampires are cursed, as are werewolves. You cannot feel what a *human* can." She felt the natural disdain of her people speaking through her words.

"You are mistaken. As I have already said, vampires still possess a bit of humanity. Although it tends to fade with time…however slowly. But as I was saying…I allowed myself to become entranced with her for almost a year. I fed all around her, at times taking her friends without guilt, but I always contained myself around her. I visited her after feeding and never before. Otherwise I knew my thirst would overcome the feelings I had developed for her. And so this continued, and I never allowed myself to taste her blood. I had distanced myself from her, for I knew how dangerous I was. But my feelings for her had begun to intensify even beyond my own understanding. I allowed us to get much too close, and still she never suspected what I was. I was playing a dangerous game indeed."

At this he paused and shook his head slightly. For the briefest of moments, he closed his eyes, but when he spoke there had been no weakness in his voice.

"What happened next?" she asked.

"My feelings, as I should have known someday they would, overcame my judgment. I grew reckless with my own power. I thought I could master myself and my thirst. I was wrong."

There, she had seen it. A glimmer of vulnerability, but it had faded into a mask of cold indifference as Arkadith continued.

"It happened soon after, much too soon. I had strayed much nearer to her than ever before, overconfident as always. Had I learned nothing of the vampire's will?" he asked bitterly.

"She never saw her death coming. It was quick. For that at least I am grateful," he said with finality, and Natalya asked him no more about Elizabeth. Arkadith's eyes moved past hers again, seemingly staring past the stone walls and into the trees he knew lay beyond the castle. He seemed to be absent from her, enfolded in his memories. Natalya allowed him a few moments musing before bringing him swiftly into the present.

"I must know what happened to my mother."

Arkadith's eyes latched onto hers, and he laughed. It was a hollow, mirthless sound.

"And what good would that do? Is your soul not troubled enough?"

"I wouldn't expect you to understand. Anesa never told me much, only that you killed her." He held her gaze for a long time before speaking, watching her oddly.

"Very well," he said finally. "If you truly wish to know I shall show you all that occurred that night."

"Show me?"

"Yes. Look into my eyes Natalya." This time it was a request, not an order, and now Natalya was only afraid of what she might see. His eyes seemed to expand, and she found herself lost in them. The images that she saw continued to grow until they had become reality.

Arkadith and the room had vanished. It was twilight, the sky dotted with thousands of stars. She was looking down from a high roof, overlooking a small, fine house within the city. Her eyes were suddenly much sharper, picking through each detail with ease. And she realized she was seeing through Arkadith's strong eyes, for this was his memory.

His head moved and her vision followed toward the top window. A woman was preparing herself for bed within the house. Something was hauntingly familiar about the scene, and he knew with a predator's confidence that this night would be her last. From his perch, Arkadith could see her silhouette through the window, her form against the yellow light of the room. Something like lust rose in him, but although her features were soft, her beauty held nothing for him. She lifted her hands to her head, and a moment later, her hair had fallen free in curly black waves down her back. Inwardly, he reveled at the fact that he could see her, but she remained, even now, oblivious to his presence. Natalya shared his giddiness. He followed her motions, transfixed, until she had disappeared from his prying gaze. This did not concern him, for she was merely delaying her fate.

Concealed in the night, he cocked his head, listening hard. She moved throughout the house, her demeanor confident and assured, her breathing relaxed. He could hear her humming a tune close to his ear as if he were in the same room. Every so often he caught a glimpse of her as she passed an open window, but mostly he relied on scent and sound to pinpoint her location.

He moved closer. He disregarded the ambient sounds around him: the wind whistling through the trees, a distant bark of a tethered dog, a slamming door. Only the sounds caused by her were of any interest of him. He was now directly outside her window, and she had still not detected his presence. He smiled knowingly. Of course she would not. But now as he neared her, he realized she wasn't alone. An infant child was sleeping soundly upstairs. He could hear very faintly the slow beating of her heart and her steady breathing. Again, this did not concern him, but it did complicate matters. He turned his attention back onto the mother, and felt his thirst threatening to consume him. He closed his eyes, battling his thoughts and willing himself not to act rashly. He turned to the moon. It was low in the sky, but the stars had still not retreated from the coming dawn. The father would not be home for a few more hours. He still had time. For the first time that night, he finally surrendered to his thirst. His eyes seemed to absorb the darkness of the night and expanded over his irises, turning them to the color of coal. His teeth grew into fangs over pale lips. Almost catlike, he crept towards her door with inhuman grace. He had been stealthy; no one else had detected him either. He stood up and knocked on the door. Almost at once, she opened it, regarding him suspiciously. How odd that her face held no fear of him, only a haughty wariness.

"I knew you would come for me one day." She showed no signs of embarrassment of her night clothes and made no effort to cover herself further. She scrutinized him through narrowed eyes, taking in the way his waxy skin was stretched taut over skeletal bones. Her breathing changed. Her body tensed. Now was the time to act.

"I'd like to come in, Irena." His tone was silky, reassuring, and her eyes obediently slid up to meet his. He smiled pleasantly and the concern disappeared from her face. She stepped aside, and he entered the home. The mysterious power he emanated had left her gaze vacant and unfocused. Her senses dulled, and her movements slowed as she began to fall into a trance. But he had underestimated her. Underneath the layers of her confused mind she knew why he had come. *Had she not prepared herself for years?* He advanced, armed with nothing more than his teeth and heightened senses, but she was ready for him. He sensed her concentration, driving him from her mind with her own barriers. He faltered, and he felt her regaining control. She thought of her daughter, still sleeping. With the explosion of maternal love, the vampire was forced from her mind.

He advanced, no longer attempting to control her mentally. He pressed her against the kitchen counter with his body. His mouth opened to reveal his canines and he prepared himself to drain her.

137

In one swift thrust, the knife that had escaped even his notice had pierced his chest. He gasped and staggered backwards. The wound blossomed startlingly red against his shirt, but no blood flowed from it. Having not fed recently, there was not enough blood in his system for him to bleed.

He fell to the floor and held his shirt against the gaping hole, but his eyes were fixed on hers. They glinted with hatred. Irena didn't hesitate. She took the stairs at a blinding run. The child still slept soundly in her bassinet, and Irena rushed to pick her up. She scooped the infant into her arms and headed back down the stairs, supporting both of their weights. She ran through the kitchen, her bare feet slipping slightly on the floor, though she never lost her footing. But he knew she sensed something wasn't right. He was no longer laying on the floor where she had left him...

"You missed my heart, Bitch," he whispered in her ear. Irena stifled a scream and turned around. With only one free arm and weaponless, she turned to flee again. She threw herself up the staircase once again with the vampire in close pursuit. A stake was in her bedroom and she headed there first, ripping it from its holding underneath the bed. She placed the infant onto the goose down mattress and threw herself across the threshold to the room, guarding the entry with her body. She raised the stake upwards, poised to strike when Arkadith came into view.

With inhuman speed, he wrenched the stake from her grip. The weapon clattered uselessly to the floor and the vampire stretched his hand outwards to her throat. He lifted her to the ceiling, and she sputtered and coughed, unable to breathe. Irena cried out but it was a choked, desperate sound, and it was swiftly cut off as the Vampire plunged his fangs into her throat. The life drained from Natalya's mother as her blood filled Arkadith, renewing his.

Natalya's eyes snapped away from Arkadith's, unable to watch any more. Her entire body shook with pain and rage while the Vampire remained unmoved. Natalya's hand closed over her fork and without thought she rushed Arkadith. She hardly knew what she was doing; all she wanted was to cause as much damage to him as she could. She reached him and thrust her fork in his direction, but she never made contact. The Vampire had seized her arm and bent it sharply upwards, nearly snapping the bone. Natalya cried out and Arkadith, equally furious, began dragging her through the room by her wrist. She resisted, desperately struggling to escape his grasp and return to the sanctuary of her own room, but it was not to be. They ascended upwards across winding hallways and up more spiraling staircases until they reached a tower that had been hidden from view from the outside of the castle. Arkadith wrenched open the door and forced Natalya inside. There were no servants here, no one to hear her scream or to help her now. The vampire bolted the lock, and with eyes as black as the night he turned to face his captive.

~ Chapter Fourteen ~
The Hidden Spire

It was in this sanctuary where Arkadith did all of his killing, in the darkest and innermost turret of the castle. The room was devoid of all furniture except for an embroidered red velvet couch that lay under a large picture window. It was closed now and shielded from curious eyes by the black drapes that covered it. The walls that were adjacent were as breathtaking as the forbidden view to the outside world; from floor to ceiling they were embellished with ancient artwork. Men with spiraling horns and hoofed feet circled naked youths in an eternal dance above them. Brilliant stain glass depicted brave knights holding dragons at bay with their swords while the beasts breathed fire of every golden hue above them.

Now was the time of the predator, Arkadith thought as he strode towards Natalya. The artwork faded, forgotten from his peripheral vision as his eyes blackened and honed in on the girl's neck. Her blood flowed just under the surface like an endless river, coursing throughout her entire body. He imagined the crimson flowing towards each extremity like the roots of a tree, nourishing them and heralding the very essence of life. His canines extended in response until he felt them nearly pierce his lips. He flicked his tongue beneath them like a snake, longing to sink them into her delicate flesh, but instead he paused, savoring the moment.

He could feel her quivering under him, beautifully and fearfully defiant. Even now she did not scream within the tower. She held her gaze longer than any human before her had when faced with his visage, except for perhaps her mother.

The inebriation he felt from the anticipation of draining the girl was almost as exhilarating as the actual act of feeding. He drew back, allowing the ignited lamps to play their light across his fangs. They glistened a gleaming white as the color in his eyes fully receded into inconceivable blackness. These changes reinvigorated his senses, and they heightened until he could feel the beating of her heart as if it resided in his own chest. The sound throbbed in his ears and was like a catalyst to his thirst. He took a steadying breath to calm himself, to prolong the moment when he would finally take his drink. The vampire's frenzy had begun.

Arkadith had changed, and Natalya knew he was beyond all reason. His pupils had dilated until they had expanded completely over the irises, twin pools of liquid oil that were devoid of thought or mercy. No understanding lay in the depths of his gaze as he approached her, only the focused deadly intent of the carnivore. She was reminded of Voren on the night of the new moon. She remembered vividly her fingers caressing the fine bone of his skull under the stars and how the wolf within had nearly succumbed to her touch.

There was no such confusion here, no human kindness to be tempered by Vampiric rage. Only a cold longing to quench the thirst that ravaged his throat was discernible in his eyes. Arkadith was nearly upon her and Natalya found herself against the arm of the couch. The fork was still clenched in her wrist and the weapon now seemed woefully underwhelming against the foe before her. Still she held it ready to strike, her other arm bracing herself against the cushion. He was only inches from her now and her muscles released the tension they had been holding. She threw herself at the vampire and the fork caught in his flesh. With an animalistic cry of rage he wrested the prongs from his shoulder and threw the utensil to the ground, beyond Natalya's reach.

His hand closed over her neck as her arm reached helplessly for the makeshift weapon. Her hand groped desperately at nothing as his grip tightened around her throat. She sputtered, not ceasing her futile attempt at recovering the fork. She could feel his weight upon her now, and she cringed, wincing as his rank breath stroked her cheek.

Her eyes circled the room but neither a means to her escape nor a suitable weapon presented itself. Instead, her view rested on a bronze eagle that stood on a pedestal in the center of the room. It was captured in midflight, its beak torn open in a shrieking cry. Natalya felt like the forever frozen bird, immobilized and unable to give life to the screaming warning that was gathering in her chest.

At this she closed her eyes, but they flew open again as Arkadith plunged his teeth into her neck. She gasped as her flesh was opened and her blood began to spill into fine streams of deep scarlet. The rivulets ran down her neck, over her chest and seeped into the red of the couch, and still the vampire drank. She gasped, clenching her teeth in agony and still trying to scream, but she could not make a sound. The noises the vampire made as he fed were terrifying, a wolf eagerly lapping up a river of blood or a venomous snake hissing its delight.

She began to weaken. The corners of her own vision also blackened, and she felt herself slipping in and out of consciousness. Strange memories flitted before her like butterflies she couldn't quite catch. Dancing firelight reflected on somber werewolf faces around the campfire, then blurred until she could no longer recognize them. A fleeing beast that had been Voren only moments before was tearing through the trees until he disappeared altogether. The vampire she had hunted down was desperately clawing his way towards the shadows before exploding into a burst of brilliant dust under the sun. A ghastly white owl's face, glowing in the darkness as it flew in slow motion towards her. It turned its face nearly all the around as it passed, its eyes blinking languidly at her until it too faded. The next memory was different.

It was twilight. The sky was dotted with thousands of stars that held every color imaginable. The nighttime blues were of every shade Natalya had ever seen, and when her vision swooped toward a small, fine house, she was immediately filled with dread. The house was *hers,* and she realized as her eyes picked up every grainy detail of every interlocking shingle that she was seeing through Arkadith's eyes. Natalya could hardly stand to relive the memory again but she was powerless to stop it.

It played on, the vampire pinning Irena against the counter, her mother stabbing Arkadith's chest through with the knife, her desperate bid for the sleeping infant upstairs. Natalya struggled to close the eyes that were not hers as her mother's final scream rent the air. Her enthralling blood began to spill as they shared in the ecstasy of the drink. Her skin paled as more of her blood disappeared past Arkadith's lips, and when Natalya finally screamed, she could not differentiate her own blood from her mother's.

The exchange in memories had left Natalya's mind reeling as she continued to get flashes from his mind. People were dancing in the large cathedral, seductive eyes that beckoned them forward from behind feathered masks of reds and blues and greens. As one, they took the hand of one such girl and the memory flew forward. Arkadith was above his beautiful Elizabeth, her arm draped over his while her head lolled to the side, unsupported by her bleeding neck. Anna, dripping red from his bite and her euphoric smile.

Finally the images receded, and Natalya felt her own body lowering to the floor. Her head throbbed as the room faded from her focus. She hardly felt the vampire withdraw his fangs from her skin. Blood was still gathering at the holes in her neck, and she tried to stem the flow with her fingers. Her arm, spent of energy and devoid of enough blood to give it movement, fluttered to the floor, and she merely lay where she dropped. The vampire walked away, his footsteps echoing loudly throughout the room. She heard the door creak and crawl open and she tried to lift her head, but she was too weak. She faintly heard the lock click behind him before the world went black.

With the arrival of blood, Arkadith's dead heart began to beat. Slowly at first, thudding weakly until it picked up speed. His chest expanded, but still he did not breathe, though he felt more alive than he had in days. He lifted his hand until it was illuminated by the torchlight above him. He cocked his head curiously, marveling at how his skin changed, starting at the fingertips. The pasty white was ebbing into the flush of pink color, and his veins protruded with the life giving blood that swelled them.

But he was not satisfied. His bemused expression gave way to an angry snarl as his skin reversed; the white now dominated the human pink, and his veins sunk back into oblivion.

The effect had been temporary. He would need to feed again this night if he wished to remain strong. His thoughts drifted back to Natalya. It had taken all of his resolve to stop. He had given himself up almost entirely to the predator within and felt the raw thirst that had rendered him incapable of human thought or emotion. But one small part of him held back, and this he had clung to, his one shred of humanity. And it was this that had made him capable of stopping, making him able to stay sane while he eagerly fed. He nearly laughed at the irony.

She was not merely prey to be immediately devoured, but a vampire huntress that had slain far too many of his own kind. Many of the fledglings had been created by his own hand, and their deaths stirred a deep confusion within him that could not quite translate into true grief. He did, however, feel a measured need to utterly and completely destroy this huntress.

Her death must be a lasting experience and life only a fleeting whisper that will not answer her desperate calls for release from the unceasing pain. He smiled cruelly as the colorless white of his skin returned, and he felt the thirst again. Now her death would be properly drawn out, and he could exact his full revenge onto Natalya.

~ Chapter Fifteen ~
Fang and Claw

The night was motionless except for the eyes. They smoldered, casting luminescent beams that made the sparks that flew from the men's campfires sparkle in the twilight. Darting in and out of view, they disappeared behind trees and bushes only to reappear a few steps closer as the creatures wended their way through the forest's edge.

Here the werewolves would go no further, their deadly fangs and claws held at bay by the flaming branches that were flung at them and the sight of the muskets that lay across the men's laps. The men too were at a standstill, unwilling to venture into the unfamiliar land and crippled by eyes that were nearly useless in the late hour.

In the weeks since Natalya had left them, the men had begun their campaign into Claw Haven. But now, bound by their weaknesses, the two enemies could do nothing but wait until the day to break above them. The werewolves settled within grassy clearings, their tails furled over their noses while they watched the men in their wakeful unrest. Others paced restlessly. The men caught snatches of sleep as they sat in the fire's glow in between tending to the blaze. Their horses squealed nervously and pulled at their tethers whenever the werewolves grew bolder, but a shout from one of the men and the sight of him brandishing his gun would send them fleeing into the trees once more.

Another pair of eyes was also watching, twin obsidians that held all of the night's stars in its unblinking glare. They were fringed by feathered eyelashes against the ghostly white feathers that rimmed its face. The owl had returned, casting his and Arkadith's vision to every corner of Claw Haven. He alighted from branch to branch, sweeping his silent wings into frayed arcs as he took flight. With his supersonic ears, he could hear every fragmented conversation between the invading men and every growl and snap of the werewolves, though he could not discern their meaning.

The owl glided overhead, a spectral phantom in the silence before battle. His wings flapped lazily over the soft currents of air as the first shades of pink and orange flooded over the horizon. The crescent moon was growing faint now, a shadowy glimmer that held little of its former glory as it settled back into space.

The owl, so attuned to the night, was not meant for the day, and neither was the vampire he was tied to. As the sun's flares warmed the morning air and illuminated the owl in brilliant hues, it turned its great wings and wheeled back towards the castle.

Claw Haven at sunrise was breathtaking; the owl took in every detail of the gold and red trees that rose and fell with the land's gently rolling hills. Many more were unburdening themselves of their foliage, and the scattered leaves were tossed to the wind where the owl now flew. He followed the line of the river that snaked through the forest and up the great hill where Arkadith's castle lay. The bird encircled the iron fence and flew through one of the great windows of the main turrets. The waiting vampire's arm was outstretched, and the owl splayed its talons as it landed on Arkadith's closed fist. The vampire pulled the window shut against the deadly sun's rays and drew the black curtains before his flesh could be burned. The owl fluttered to a waiting perch and closed its somber eyes. Arkadith too fought his own fatigue and retired to his room. Having stayed up too early already, he gratefully climbed into his coffin and collapsed into the hold of day sleep as he considered what the owl had shown him in his dreams.

For the werewolves and the men of Valwood, the morning did not bring peace. Freed from the bonds of invisible darkness, the men continued their march through the woods. They had already secured the Ruins. Flames licked the sooty edges of the buildings, and smoke poured from the shattered windows. The place lay abandoned for not even the rogue werewolves visited it now.

The inner camp was the only stronghold left in Claw Haven, and the men were closing in. The day had awakened with gun shots, and the howling cries of the fallen werewolves. Occasionally, the stillness was punctured by the startled scream of one of the men, as they too were leapt upon and dragged into the woods to be torn apart.

But not all of the werewolves had been discovered. On the other side of the forest, Voren sprinted through the trees. Others

149

followed behind, surreal in their silent run. He could just make out the forms of more werewolves ahead of him, their tails streaming behind them and outlined in silver light.

Under the waning moon, the werewolves were nearly skeletal; their bones flared outwards from their bodies, draped in tattered flesh and hair. Still more fur rolled from their bodies as they ran, caught in the bushes as they scraped alongside them. Despite their undead appearances, they did not tire. They ran as one indefatigable being, each paw step brushing the ground and then extending in complete and beautiful unison. They continued for an hour this way until Voren broke from the line and stopped.

The others slowed and turned towards him, their ears pricked curiously. Voren's nose twitched, and his tongue flicked outwards, trying to recapture the fleeting scent that had filled his nostrils only a moment before. The smell had been faint but vaguely familiar and carried a hint of the men that followed them.

Another werewolf, Moira, nosed the ground behind him, trying to pick up the scent she had caught, but her senses had lost much of their acuteness in her old age. This werewolf moved much more slowly than Voren, though she walked with much dignity. Apart from the abundant white hairs that lightened her muzzle during the full moon, the two werewolves were nearly identical. But under this silver crescent her skull was as bony as his, and she lifted her cloudy gaze to Voren. Only a tiny light flickered in her questioning eyes, but Voren had no answers. The scent had been lost to the wind and not even his strong nose could pick it up again.

A baying sound, unlike anything the werewolves had ever heard, sounded in the distance. The scent had returned, and suddenly Voren realized.

Dogs! We're being tracked! He snarled in each of the werewolf's heads. Moira growled nervously at his side. Voren's hackles were already beginning to rise, and it took much of his effort to lower them and to appear calm. He looked towards the source of the sound, but nothing was discernible through the morning fog.

Protecting the rest of the pack was his charge now, and he sprang back into line. The werewolves that accompanied him now were made up of the young, the old and infirm. Only their immortality would protect them from these creatures now.

They resumed their running, but it held none of the synchronized beauty that it had before. Now, they poured through the trees desperately, trying to put as much distance between them and the dogs that followed. The baying grew louder and more frenzied as more of the hounds had caught their scents and joined into the chase.

For a while, the fleeing werewolves were able to keep the dogs at bay, but even the undead began to slow eventually. The hounds had grown more ambitious as they closed in, snapping their muzzles, eager to sink their fangs into their quarry. Voren ran behind his brethren, willing them to keep running, but the pack was slowing despite his efforts. As the hounds came into view, he resigned himself to battle.

The dogs were monstrous, much bigger than any he had ever seen before. They were a far cry from the lumbering, low to the ground curs that he had seen before when they occasionally strayed too far from their homes. These were nearly as tall as him with sleek brown and black hair and massive jaws. They had come to a large clearing, and the werewolves whirled to face their enemies, snarling at the sight of each other. Steely brown eyes met translucent white orbs, and although the dogs must have been fearful at the sight of these decrepit aberrations of nature, they did not back down. Both sides were still for only a moment before the clearing was alive with writhing, grappling bodies.

In the center of the chaos, Voren was sparring with a huge dog. Both of them stood on their hind legs, their front paws hooked in each other's necks, trying to gain purchase, while their jaws snapped at each other's throats. Voren was healing nearly as quickly as the dog could inflict damage, but he was unused to fighting an enemy that could outmaneuver him so easily with a body that was overflowing with pure, untarnished life. The hound's frame rippled with solid muscles and sinewy speed to score bloody wounds down the werewolf's neck.

His own flesh was vulnerable under the weak light of the moon, and sweet death beckoned to him, but he could not answer her call. Although his physical strength waned under the tiny crescent, the full power of the fallen werewolves before him flowed through his body. He could almost see the specters as palpable beings that fought with him. The silver phantoms were breathtaking in their realism; in death, they had shed their horrifying skeletal forms to become pure wolves. They were only an illusion though, and they faded into a fine trail of silver mist. Far from helping them win this fight, the phantom members of their pack only served to remind the remaining werewolves of their curse and their futility in breaking it. As Voren fought bitterly against the dog, he struggled to clear one particular phantom from his mind.

He was unrecognizable from the skull that decorated the great wall. The image of Sakarr did not leave easily, and Voren had no trouble recalling his powerful form. His empty eye sockets, old and devoid of emotion, now brimmed with ferocity and vigor behind each amber layer. His penetrating gaze never wavered from Voren's eyes.

It is not your time to join us, Voren, the Alpha's voice echoed in the werewolf's head. *Our kind stands on the verge of extinction, and you must not let this come to pass. We once found peace with the other packs under Zulae's moon. Perhaps harmony can be won again. Do not allow that creed to burn with Celestial Hold. Now fight!* The specter of his former leader released him, and as the dog buried its fangs into the side of his neck, and his blood welled to the surface. Voren closed his eyes.

He had felt it before, the ebbing of his own life as it flowed from him, but his body was already closing the near fatal wound. Invisible stitches seemed to wend their way upwards, zipping the gaping hole shut, and with it came mental clarity. *This tamed wolf could not destroy him, and he felt Sakarr's spirit lending his body strength.* His curse could not be broken this night, but he would seek to end it one day.

The dog grabbed his foreleg in its jaws, and Voren plunged to the ground, dragged down by the beast's weight. He struggled on three legs, wresting his fourth from the dog's grip when he saw his opening. The dog's fleshy throat flashed before him for a second, and Voren dove for it, his jaws snapping wildly. His teeth connected with the hairy folds of the dog's neck, and he clamped down. The dog yelped, and its paws foundered in the air, but he could not stop the inevitable. Sweet hot blood bubbled at its torn throat, and there was nothing in body that could heal the terrible wound. The dog's blood ran to the earth as its eyes became sightless in death. Voren worried the dead dog back and forth in his jaws before he released him. He howled in victory before he turned his attention to the rest of the battle.

Despite their disabilities, his fellow pack mates dominated the clearing, and more dead dogs joined the first. Voren scanned the clearing, looking for any injured pack members, and he barked in horror.

Moira was laying on her side, bleeding profusely. A dog tore into her flesh and scrabbled at her exposed belly with its claws. She was gasping for air under the dog's weight, and she twisted beneath him. She struggled to rise, but her age now failed her. The livid gash in her side was healing as well, but at a much slower rate than Voren's had. She shuddered, and Voren saw the starlight that was caught in her weak cloudy gaze begin to fade.

He ran to her, his paws kicking up the earth as he willed himself to go faster. A dog's teeth grazed his shoulder, and he snarled, but he did not turn against his attacker. Instead, he rushed at the dog that was still on Moira. He plunged his fangs into the dog's side and buried his snout deeper until he reached bone. The dog's femur cracked under his jaws, and its cry was a stark agonizing howl that tapered into a shrill whine. Its fangs released their grip, and Moira stood up, panting. She swayed on her paws, her eyes still flickering with nearly quenched life. Blood dripped from the wound, but the flow had ebbed somewhat, and she limped to the forest's edge.

The dog now turned on Voren, and they met with a clash of animal fury. Killing the first dog had taken much of the werewolf's strength, and he felt his muscles tense with exhaustion. The exposed sinewy strands that held them together were stretched taut with the effort of keeping the dog's teeth away, and he felt himself tire considerably. But the crescent moon blazed overhead, basking him in her gentle, silver warmth. The moonlight poured into his body, giving the dead an undead strength. All of the werewolves felt it, and the dogs nearly retreated at the sight of their swelling power. Their gazes were no longer blank and lusterless; instead, they gleamed with yellow eye shine. Their united energy became a tangible thing, much more real than the ghostly wolves of before. Together they fell onto the dogs, gradually driving them back towards the men. Visibly

154

mystified and exhausted, the dogs hesitated before the werewolves. They seemed to sense the supernatural strength that coursed through their veins and the heightened senses that the moon had given them.

Some of the dogs paid for their hesitation with their lives; for the werewolves did not pause before tearing into their throats. The others began to flee and the werewolves gave joyful chase. Under the power of the moon, their only true refuge from their unfulfilled existences, they ran as true wolves after their prey. They snapped at the heels of the dogs, worrying them further, and only stopping once the faint scent of man had filled their nostrils. The remaining dogs fled into the woods beyond Valwood, never to return.

Their tongues lolling, the werewolves turned, and like their ghostly counterparts, they too faded from view, though nature did not cloak them entirely. When he was sure that he would not be seen, Voren slowed to a stop. He reflected on the battle and the spirit of his former leader.

Thank you, Sakarr, Voren growled. If one of the men from the camp could have seen far enough, they would find the faintest amber lights flickering like fireflies, before dimming into a translucent white once more.

~ Chapter Sixteen ~
The Point of No Return

Natalya was growing weaker as the days progressed into weeks. She had only a limited sense of time by counting the number of suns and moons that lit her room, and by the snow that had come to the land, she could estimate that she had been held at Arkadith's castle for about two months.

The vampire kept no clocks, or at least none that she could find, and she attributed that to the dead's lack of needing to measure their unlimited time on this Earth.

There were still some gaps in her memory. She still did not know how long she had remained unconscious in her room when she was first captured. Some nights, too, were blurs that ran into the next, after particularly draining feedings from Arkadith.

She no longer flinched at these disturbing thoughts, instead they seemed to sustain her in some way. She imagined that they kept her constant fire to defeat him fueled when the rest of her was slowly giving up. Natalya shook her head. Practicality ruled her above all else, and she could never succumb to the fortune that he had laid out before her.

Perhaps, comfort in her confinement could be taken in small snatches, or the ease of a repetitive pattern in the day. But she would never find herself *giving up*.

A faint flicker of hope still burned in her chest, and she could do nothing but nurture these thoughts of herself escaping, lest they became fleeting visions that she could summon only in her dreams.

The plan. She could not waste any more time. She abruptly climbed out of bed only to collapse onto it once more. *Careful,* she thought to herself, as throbbing stars flashed before her vision. She tried again, this time more gingerly. She was still unused to the reluctance with which her body responded to her desires.

She went to the door and opened it, this time unimpeded by a lock or crossbar. By now, Arkadith was more than confident in his ability to keep his captive and allowed her free reign of the castle, except for of course, his own room. The grand front door too, was left unlocked, a tempting portal to the outside world.

Even as it beckoned her forward with temptations of an easy exit, it stood guarded and mysterious as it withheld its secrets of what lay beyond. Natalya had little sense of proximity to her home; the journey up the mountains could have lasted hours or days.

She only knew that uninhabitable forest surrounded them on all sides, and in her weaponless and weakened state, she could not hope to hunt for food or defend herself against rogue werewolves.

It was almost mid-afternoon now, and Natalya knew the vampire was locked away upstairs, vulnerable in his state of day sleep. The door to his bedroom was guarded by two men that

Natalya rarely interacted with. She ignored them, and they in turn regarded her with utmost indifference. When she did happen to catch glimpses of them, she could tell they were human, but how they came to be of service to the vampire, Natalya did not know. She did know that at this moment they stood at either side of his door, dressed in all black cloaks that obscured much of their faces. She had walked by them once, and one of them had parted his cloak just enough for her to see the metallic glint of concealed daggers and assorted knives. His message needed no elaboration; apart from the subtle reveal, the man had not moved a muscle. Natalya knew his meaning to be clear: the two of them would swiftly bring a violent end to anyone foolish enough to attempt to assassinate the vampire while he slept.

Natalya closed her door as quietly as she could before taking a right down the hall. Even though the inhabitants of the castle had grown used to her presence, she still did not wish to arouse any suspicions.

Many of the rooms had become familiar to her, and she passed by these, having already searched through their contents. It had taken her a couple of days to explore most of the rooms on this floor, and still, she had not located her weapons or her amulet.

Since running into the two men, Natalya had avoided the upper levels completely, leaving the vampire's room and the rest of the spires undiscovered. She assumed her belongings were there, under lock and key. Regardless, it would be impossible to get past the two guards, unarmed as she was.

She came to another closed door, and she gently leaned into it, prolonging the moment to when it would finally open. She allowed her anticipation to build, feverishly hoping against hope that this room would be the one.

The door creaked open, and a gust of wind immediately chilled her. She nearly closed the door again at the gale, but she held fast and peered into the room.

It was open to the sky and floorless. Only straw covered the dirt bottom, under a fresh layer of powdered snow. In the center was a single leafless tree, twisted and gnarled as it curled its way upwards towards the waning sun. Its branches were laden with snow as well, though it was still early in the season. But it was what was on the tree that had caught Natalya's interest.

The owl from Celestial Hold. The bird was sleeping now, its head tucked beneath one wing, and its closed eyes facing her. Its face seemed grey against the white background while its ashy body seemed to be flecked with snowflakes. It was only the pattern of its feathers though, Natalya realized when she examined it closer. The bird seemed to sense her presence and opened one eye to watch her. It seemed to be staring *through* her, and the feeling unnerved her.

She could not be sure that it was the same owl that had she had seen among the destroyed buildings, but she had an odd feeling that it was. By now, both eyes had opened, and they seemed to hold an entire starry sky in their glare. Natalya and the owl watched each other. Natalya felt paralyzed as the sky in the birds eyes seemed to expand, and she felt like a mouse held sway below it.

Owls are fascinating creatures. They can see for miles and can hear across great distances. And when they swoop in for the kill, the air flows silently over their wings. Arkadith's words echoed in her mind, but they brought no revelation.

She broke off eye contact with the owl, and the sensation ceased. She shook her head, wondering if she had not imagined the feeling.

159

Abruptly, she closed the door on the bird and leaned against the hall inside the castle. Seeing the owl there had distracted her. It nagged at the corners of her mind, something important, but she could not see how. She remembered it flying through the destroyed remnants of the werewolves' buildings, and she speculated to herself why such a creature came to live at the vampire's castle.

She lowered herself until she was sitting on the hallway carpet, her head cupped in her hands. She felt like a pawn in some twisted game that she could see no end to. Each mystery that she stumbled on within the castle seemed to bring her more questions than they answered, and each room that came up empty seemed to be pushing her towards some climatic end with Arkadith. Without anything to even the odds, she felt herself growing desperate. Tears began to streak down her cheeks, and she wiped them away with her sleeve.

The next room, her mind prompted, and she obediently stood up, sniffling slightly. Her own psyche would not allow her to retreat to the dark recesses of black thought.

She walked further down the hall until she reached a dead end. The door to the right was nondescript and so plain that Natalya almost walked past it. She pushed, and it opened easily, swinging noiselessly as if the hinges had just been oiled.

Inside was a bedroom, not unlike her own. The comforter was black and white, and the black curtains on the window matched hers. The oil lamp was lit, and the fire within shrank and grew, casting a flickering orange tinge over the room.

The pale green vanity was flaky with peeling paint, and the old fashioned décor made Natalya feel as if this part of the castle were far older than the rest.

An elaborate family crest was mounted above the vanity. She was drawn to it, craning her neck to take in every detail. It was of two peacocks facing one another, their beaks open and their wings flared as if caught in battle. Their tail feathers were fanned out brilliantly. A hundred dazzling eyes amidst the iridescent greens leered down at her. Their feathers were colored with painstaking radiance, as if the artist had dedicated many years to this one piece. The name *Springard* was printed onto parchment paper along the bottom of the crest, though it held no meaning for her.

It was a moment before she remembered her weapons, and she began sifting through each drawer of the vanity. A few chips of paint were shaken loose, and they fell to the ground, but they were unnoticed by Natalya in her haste.

She rifled through old photographs of a beautiful young woman amongst combs, brushes, a cracked golden hand mirror and more hairpins.

Natalya picked up the mirror and held it to her face, her hand trembling slightly. The shards were mostly intact, as if the attempt to completely shatter it had failed, and she cradled it in her hand as if it were a baby. It had been about a month since she had looked upon her own reflection in the elegant blue dress, and apprehension stilled her hand. The next moment, she had thrust herself into view and gasped slightly.

Her face, slightly distorted by the large crack that plunged down the middle, held all of the familiar features she remembered. Her slightly upturned nose, naturally arched eyebrows over honey brown eyes that were framed with long, dark lashes and soft round cheeks that betrayed her young age, were all unmistakably *Natalya*.

But the mirror also revealed a sunken collar bone that stretched to slightly protruding shoulders. The blood that Arkadith had taken had weakened her considerably. Her eyes, once brimming with life, were now weighed down by shadows

161

underneath, and her normally olive skin was pale with nothing to redden it. Her veins seemed to age her prematurely; they bulged like engorged snakes beneath her flesh. In them, she saw a similarity to Arkadith's skin that she could not even bring herself to voice in her own mind.

She slammed the mirror facedown into the drawer and begun forcibly opening the others, throwing herself back into her task.

One of the lower drawers contained a wide brimmed hat that was adorned with pink flowers and nothing else that could be used against a vampire.

She slammed it shut and turned to the closet. She sorted through lacy white dresses, tattered blouses and floral robes. Worn dress shoes littered the floor, and boxes containing perfumes and more hats were stacked behind the clothing, but no knives or swords revealed themselves. She was just pulling the closet door shut to check underneath the bed when she heard the door begin to open.

Natalya froze, the liquid fear chilling her blood as the door crawled open. A shot of adrenaline threw her muscles into movement, and she revolved towards the sound.

Anna stood in the doorway.

"I'm sorry, I…" Natalya trailed off when the old woman did not turn to look at her. She finished closing the closet door, and the sound throbbed and died in the silent room. Anna's red neck shined in the lamp's glow, and she turned to the vanity, arranging the strewn photographs on its top back into their proper places. Her back was to Natalya, and Natalya felt trapped between the chilled wooden closet and a woman who could shatter in a violent furor at a moment's notice.

But Anna did not acknowledge her after the photographs were neatly organized, nor when she smoothed the comforter over the bed. She blew out the lamp and turned towards the door, leaving Natalya alone in her room. Only when she had passed the threshold did she turn to the girl and smile. It was a wide grin that bared many missing and decaying teeth.

"Arkadith will see you for dinner now child," she said, laughing as she went.

The sight of the vampire never ceased to drive bolts of fear down Natalya's spine. He sat at his usual place at the head of the table, his hand casually outstretched, motioning for her to sit down. He smiled; even his onyx black eyes had caught the light of the chandelier.

The spread was grander than usual today. Steaming dinner rolls were piled high amongst a full chicken, accompanied by purple and green grapes, with a full suckling pig roasted in the table's center. Vegetables that Natalya couldn't identify were beautifully laid out alongside cheeses and more red wine. The many aromas blended into one irresistible scent that brought waves of hunger to Natalya's stomach.

"Sit," Arkadith said when she still hadn't. She hesitated for only a moment, and the vampire tensed. Not wanting to pique his anger with outright defiance, Natalya settled into her chair opposite his. He relaxed again and drank deeply from his glass.

She took his action as permission to tuck in and reached for the nearest food.

Arkadith too made himself a plate and speared a bit of meat onto his fork. He lifted it to his lips and chewed slowly, as if savoring it. Natalya watched him before she could contain herself no more.

"This is quite the feast you have prepared for us," she said. "Especially for someone with such a *limited* palate."

"Indeed it is," Arkadith answered smoothly.

"May I ask why?"

"May I ask why an oxen is fattened prior to its slaughter?"

"It is so there is more meat, but that doesn't answer my...*oh, God,*" Natalya whispered. Arkadith only smiled again in reply. She swallowed deeply, feeling as if she were choking on her own saliva. She held a hand to her chest, stifling a cough. Her breath quickened, her hunger departed.

"So you intend to fatten me and kill me?" she asked when she had finally found her voice.

"In a manner of speaking," the vampire answered. His canines had grown and they now rested on his lower lip. "The blood is richened with excellent food. It will be a great pleasure to drain you dry."

"When?" she managed to ask.

"I expect very soon," he replied.

Natalya could only blink at him in horror. She had always known this was his plan, but to hear him say it aloud had shocked her to her core. No clever retort that could sway his mind came to her, and no weapon fell into her lap. The pivotal end she feared with Arkadith was looming just before her, and she was not prepared.

She longed to run, but she stayed rooted to her chair, gripping the edge tightly. She could not escape him, and even now, it was against her nature to run. Her eyes swept over the dining room, gracefully avoiding the eating vampire.

She began to think. The room's window had been curtained shut, letting none of the sun's light into the room. The sky had already darkened in response to the colder weather though, and merely opening it would not be enough to burn the

164

vampire's flesh. The kitchen, and all of its sharp holdings were locked away, and Natalya did not wish to engage the staff into battle. Her eyes returned to the table, and she examined the food again.

The threat of death was not enough to contain her hunger, and it returned in full as she took in the feast. Her eyes were drawn to the crisp piglet and the knife that rested beside it. She reached for it and sawed off one of the pig's legs, allowing it to fall onto her plate. She returned it and the knife to her setting.

"Eat," Arkadith said, and she complied, rooting the severed leg to her plate with her fork and slicing it into smaller pieces. She was sure it was delicious, but to her troubled mind the meat was tasteless.

"Good girl." Natalya did not reply. She was beginning to plan. She ate now with much gusto, feeling the strength pour back into her famished body.

"How is it?" Arkadith asked.

"Excellent," she murmured through a full mouth. *Yes, keep him talking*, she thought. She reached for grapes, bread and cheese, filling her dish with as much food as she could. She planted both of her elbows on the table, smacked her lips and even forewent the napkin choosing instead to lick her fingers clean.

"Why are you making a mockery of my dinner, Natalya?" he asked, but she barely heard him. The vampire leaned over the table now, and she knew she could not ignore him any longer.

"What do you mean?" she asked innocently. The knife was sitting by her plate. Careful not to arouse his attention, Natalya slowly slipped it onto her lap. The cold metal felt uncomfortably sharp against her skin, reassuring her of its deadliness. Arkadith had stood up now and strode towards her. She fancied she had seen his eyes flicker towards her plate and to the missing knife for the briefest of seconds, but his eyes had snapped back towards her, and she realized she must have imagined it. She fought to keep her face perfectly neutral as he neared her.

She held the knife under the tablecloth and waited until she could see the whites of his eyes behind the ever expanding black and feel the warmth of his decaying breath on her cheek. All of her desperation and will to fight for her life was contained in the one movement to thrust the knife into his chest. She plunged it upwards, waiting for it to break through his flesh and into his long dead heart, but Arkadith's hand had closed over her wrist. He twisted until the knife now pointed towards her own fragile heart and squeezed until she cried out. Natalya's eyes widened in shock, and in that moment, she knew he had never been fooled. She had underestimated him again. The weapon fell from her hand with a loud clatter, and she watched as it came to rest underneath the table.

He still held her arm, and she grabbed his wrist with her free hand, trying to pry it off the other, but he was much too powerful.

"Have you learned nothing from the fork, Natalya?" he asked in her ear, and she struggled helplessly in his grasp. He twisted even more, and she was sobbing now as she felt the bone bend almost to its snapping point.

Without another word, he strode to the great banister, and Natalya could only follow, her wrist still clamped in his grip. She did not dare ask where we they were going for she already knew, and the thought filled her dread. They climbed higher and higher until they had reached the inner spire.

He opened the door to the feeding room and performed the ritualistic locking and securing of the room while Natalya stood shaking in its center. Her head was surprisingly clear, and her thoughts too impassive for any of this to be real.

No preamble marked the beginning of his frenzy; he simply turned. His fangs were now fully extended past his lips, and his eyes had blackened until even the whites had faded, and his face contracted.

He gripped Natalya's shoulder with both hands, his curved nails digging deeply into her skin as he went for her throat. She did not have time to prepare herself before he attacked. She felt her skin tear at the neck and heard the familiar sounds of his drinking. This was Arkadith at the height of his bloodlust, and while he fed all her hopes of defeating him had finally been quelled into nothingness within her. He drank ravenously, cruelly ripping more skin than necessary in this state. The primal sounds he made now were nothing like the past feedings, and it terrified her.

Stop, please, she wanted to beg, but she could not make a sound.

The room darkened, and she felt herself swaying on her feet as still the vampire drank.

Her eyes rolled into the back of her head, and her legs gave out, and she fell to the floor. Arkadith lowered himself with her, his fangs still rooted in her neck as she passed out.

Arkadith had always restrained himself, but not tonight. He was tired of his game and already he longed for new blood. He stopped feeding to savor the steady beating of his returning heart beat and it seemed to throb with delight.

He looked down at Natalya. Her hair had fallen over her face and disguised the disfiguring wound in her neck. A weak pulse still lingered and sweet blood still ran its course through her veins. He lowered himself to her once more, and her blood leapt to his call.

He went further than ever with her tonight, to her death. She collapsed, almost as pale and white as he had been only moments before, completely drained with her eyes blank and lifeless.

But a thought had occurred to him as he drank, and it exhilarated him. He stood, leaving the dead girl crumpled on the unfeeling floor. He turned to leave the room and extended his hand, about to unlock the door when he lifted his wrist to his lips instead. A smile graced his lips, and he looked at Natalya once more. It had been a *marvelous* thought indeed.

~ Part III ~

~ Chapter Seventeen ~
The Siege

The stillness settled over Valwood like an impenetrable fog. The quietness pulsated through Elder Greg Vrushko's ears, and he wanted to scream, to cry out and break the silence, but he made no sound. He looked to the orange streaked sky and could see the spreading of stars over the coming dusk.

Over the past month, he and his soldiers had been pushed back to their own borders after their attempts to secure Anraq's village had failed. Now, that the werewolves had drawn back to wait for their strength to wax under the moon, the men of Valwood had precious little time to prepare for the impending onslaught. Most of their women and children had been loaded up on horse drawn caravans headed towards Dark Cliff Bay, the nearest town. It was several miles away, but the winter was mild, and it was unlikely the werewolves would be able to reach them there.

They could pursue peace and a new life there if things here ended...unfortunately, Greg thought darkly. It was a bustling trading town that had enriched many of Valwood's citizens with exotic seal furs, whale oil, and fish meat. The people were cheerful and unreserved with their pleasantries, and Greg felt relief that at least some of Valwood could survive and assimilate there.

He took a long draught from the tankard of ale he had brought up and looked out over the forest. He scanned the trees below for movement, but only their naked limbs waved innocently in the breeze. He did not relax. Now that the clouds had darkened and night was falling, he knew the werewolves would come.

A gong sounded then another and yet another as Greg counted them. He waited until nine resonated and blended into an echoing union before he stroked his own. They all rang out across the city, a message to all the citizens that remained. The men were ready. Greg picked up the musket that had been leaning against the wall of his tower. It was heavy in his hands and primed to explode with great power, but he was not altogether comforted. He closed his eyes. He had seen too many of his men overtaken by werewolves in the last few days despite their heavy guns. Hardworking, good men that lay buried in the fields with their throats and hearts torn out by the savage beasts. He opened his eyes, but the dead men still stared at him from atop the snowdrifts, their eyes hard and accusing, blood streaming from wounds in their necks and chests. Guilt plagued his stomach with pain and spinning tales in his ears until he hardly knew what was real and what wasn't. He shook his head, and the images cleared. The bright snow shimmered innocuously.

He laid the musket back against the wall and rubbed his hands together over the fire. He knew that each of his men had

171

fought with him out of a unified drive to rid Valwood of the threat of werewolves. But they had still died at his command, and his own hand it seemed, and this did not lay easily on his mind. He and his men had killed many of the werewolves as well though, and they had left their bodies in the woods to rot. This brought him a small comfort, but he knew many more were still lurking in Claw Haven. He leaned over the side of the tower, his head in his gloved hand.

But he had not found his daughter there. His search had been in vain, and he had only been able to exact justice on a few of the werewolves before they had been driven back here. Bringing her home safe would be the ultimate victory, but he was starting to lose hope. It had been almost three months since the werewolves had taken Natalya.

Losing Irena had broken him, but losing Natalya too would shatter everything he had left. Irena at least had chosen her fate, and many vampires had fallen to her stake.

His sweet Natalya though…she had been innocent. Remaining happily unaware of her mother's occupation had failed to keep her safe. He was growing resigned to losing her and only his feverish hope kept him from losing himself entirely.

Stars now dominated the dark sky. A flicker of movement had caught his attention, and he looked up, squinting into the woods.

The werewolves had come. Greg lurched backward with a sharp intake of breath.

Under the new moon they were chilling. They walked purposefully towards the watch towers in a long line that spanned across the forest. These brutes could never be mistaken for true wolves. They were identical, skeletal forms with rotting flesh that fell away from their bones. Their breath rattled as they panted, their tongues lolling from open mouths. And when the creatures faced the men their faces were ghastly, for they had no eyes. Only empty sockets turned their somehow seeing gazes on the men.

The others in the watchtowers must have been similarly petrified and unable to move because it was a while before the call to shoot had come.

A moment later, the still night was cracked with gunfire. It exploded from the muskets, and silver bullets tore through the werewolf's ranks. They marched forward, as close to one another as the trees would allow. And even as the deadly silver had pierced through them, they continued their stride onwards. The werewolves yelped, cried and howled as the silver lanced through their bodies. Some fell dead on the spot but most continued on with gaping wounds where the silver had failed to destroy them. They could absorb some of the silver and heal, but many of the werewolves were shot multiple times. One lay dead in the snow, its skeletal face peppered with small silver infused pellets in lieu of balls. Another's heart had exploded through exposed ribs, and yet another clawed its way forward with its front paws, its hindquarters riddled with smoking holes that hissed as they still devoured its flesh.

The sight sickened Greg, but he thought of Natalya, dead in the woods somewhere, and his heart knew no pity. He picked up his musket and took aim at one of the werewolves himself and pulled the trigger. The spray mostly sprinkled the snow, but one of them hit the werewolf in its forepaw. He waited for it to spread and the werewolf to slump over dead, but instead it turned its blank gaze on him. The silver had made it pause, and Greg smiled grimly in satisfaction. But a moment later, the werewolf simply dragged the useless appendage along and continued towards him, unheeded by the paw or pain.

This wasn't working. He stole a glance at one of the neighboring watch towers and was met with a similar situation.

173

Though many of the werewolves had gone down, there were simply too many of them.

Greg reloaded and sighted the werewolves once more, this time aiming a touch higher. His hit was successful, and the targeted werewolf sank in the snow with a strangled *yip* and did not get up.

"There you go, you bastard," he muttered, retrieving another bullet from the extra box of shells that had been stored for this purpose. All of the watch towers had been outfitted with boxes of ammunition; some of them contained powerful single projectile bullets and others like Greg, favored the devastating but less accurate spray of silver pellets. He checked his count; he would be good for another few rounds at least.

He felled another four of the beasts before pausing to see how the other men in the watch towers fared. The men on his left seemed to be doing similarly well, though there seemed to be no reduction in the number of werewolves they faced.

A startled bellow from his right caught Greg's attention, and he jerked towards the sound. Some of the werewolves had reached one of the men's tower and were attempting to climb its wooden ladder. Others gnawed at its supports, the wood splintering under their bone crushing jaws.

The man shot at the werewolves blindly, and a few of them whimpered in the red snow, licking their wounds. One of them had nearly reached the man, and it snapped its muzzle inches from his face. Greg heard the blast of the man's shotgun, and he could see the dark shadow of the werewolf plummeting backwards off the tower to its death.

Greg's muffled cry of jubilation at the man's harrowing escape of death tore from his mouth as he continued to watch in horror. At first, the man had kept the werewolves at bay, shooting each of them as they climbed the tower and tried to reach him.

174

He watched him frantically reload again and again until he had finally run out of bullets. Desperately, he had resorted to using the musket itself as a weapon and had brained one of the savages on its head, but the immortal was not to be killed that way.

One of the beasts that had its jaws closed over the legs of the tower had finally snapped through it, and the tower shifted dangerously to one side. The other legs held, but the man had been thrown off balance, and his musket fell over the side. The werewolf that he hit was momentarily stunned but it quickly recovered, swinging its massive head from side to side. Then, as the man backed to the far end of the watch tower, the werewolf leapt at him. Greg could see the soulless creature, outlined in hellish red and orange firelight, its slavering jaws open for the kill. It was over quickly, and for that Greg was grateful at least. The man lay in the corner, his arm slumped over the railing. Greg couldn't see, but he imagined the man's throat had been bitten out, and he turned away.

Seeing the man die had given him a surge of energizing adrenaline, and he slammed more ammunition into his musket. He cocked the gun, ready to kill more of the savages. They had breached the tree line and were surging below, and then past him. He fired into their ranks and one of the werewolves flinched, blood spraying from a hole in its lung. It fell to the ground, but the others were already out of range of the musket. Rather than stay and risk the rain of musket balls and pellets, the werewolves had evidently decided against killing the men in the remaining towers.

Greg pounded his gong again, and the sound was repeated back to him eight times. Their meaning was clear; they would have to follow the werewolves into the city.

Nine horses had been led to the base of the towers, and Greg gathered the last of the bullets into his vest. He threw his gun over his shoulder and began the laborious descent to the ground, leaving the remainder of his ale. He would need a clear head now.

His feet touched powdery snow, and he turned to his horse. It was a stallion, coal black and stocky with a fine, intelligent head. His own gelding had been retired to his stables; this horse was fresh and ready for battle. A layer of chainmail draped over the horses' chest and back, but its head and legs were left uncovered to move freely. It pawed the ground with one feathered hoof, and Greg wasted no time climbing onto its massive back. He squeezed his legs together, and the horse surged into a surprisingly graceful gait for its size. Horse and rider merged with the other nine and they charged into the city.

Their horses' hooves pounded on the cobblestone, their front legs spanning forward to gain more ground on the werewolves. Their manes and tails fanned out behind them and white froth gathered at their lips. Their protective chainmail clanged in a collective sound of clinking metal. When they came to the buildings, nine separated into threes, and they split off in search of the skeletal beasts.

Greg heard a gunshot in the distance, and he knew one of them had been found. His eyes searched between the buildings through the darkness, but they were not powerful enough to discern shadows from beasts. When no savage leapt to meet them, he and his companions turned their mounts to look elsewhere.

They came to another alley, and shining yellow eyes met them. The werewolf growled deep in its throat, revealing white fangs. Although it was alone, it walked boldly towards the three men on horseback, with what was left of its fur rising along its back vertebrae.

"Go!" Greg shouted to his fellows. "I'll take care of this one, find the others!" With a nod, the others pulled on their reins and galloped away. Greg reached over his shoulder for his loaded gun and trained it on the werewolf. His finger rested on the trigger as the beast paced in the narrow alley. He was ready to apply the killing pressure, but the creature never stopped moving, its eyes locked on his.

The werewolf had changed just enough for its eyes to mimic a humans but its body still held the undead qualities of the wolf. Looking into the beast's eyes was unnerving; the yellow was claimed by wild instinct while the black irises mirrored an intelligence so like his own that his finger hesitated on the trigger.

Greg did not know how long he stood rooted there before he heard the voice in his head.

Are you going to kill me now human? The werewolf's voice asked in his head. Greg squeezed the trigger and the exploding blast in the alley was amplified before his brain had registered the action. He steeled himself against the recoil of the musket, his boots still tucked in the stirrups. He closed his eyes, and when he opened them the werewolf lay on its side, its lungs shuddering between shattered ribs. Shaken slightly, Greg turned his horse and galloped after the others.

He could hear the commotion in the streets before he reached them. One man had been dragged off his horse and it fled, dragging its shifted clinking armor behind it as unarmed men began trying to corral the terrified animal. A werewolf stood over the man, one paw planted on the man's chest, its maw open in victorious fury. Men shot at it from a distance, but none wanted to get within range. The fallen man's musket lay just out of reach, and he shifted his weight, trying to get closer. Finally, his hand closed over the trigger. The gun went off, the bullet ricocheting off a building and into an oil lamp, scattering into tiny exploding shards. Drops of burning oil rained from the air and onto the streets, hungrily devouring strands of loose straw.

The fire began to spread and flames licked the sides of the wooden buildings. The werewolf threw back its head and howled loudly enough for all of Valwood to hear its call.

As the flames writhed with burning energy all around, the werewolf paused, then bit deeply into its victim. The man cried out, blood bubbling at his mouth. He tried to get up, but the werewolf held him pinned where he lay. His movements grew weaker and weaker until his head rolled to the side, and he was still. The werewolf snarled in each of their heads.

Hear me now humans. The war is raging and now your grand city is ablaze. Surrender now or we will not stop until every one of you lies dead!

~ Chapter Eighteen ~
The Fall of Valwood

For a moment, all of the men stood speechless, unable to move. The werewolf's words echoed in their minds until the threat seemed to linger like a tangible being over their heads.

Amidst the fearful silence, one brave man strode to the center, and fired his musket at the werewolf. The creature rose to meet the blast, its claws fully extended, but the gun was faster. The werewolf's exposed heart and lungs imploded from the point blank shot. With a tortured cry it fell to the ground, the life already ebbing from its white eyes.

The shooter emerged from the shadows to stand under one of the street lamps. His face shone under the light, and Greg recognized him as Chief Elder Olek. Olek put a hand on his knee and leaned onto the musket, breathing heavily.

"That is what I say to that," he chuckled wearily, running a finger through his dark beard. The men laughed, seizing the humorous moment in a tumultuous time.

But as the nervous laughter died off the men froze, only their eyes searching through the shadows. Faint white orbs could be seen hanging in the distance, and Greg remembered the fallen werewolf's ominous words. The eyes seemed to multiply before them, shifting and disappearing behind trees and buildings to reappear several feet ahead. The cursed creatures paced in the woods, taunting the men with eyes that glowed from their previously empty sockets.

"Ready yourselves men," Olek whispered, but his voice nonetheless carried to the trees. They could see a mist forming and rising, the evaporating moisture that rose from the werewolves' open mouths. Their skeletal forms were materializing; the cracked bleachy white of their bones shined ivory when they caught under the lights of the fire and the city. Tendrils of hanging flesh and sinew held their forms together, and when they breathed their entire rib cages shuddered and shook.

The men wished for nothing more than to drop their guns and flee from the strange apparitions, but instead they looked to Elder Olek.

He no longer leaned on his gun, instead he held it at the ready, his breathing deliberately regular. Even as one of the creatures approached him, he allowed no visible indication of fear to slip past him.

This one was larger than the others, standing nearly as tall as Olek on four legs. Hand crafted beads of every color and small feathers hung from what was left of the werewolf's mane. He drew himself up to full height, meeting Olek's gaping stare with eyes that had stopped spinning and regarded him with all of the human's intelligence.

I am Anraq, Alpha of this clan, he projected into every man's head.

180

"Anraq, I am Chief Elder Olek of Valwood," Elder Olek said. The werewolf dipped its head in response, but his narrowed white eyes never left Olek's.

"Your werewolves have suffered a great loss Anraq. I suggest you leave if you do not want any more of them to suffer the same fate."

Your men have invaded Claw Haven to destroy us with burning silver and threaten us once more without cause. I should tear the flesh from your bones where you stand Chief Elder Olek. Elder Olek listened without interruption and slammed the butt of his gun in the snow, bristling with rage and indignation.

"You dare to threaten me, mongrel!" he managed to answer, spitting out each word as if it were an abomination that lay on his tongue. The other werewolves had stopped their restless pacing and formed a semicircle around the two. The men too, held their unwavering positions, their hands on their weapons.

The words ceased to sound in the men's head, and once it was clear that the Alpha had words only for their leader, both sides stood in eerie silence, prepared to act at the slightest need.

"You vile creature dare to fill my head with lies! Anesa! Elder Tomas Edrich! Both of them rest forever in the ground because of your disgusting species!" Olek answered, spittle dribbling from his mouth at his frenzied accusations. He pointed a stubby finger at Anraq's chest. "You who have taken Natalya and probably killed her as well!"

At Elder Olek's words, Anraq began to snarl, and it was a horrifying sound. His hanging vocal cords vibrated visibly as the growl began low in his throat. His jaws quivered with the effort of containing the awful sound, and saliva dripped from his fangs. His entire body shuddered horribly, and when he was done, he had shifted his gaze to meet every man's in the street. This time when he spoke, they all heard his words echo in their heads.

It is you humans that are filled with lies. Our attempts at peace have been shortsighted, and they end now.

Elder Olek began to laugh, quietly at first until his entire body quaked with laughter. It had the manic quality of one who did not believe his own eyes or ears, and his chortling seemed to hang on the verge of insanity. The men could only stare in disbelief at their leader; it was as if he had lost his mind completely.

"You have spoken your last words, Anraq." Elder Olek pointed his gun, positioning the barrel so it rested between the werewolf's eyes. He lowered his eye to line his sight, but Anraq had already crossed the distance between them. He opened his jaws as he attacked and closed them over Elder Olek's arm as the musket went off. Elder Olek cried out, his musket falling from his grip, and Greg watched as if in a trance, reminded of the man in the watchtower. Anraq loosened his teeth from the elder's arm only to sink them into his shoulder while all looked on.

The men hastened into action and began firing their guns, and the next moment the neat cobblestone streets of Valwood descended into chaos. A torrent of balls and pellets fell just short of the ring of werewolves. The savages charged into the deluge of silver, howling in rage when their legs, tails and ears were hit, or falling to the ground when their vitals burst into bloody fragments. The men, pausing to reload their weapons between attacks, had their muskets seized from their grasps by waiting jaws. The werewolves ripped flesh with their claws, bit through sinew and bone and tore throats from necks in the fray. Blood ran into a thousand rivers that gathered in the creases of cobblestones, and the snow was littered with bony shards, clumps of hair and fur, singed flesh and human skin.

In the center of it all, Elder Olek still lay pinned beneath the Alpha's grasp, and the werewolf lowered his fangs to the man's chest. He opened his jaws and clamped them shut, and Olek screamed a heart wrenching sound. His ribs had cracked under the pressure of the werewolf's weight and jaws, and his still beating heart thudded in its place, oblivious to the imminent peril. Anraq bit into his delicate heart and blood sprayed from the body. Olek closed his eyes as he exhaled, but another inhale was never to be achieved. His corpse deflated, all signs of life gone, and with his death a piece of Valwood seemed to die.

The men, so successful at first with their rain of burning silver, began to pull back into the inner core of the city. Their supply of bullets was running dangerously low, and moral had dampened into a nearly defeated stupor.

With their leader dead and no time to pray for his soul, all of the men now looked to Elder Greg. He lowered himself out of the saddle to face his men.

"Chief Elder Greg Vrushko, what are your orders, sir?" a man asked, kneeling. He removed the sword that had served as his back up weapon from its sheath. He held it by its blade, offering the handle to Greg. Tentatively Greg reached for it and stared at the proud weapon for as long as the battle would allow, feeling honored. He mounted his stallion and began issuing commands from atop his horse. The sword he sheathed, still favoring the musket while the ammunition lasted. He no longer fired as often as he could. Instead, he waited until his short range spray of bullets would be most advantageous to him.

Some of the men abandoned their guns after the ration of bullets came only to those who had shown they could effectively hit the creatures consistently in their vitals. The farmers, cobblers, potters, writers and others that made up Valwood took up swords, maces, sickles and whatever other weapons they could

183

scrounge together. They held them upright, the weapons strange in their nervous hands, but their faces were tight and determined.

Those that were still weaponless fought the flames that were slowly gaining ground.

The blacksmith, having never preferred the gun, made excellent use of his hammer, swinging it at the creatures' heads and keeping them away from his body. Some of the ranch hands gathered pitchforks, and more than one werewolf met its demise on the pronged end through its heart.

The beasts had scattered all throughout Valwood, leaving a trail of bloody destruction in their wake. The city was rent with anguished cries and howls as each side grappled desperately for a hold on Valwood. Meanwhile, the number of dead climbed higher on both sides.

The werewolves stuck to the shadows, no longer engaging the humans in direct combat. They eyed the various weapons with respect for their immortal hold on this earth could be broken by a single stab to the chest or silver bullet to the brain. They were tireless in their invasion, crashing through windows and destroying anything they could get their jaws around.

Some of the werewolves ran into the trees at the sight of the men and their weapons, and the men cheered, thinking they had driven the beasts away. But when the werewolves returned with dry branches clamped in their mouths, they could only watch in horror. Their nightmare faces swayed back and forth into the many embers that the men had failed to contain, the reds and oranges dancing in their incandescent eyes. Sparks from the burning wood flew to their faces and singed their fur and flesh, but the werewolves took no notice. Once their branches had caught fire, they sprung to other buildings and rubbed their burning kindling against their sides, urging them to catch flame. The embers flared and leapt to the roofs where they quickly spread, hungrily devouring the wood. Plumes of smoke rose from the city, obscuring the stars behind a smoky veil. A black cloud, alive with a million flapping wings, ascended into the air. The birds' desperate cries deadened all other sounds as they sought to escape the blaze. Soon, nearly all of Valwood was aglow with dancing fire, and just as the once glorious Ruins had once burned, so too did the humans' great city.

Naktor prowled along the tree line, his nostrils assailed with smoke. The gritty odor of ashes clouded his sensitive nose until he was no longer able to pick out the human scent he had been tracking.

He shook his head, sending a gelatinous tendril of saliva flying into the woods. One of the rotating ears atop his exposed skull had been slashed to a fleshy strip. It hung loosely, bleeding freely, but his hearing was unaffected. They twitched as he relied on his hearing to stay on the trail. Other than his ear, he was unhurt, and his body pulsed with undying stamina and strength.

Naktor snarled in the darkness and another werewolf appeared behind him. This one was larger than he, with great size even for their kind, and when he turned his head, only one glowing eye glared at him. That socket was empty, only a gaping black hole in his cracked skull, for the other had been lost in the battle. *That visage must have surely had the best of the humans fleeing for their lives.* Naktor growled at the thought, amused by the fear his companion must have evoked in Valwood.

But rather than fleeing, the humans had put up a remarkable fight against them. Even as they were torn apart, their throats ripped viciously from their necks, they had managed to kill many of the werewolves' number. Naktor cleared his thoughts, and his ears scanned through the various howls, shrieks, pleads and cries for this particular human, and he locked onto his unique voice.

Got it, he growled to his fellow, and the werewolf behind him dipped its head keenly. They surged from the trees into the outskirts of Valwood, splitting up to avoid flaming debris from collapsing buildings, and then returning to each other's side as they charged through the snow. They never deviated from their mission, their ears always strained towards the man's shouting lest they lose his voice amidst the mayhem.

The pair ran in perfect stride, their footfalls timed in a rhythm as old as the pack itself. They did this instinctually, seeming to revert almost back into the true wolves from which they came. A voice as ancient as the wind whispered to them, and although their need for prey had long been rendered unnecessary, they still retained the synchronized grace of the cooperative hunter. The two specters ignored the fighting all around them, their concentration never wavering.

They heard the voice, raspy from delivering endless orders, before they saw the source of it. The man was on horseback, and he had not yet seen them.

As quiet as ghosts, the two werewolves streaked into opposite directions, slinking into the shadows where the man's human sight was not discerning of their shapes. They waited on either side of him, stalking forward when they were certain they would not be discovered.

The man, oblivious to the threat, plunged a sword into the chest of a werewolf that had thrown itself at him. He had clearly run out of bullets; the empty musket lay abandoned in the street. The she-werewolf went limp on his weapon, and Naktor's other growled in the darkness as he recognized Henovi's fallen form.

186

Silence, Lehova! Naktor snapped in his head, and the werewolf's growl tapered into quietness. Luckily, the noise had been lost in the din, and the humans around them remained unaware of their presence.

From their opposite positions, the two lowered themselves into the slushy snow, their mandibles resting on their paws in mutual grief. Lehova's muscles and tendons were straining, as if he were still keen to come to Henovi's aid, but Naktor's glare held him where he lay. They could do no more for the dead werewolf.

The two waited for the opportune moment to act, when the new Chief Elder Greg Vrushko was sufficiently distracted. With his back to them, they closed the distance, their jaws opening. Lehova had gone for the horse's unprotected belly, while Naktor plunged his canines into Greg's leg. The man cried out and slashed with his sword, glancing Naktor's foreleg. He released his grip and landed squarely on his paws as Greg's stallion stamped his hooves, narrowly missing him.

The black war horse reared onto his hind legs, neighing defiantly, his deadly hooves flailing. Lehova leaped upwards like a spring uncoiling, his jaws maneuvering between the horse's kicking legs and the protective chain mail. His teeth pierced the horse's flesh, and the stallion's agonized squeal echoed jarringly in the werewolves' ears.

The stallion fell on its side, its legs kicking as it struggled to regain its footing. Greg cried out for help, his leg pinned beneath the street and his fallen horse.

Lehova and Naktor circled them, preventing the other humans from getting close to Greg while he swung his sword madly. They eyed the weapon, springing clear of it but could gain no land on the human.

Instead, they worried the horse, darting in to nip at its flanks, and then dodging its legs. The horse began to weaken, and it was not long before a final bite to the throat had killed Greg's stallion.

The other men watched helplessly as the werewolves began to close their circle on Greg. Just as they had defeated his horse, they worked as a pair, one drawing his weapon while the other bit in rapid succession with his fangs, whirling away before Greg could make contact with the sword.

As he too began to bleed from numerous bites, Greg's speed with his weapon faltered. He had quickly exhausted himself, and when one of the savages charged him, he could see his own death in its expressionless eyes. Adrenaline flooded his body, but with him still pinned, this reckless energy had no outlet. It had one blessing though, the endorphins that had shot through his blood stream made him numb to the werewolves' bites, and his thoughts turned to reflection.

He no longer considered his own life, for in his mind it was already lost to him. But he did think of Valwood and hoped his short leadership could carry his men to ultimate victory. He remembered the honor and valor he had felt when he taken Chief Elder Olek's sword, and he knew he had done the dead Elder proud.

Then his thoughts shifted to Irena and the love for her that had never faded even when her life had. He remembered her as she was, his beautiful bride and accomplished vampire huntress. And when he thought of his daughter, he felt a sadness he had never known. Natalya, his light. He hoped he had been a good father, despite the absences that his duties had demanded from him. And he wished bitterly that he could have saved her, could have stopped the beautiful light she had brought to the world from dimming into darkness. When his eyes began to close for the final time, and the black that brimmed at their edges began to grow, he found himself also lost in unending darkness.

~ Chapter Nineteen ~
The Birth of Dissent

    With the human Chief dead, Lehova and Naktor ran together again under the new moon. With the werewolves' victory seemingly assured, most of their kind had spread to the far corners of Valwood, and the pair followed. The men rushed them with swords and pitchforks, but their paws were fast and their legs swift, and so they reached the farmland unharmed.

    The distant hills and crops were untouched by the fire, and the two werewolves slowed their pace to a lope. Here, only a few houses, ranches and barns were spread out over the miles, and they were finally able to catch their breaths.

    The new moon was waning into the spreading light of morning and with it, their tireless energy also began to wane. Their tongues rolled from their mouths, and their bodies shook as they panted. And just as the day had shed the moon, their undead appearances were also shed, like a worn snake skin.

Hide grew above their exposed bones and muscles, and fur rippled above that. Their rigid skulls were replaced with shorter hair and whiskers. Noses as black and shiny with moisture as wet obsidian, grew from the bone. Now they could have passed for true wolves except for their glowing white eyes.

Their injuries healed too; Naktor's ear seemed to mend with invisible stitches until only the dried blood remained, and their scratches faded to nothing. But Lehova could not regrow his missing eye. The socket remained a black abyss from which only a faint glowing light shined from within the deep recess. He gazed mournfully at Naktor.

May Zulae take Henovi in her paws, he growled.

And her spirit be forever transformed, Naktor finished, referring to the prayer that the werewolves always said over their dead. The words could give no comfort, only the hopes that their curse could be ended with their passing.

They bowed their shaggy heads, wondering how many others of their number had died without anyone to say those words over them. The moments passed in silence when Naktor finally spoke.

We should slaughter all of the humans for what they have done.

Lehova growled softly in his throat with sympathy, but as he looked at his pack mate, he could think of no words to soothe his anger.

The two ranged over the hills, relieved to be alive but without reason for their feelings. Their biggest curse was to fight bitterly for a life that was not worth living, a life that brought them no meaning and gave them little pleasure. And while each of them secretly longed for Henovi's fate, they feared it greatly. Perhaps Zulae had left Henovi in a world more desolate than the one they walked in now. Or perhaps the moon Goddess did not even exist, although they dared not utter that possibility aloud.

They crested a hill and startled a flock of crows that had sought refuge within the rows of sparse corn stalks. Their cawing echoed all around them in unison as most of them took to the nearby trees. But one crow settled onto a scarecrow and turned its head to stare unblinkingly at the pair of them. It was an ominous sight, the bird silhouetted against the streaking pinks and blues of the morning sky, perched on that mockery of a human body. The crow stared at them intently with an eye filled with unearthly brilliance, even as the other birds had disappeared from sight. The werewolves had made a full circle, and the creature's eyes still followed them, its neck revolving like an owl's in a supernatural position. The werewolves turned back to watch, waiting for the bird to succumb to the pain in its neck and fly away, but the three of them seemed to be caught in a strange battle of wills.

The next moment, the bird gathered air beneath its wings and it rose too, its neck still bent unnaturally to shriek malevolently at them as it turned towards the woods.

Lehova and Naktor walked onwards, all too aware of their effect on nature's creatures. They were an aberration, a mistake that should have never been, and they fit in with neither animal nor human.

They reached the home of the humans that had planted this cornfield. They could smell them inside, their fear wafting invitingly towards them, and they paused outside the door.

Lehova began padding towards the forest, but he stopped and turned when he noticed Naktor had still not moved. The other werewolf was staring intently through the front door as if he could see the humans inside, his ears pricked forward.

Naktor, what are you doing? Let's go, Lehova growled and resumed his walking.

The enemy lies behind this door.

It is our mission to secure the borders now that their leaders have fallen. No human is to be let in or out of Valwood. Those are our orders.

I will not stop until every one of them lies dead!

I grow weary of battle. This war has forced us to abandon our journey towards ending our curse, but now it is time we continued it. I wish for no more death on my paws.

You have grown soft, Lehova, Naktor snarled in disgust. Lehova did not reply. Instead, he tilted his nose to the sky and howled. The crescendo was beautiful and haunting, and as it tapered to a low moan, he cocked his head, listening for a reply. He did not have to wait long before another werewolf answered the call.

There is Anatuk, about four miles away. We are needed there, Lehova growled, and began walking towards the answering howl.

Naktor had backed up, his eyes narrowed, his tail lashing back and forth behind him. Without warning he leaped straight towards the glass window. Lehova turned, and realized too late what he had intended and tore after him.

Naktor had passed through the window and it seemed to shatter in slow motion, showering him in a million shimmering fragments of broken glass and timber. The only thing Lehova could hear was the tinkling of the window bending into the werewolf's weight, amplified by his own desperation to reach him.

Naktor landed deftly on his paws inside the house, and began sniffing for the humans. His pelt was streaked with blood from a thousand cuts, but he did not wait for them to heal before heading towards the humans. Lehova leaped through the window as well, but without his full sight, he had trouble measuring the distance. He landed hard on his foreleg, and for a split second, he lay disoriented inside the human house. He quickly recovered and shook himself before following the other werewolf into the next room.

Naktor had cornered three humans, a female and her two young children, onto their couch with his snarling. They sat terrified, their legs pulled up as far from the werewolf as they could get. One of the children was crying, and the mother tried to calm him, though silent tears were running down her face.

"Please," she moaned. Her arms were spread out across her children, shielding them from the werewolves with her weak, frail, human body. Naktor was pacing the length of the room, his ears flat against his head, and his tail scything the air behind him.

Naktor they are only children! It is against Zulae's law! Lehova snarled but Naktor had already thrown himself at the human family.

Lehova had misjudged Naktor before; he did not make the same mistake a second time. He intercepted the smaller werewolf, and they were both knocked against the wall while the humans watched, frozen by their terror. Lehova recovered from the impact first, and as they struggled, Naktor's throat flashed below him.

Lehova clamped his jaws onto Naktor's neck, shaking it hard enough to taste hot blood, and for droplets to fall from the wound.

Enough, Lehova snarled, biting deeper still until Naktor's agonized whines filled the room. He released the werewolf, and Naktor coughed deeply. The humans watched in horror as he lay in the corner, blood welling from the tear in his neck, while his body shook violently. Lehova drew himself up to his full height and addressed the humans, his eyes locked onto the shocked mother's.

Your kind have denied us, persecuted us and hunted us like wild dogs from the lands we have so fiercely guarded from man's hate. Though hate grows in us too, for we are not unlike your kind. But we possess all of your capacity for understanding and peace as well.

His gaze lowered to the youngest boy and though tears still shined on his round face, he wiped them away with a tiny hand. Like most children who possess more understanding of the world than adults could ever know, he met the werewolf's eyes boldly.

You have been thrust into a war that you have no part of, and now we shall go from this place. You and your mother and sister shall flee, for we do not kill innocents; nor do we bite a child who has not yet wielded a sword. So go from here just as we will go, and may harmony someday rule this land again.

Lehova broke the eye contact, and the light from his eyes dimmed from the room as he turned to leave. The little family watched him go, unable to speak. He padded through the empty doorway without needing to check if Naktor followed. The smaller werewolf was indeed close behind him, the wound in his bloodstained neck fading. He snarled deeply, but Lehova had drawn blood from him, and he did not draw blood in return. His throat had been bared, waiting for the larger werewolf to kill him. But Lehova had not, and Naktor was defeated.

Now pack ritual and honor prevented him from attacking Lehova when he had his back turned to him.

They leaped out of the house through the ruined window in single file and continued towards Valwood's border. They converged and ran once more together in a steady lope, but their heads were empty of one another's thoughts.

Naktor's head brimmed with thoughts of his own however, dark images of traitors and blood, and he shot a sideways glance at his pack mate.

Lehova was weak and unwilling to do what was necessary. He, Naktor could do it; he could drive every man away from Valwood, leaving nothing left of the human civilization that had bordered their lands for hundreds of years. Their beloved home, and their very clan depended on them now, and there could be no room for weakness.

~ Chapter Twenty ~
The Calling

The fires of Valwood had finally burned themselves out, leaving the city shrouded in a smoky haze. The buildings that had not been felled were scarred with vivid scorch marks, scars that could not be washed away. The charred trunks of the bare trees stood like slightly waving sentries along the borders. To Kaima, they were deceitfully benign in their gentle swaying, in stark contrast to the turmoil that had descended over her dear city.

She lifted her hand to her forehead and wiped away the sweat that had collected on her brow. The sun had not yet graced the sky, and she had already made several trips here to her family's well to collect water. Now she cranked the pulley again, lowering the bucket into the abyss, and she focused her eyes on the task. The farmland was remarkably quiet, away from the screams, howls and halting gun shots. The outlying fields too were mostly untouched by the smoke and fire in their snow laden serenity. Only the odd cawing of a crow or the shrill grinding of the bucket along the rope punctuated the disconcerting quietness. As Kaima drew the sloshing bucket up again, a peculiar feeling stole over her. She sensed that she and Valwood lay on some proverbial brink, and she did not know which way the tides of action would throw her. *Would she be called upon to take up arms, to protect her homestead in the face of marauding death or would her courage lie in her fleeing feet, aboard a caravan to new life that she and her surviving family would have to rebuild on their own?*

She sighed and unhooked the bucket from the rope. She could not answer that question now, but she could get this water back to the house. She walked slowly so as not to spill, and it was then that she heard the noise.

She froze, halfway between the well and her home. It had been a fleeting sound, one so subtle it could have been the winter breeze or a pine tree rustling. She looked to the pastures at the other end of her property, but the horses were locked safely within the barn. She turned back towards the house and walked briskly towards it, her ears sill listening. She had reached the front porch and set the bucket down to open the door, when she heard it again.

This time, the noise was not so subtle. Something was behind her, and she hesitated, uneasiness inhibiting her desire to turn around and meet whatever faced her. After a second, her curiosity deadened her fear to an elusive spook, and she whirled around.

A werewolf stood in the center of the snowy field, its jaws quavering. Its fur was such a deep gray it appeared almost black, and it was looking straight at her. Its eyes were narrowed, but the glowing white that radiated from its stare was undiminished.

Kaima gave out a tiny cry of surprise, starting for the house. Her hand had touched the handle when she heard his voice in her head.

Wait! Do not be afraid. The sensation of her thoughts being invaded by another alarmed her, but she did not react. The voice had been of a young male's and rang with the desperate truth of one who begged to be heard. She turned back to him and answered in a clear voice that bordered on defiance.

"I'm not." She knew her words and tone were convincing but she could not hide the faint whiff of fear that emanated from her in his direction.

You carry Natalya's scent. You must be her friend, he answered and now she grabbed a garden hoe that had been leaning against the side of the house. She held it straight out before her, keeping as much distance between her and the werewolf.

"What do you know of Natalya, beast?"

The werewolf seemed almost amused at the red headed girl with the makeshift weapon before him. She wielded it clumsily, but nevertheless like a two handed sword. A saddle of freckles across her nose and rosy cheeks betrayed her youth, and vivid green eyes failed to disguise her wariness.

I know many things, he answered. *She has spent a good while with us, seeking peace between humans and our kind. Now the war rages on with no end in sight, and Natalya is nowhere to be found. I fear something has befallen her.*

"I thought she was safe with you," Kaima answered, and now there was fear in her voice. Her grip on the pitchfork slackened, and she lowered it slightly.

She had succeeded in dissuading our Alpha from immediately attacking your people. She was on her way towards Valwood to stop her father's attack. She must have never made it back, he growled sadly, and now the glow from his white eyes nearly dimmed completely.

"Why do you tell me this, werewolf? Why do you concern yourself so much with one of our own? I cannot trust you."

Oh rest assured, human girl, that your death would be a minor exertion on my part, even with your weapon. *But I have no desire to kill you. We have suffered and lost a great many of our pack members, and more die with each passing sun. I know that it is the same for you and your people. Now I seek to finish Natalya's vision and end this war.*

"Ok...but why ask me?" Kaima asked, withdrawing the hoe. "I am a mere farm girl, and I doubt the men would listen to me even now."

You know Natalya, just as I do, and I believe that she may still live. Kaima looked at the werewolf strangely now.

"What is your name werewolf?"

I am Voren.

"I *knew* it," she whispered shakily. The hope that she had been fostering for Natalya's safe return had long been doused, and here a strange werewolf had come to breathe life into the flame once more.

You have heard of me then?

"Yes, Natalya has mentioned you," Kaima answered.

What has she told you of us and our kind?

"She seemed...to feel that she could trust you."

Your friend's instinct has been a great boon to her. If she still lives, bringing her safely back home may be the key to ending this war.

"What do you think has happened to her?"

I do not know for certain. I have only my suspicions, but I do know this. Her scent, although it permeates throughout Valwood, is stale in my nose. It lingers here but like a stagnant pool, never flowing either in or out of the city. I plan to track her scent from Claw Haven to see if I can piece together what may have happened. You have confirmed she is not here, and I thank you for your assistance.

Voren turned and began to walk away. Kaima watched the werewolf slink away until he had nearly reached the distant trees. Without hardly knowing the reason, she called the werewolf back.

"Wait!" He slowly turned his wolfish face to hers. "You will need help. I am coming with you, Voren." The werewolf gazed back at her, surprise now widening his eyes. He thrust his muzzle in the air, sniffing fixedly before he answered her.

All is not well in your home. Your father and brother lie inside, dependent on the water you have brought and the tending to their wounds as they should be. I appreciate the sentiment, but I shall bring Natalya back home myself.

"You need me," Kaima said stubbornly, raising her head hesitatingly, but with pride. "Natalya is my friend and if she still lives I owe her this. You risk death at the hands of our men with silver guns everywhere you go in Valwood. I can afford you some protection there. I am strong too and will not hold you up."

I admire your courage Kaima. The men's wounds are not fatal, but they will need some attention. Make your arrangements, and meet me here then at dusk. We shall leave immediately, and may Zulae help us all.

201

~ Chapter Twenty-One ~
The Pack's Discord

The city that had never known the cries of the wolf now sang with their howling. It started with a clear single voice, raised to the waxing moon in victorious sorrow. The sound was searching, longing to find its pack mates, and others soon rose to the call. Their songs were taken up by werewolves from all corners of Valwood while the human citizens hid behind boarded up windows and doors.

The blizzards that had passed the city by in days past, now unleashed their fury with an assailment of sleet and driving snows that only added to the din. With no one to light them, many of the city's lamps had died, and the storm darkened Valwood even further. Most of the light came instead from the many pairs of glowing eyes that were drawing together in the streets.

The creatures leaped from the ruins of broken buildings, their paws shattering windows while fallen doors bent under their weight. Soon, they had settled on a low rooftop that was overlooking the city, looking as strange as any wolf pack that had been caught out of its natural habitat.

One werewolf rose to its middle as the others parted respectfully to allow him in.

Anraq, one of the werewolves said telepathically, dipping his head into a low bow.

The Alpha nodded his head in return, before taking his place in the center of the roof. He sat back on his haunches, his tail swept neatly over his paws. One by one the others turned their heads to look at him expectantly. When he had the enraptured attention of every werewolf in the clan, he began to speak.

We have achieved a great victory over our enemies. Our kind has spread throughout Valwood, and its men quake in fear at the mere mention of our names!

The werewolves threw their heads back and howled in agreement at his words. Others whined and barked excitedly at one another. Anraq waited until they had quieted down before speaking again.

But the earth screams with the heart wrenching cries of our dead. We have lost so many...and I fear for those that have not had the prayers said over them. How many spirits have been lost to the winds with no way of finding Zulae?

This time there was not a howl or a yip of joy among them. All of the werewolves' heads were lowered in shared grief and mutual loss. They looked to Anraq silently now with guidance, their eyes searching his.

We must restore contact with the humans and offer them peace.

His words were met with shocked growls of dissent and raised lips. Glowing eyes widened while jaws quivered with shock.

Anraq, with all due respect, what you suggest is madness.

At once, Naktor raised his head when he recognized Kivah's voice echoing in his mind. He was glad the dissentient words had not been his own. Anraq began to snarl now, and Kivah met his eyes with fierce determination.

Am I not the Alpha of this Clan? Anraq asked, addressing each and every one of them. *I would be less than your leader if I were willing to condemn our brother and sisters' spirits to unrest. They scream in anguish to me in my dreams, and they are lost in the void. I will not allow any others to meet their fate if I can stop it under my rule.*

Kivah growled unswervingly in his throat, his eyes never breaking contact with Anraq's. The silver bullet that had entrenched itself into his hind leg and gaped angrily in its refusal to mend even suns later, was a livid reminder of man's hatred. The wound was shining even through the blizzard, and dried blood had formed a morbid scab over it that still hindered the werewolf's movement. He could not suppress his growling as he countered Anraq.

They have chased us from our homes and created new weapons that match us in our strength. Even my body cannot be rid of this cursed bullet. They slaughter us relentlessly, and yet you seek peace with these creatures? Celestial Hold still stands desolate in its place lest we ever forget that great injustice.

Kivah stood with his head held high, his fur ruffled in the ragged wind. His eyes dared every werewolf to disagree with him, and another voice was added to the quarrel.

Kivah has more reason than any of us to seek man's destruction. And the forest's beasts have already fattened themselves on many of the humans that burned Celestial Hold to the ground. This time they are weak, without aid from the other

*humans, and their armies are gone. I no longer fear them, for do
we not tame fire ourselves as well?*

Yes! Cried one of the werewolves.

Victory is already in our claws!

The humans shall burn!

No! We cannot lose any more of our own, shouted another,
and soon Naktor's head was filled with so many conflicting voices
that he hardly knew who was speaking. Lips were parted, fangs
were bared and hackles were raised as the werewolves challenged
each other physically now. Naktor dared not give rise to his own
objections though. Instead, he merely waited, listened and
plotted.

Finally Anraq stood up until he towered over the
werewolves, his eyes blazing.

Enough, he snarled and the voices in Naktor's head ceased.
*It was once Sakarr's vision that the werewolves could all come
together under the full moon in a monthly peaceful gathering. And
it is for all of our sakes that I propose peace with the humans now.*

The werewolves backed away from each other, just shy of
shedding blood. Anraq walked among them now. His head was
raised and his tail a waving flag held aloft. The other werewolves
lowered their heads and tails as he passed, their ears flattened
against their skulls.

Some of them were peaceful in their submission, their
fears soothed by the Alpha's words. Some thoughts of rebellion
evaporated, lost to the winds when Anraq spoke. Others harbored
their discordant thoughts, carefully fostering them into tiny
storms of oncoming change. Nakor's mind was running far
beyond his body, and he shivered excitedly at the images that now
flashed through his conscious. These images he tucked away, in a
far corner of his mind to be looked upon later. He stood after the

Alpha had passed with nary a hint of protest. *The time to act would come* he knew, *but now was that not that time.*

Anraq turned again to address the pack. He spoke with none of the paternal tenderness he had displayed in Claw Haven. Instead, his words were laced with deadly authority.

My ruling is thus. We go now to the surviving human elders. Latuk, Naktor, you two will accompany me. This war is over, Anraq growled, and now not one of the werewolves rose to challenge him.

~ Chapter Twenty-Two ~
A Quest Begun

The night was a gentle shield from prying eyes for Kaima and Voren. The freshly falling snow concealed their tracks, and the trees blocked their forms, scattering them into distorted shadows.

They had left immediately that same night, while the werewolves debated, postured and threatened. Now they ran through the forest, Voren on four paws and Kaima on Methea behind the glowing-eyed wolf. She hardly knew where the werewolf was leading her; she could only blindly trust that his sensitive nose would guide them back to Claw Haven.

Although they had reached the border of Valwood without being seen, Voren still paused periodically to scent the air. He pointed his muzzle into the snow flurries, scenting for any werewolves that may be following them. He detected none of his own kind though, and they continued on, hoping to reach his village by the following nightfall. Then they would be able to track Natalya's scent, Voren had promised. From there, hopefully they could piece together what had transpired on the way to her people.

True to her word, Kaima did not slow her horse even when the bitter cold had seeped through the layers of animal skins she was wearing or when the pangs of her hunger had grown almost unbearable. Instead, she pushed the mare to her limits until hot steam rolled off of her chilled body and her chest was heaving with the effort of drawing in the cold air. The werewolf ran in a measured lope that never differed in step or swiftness, while Kaima and her tired mare struggled to keep up with his pace.

The feeble light of the crescent moon was shining directly above them when Voren finally stopped. Only now was it apparent that the werewolf tired, his tongue hung loosely from his panting mouth, and his words were ragged in Kaima's head.

You need nourishment. There is a cave just ahead of us. We will make a fire in there for the rest of the night and continue in the morning.

"I'm fine," Kaima started to say, but her stomach groaned loudly, and she argued no more. She dismounted from Methea and pulled the blanket further along her horse's trembling neck. She walked the remainder of the way to the cave, allowing the exhausted horse to rest.

The cave's mouth was easily wide enough for the three of them, and they walked gratefully inside. Droplets of moisture dripped from forming icicles in its roof, but it was sheltered from the brutal winds, and they welcomed the slight increase in temperature.

When the mare's lead had been securely staked to the cave's floor, Kaima left to gather kindling. When she had found enough, she returned to the cave to strike metal against the flint stone that she had packed for just this excursion. When the cackling sparks had ignited into a sizeable fire, she leaned against Methea and closed her eyes.

Voren lowered himself to the ground, watching the girl and her horse. In the firelight her pale skin seemed to glow under each freckle, and the mare was spattered in every shade of silver and gold.

That horse is familiar. Was she Natalya's? He asked, and Kaima smiled somewhat hopefully.

"Yes," she murmured. "This is Methea. It may be a foolish thought, but maybe bringing her horse could help us find her." She looked away nervously, half expecting to hear his laughter in her head. Instead, the werewolf nodded somberly.

That noble beast knows more than she lets on. Perhaps it is possible.

Kaima smiled again, comforted by the thought. When she had gathered her breath, she opened her pack and pulled out a shank of meat she had brought. The werewolf was laying on the ground facing her, his head resting on his paws. His eyes never left her, and when she brought the food to her mouth, he watched her with something close to wistfulness. He said nothing though, and after a few moments he turned his body to watch the storm.

He seemed so calm lying flat against the cave floor that Kaima was taken aback. Every fiber of his being was completely relaxed; the firelight cast moving shadows across his body, and he was unmoved by the sparks that buried themselves into his fur. His ears were casually pointed toward the raging winds outside, and his tail was spread out like a fan behind him, waving contentedly like a tame dog's. Kaima was reminded of her faithful sheepdog, Obi. He had long guarded her family's flocks from the ranging mountain lions and the occasional bear. She thought of him and smiled, hoping he had remained at her farm and away from the fires that had spread over Valwood.

As they sat, Kaima's thoughts brought her back to a primal time far before she had even been born. It was a time when early man had hunted his kills and roasted them into edibility, when wild wolves had offered their protection in exchange for the fire's warmth. Submissive and cowering they had come, licking the man's hands and lying by their feet, just as her own dog did. Soon they had formed an everlasting partnership, a peaceful coexistence that transcended their times of turmoil with the werewolves.

It was an age before these strange creatures that bore such resemblance to peaceful Zulae would steal among her people to take their children and dogs to be slaughtered and eaten. She shuddered, remembering the stories her mother used to tell of the glowing-eyed wolves, and her thoughts evaporated. She looked to Voren.

For them, it seemed as if this partnership had been renewed beyond an understanding that neither of them could ever comprehend.

But this was a werewolf, and when he turned his lamp-like eyes onto her, and the entire cave brightened with their light, the illusion was shattered. Beneath his wolfish exterior was a man, buried under undying flesh and fur. Limpid human eyes shone under luminescent wolf eyes, and a clumsy humanoid struggled with the grace of four slender legs. They passed the minutes in silence until Kaima's tentative voice rang across the cave.

"Voren, can I ask you something?"

Of course.

"What will become of my people now that we are not with them? I mean…are all of the werewolves like you?" Voren closed his eyes and slowly reopened them, and it was a few moments before she heard his reply.

It is true some of the werewolves want peace, he answered thoughtfully. *I imagine some are wrestling amongst themselves for we do not wish to cause more bloodshed in the world. Nor do we go into the arms of death willingly, for just like men, we are afraid of the unknown. Perhaps even more afraid, for this curse has shown us the horrors of life more vividly than any man could experience. We fear what may come after for us could be even more terrible than this life.*

But others may not feel the same. Some of us have felt man's hatred for too long and have become hard to it. After being driven from our homes, some feel that men's persecution of our kind needs to be eradicated from this earth completely.

But you and I, human and werewolf, are proof that it does not have to happen like that. Anraq is a fair leader and he has the trust of the pack. I believe in that.

"Thank you, Voren," she said, and she leaned back into the mare's side. The werewolf had turned his head back towards the storm. The flurries seemed to grow in their angry pursuit of the three of them. But the cave had warmed to an almost tepid temperature, and they passed the time in relative comfort. Kaima watched the patterns of the fire again, the writhing blues at the logs below fading upwards into resplendent orange. They lapsed into silence, and the fire flared red against Kaima's closed eyelids. Her mind relaxed, devoid of uneasy thought. Soon, she had fallen into the blissful naiveté of sleep, while the werewolf's eyes never strayed from the raging blizzard outside.

Sometime in the night the storm had broken, and when they exited the cave the next morning, they stumbled onto a forest that was sparkling white. The dark oaks were impressive in their stature as they stood glowing, silhouetted against the yellow sunlight. Their twisting, fibrous branches were laden with cottony snow that enveloped their trunks. The neighboring pines were likewise stooped towards the ground, their boughs bent under the weight of the drifts.

The dazzling brightness drowned out the light from Voren's eyes until he looked more wolfish than Kaima had ever seen him as she followed him on horseback.

They had abandoned their reckless pace, and now Methea ambled through the banks contentedly, sounding an occasional nicker into the quiet wood. The cold air brought a rosiness to Kaima's cheeks, and her fingers slowly went numb at the reins, despite her furs.

The beauty of the winter forest gradually lost its splendor as the morning progressed into the afternoon. Although they were touched by the sun's warming rays, the chilly season still reigned over the land. It superseded any short-lived heat she could draw from her horse's body or from the feeble sunlight. The creeping iciness now penetrated Kaima's many layers to rest jarringly in her bones, and not even her constant shiver could shake it. The werewolf however looked completely at ease under his furry pelt for the frost could only cling onto his guard hairs, unable to reach his skin.

He still paused every once in a while to shake away the snow that was settling onto his fur and to bury his muzzle into the white to scent for oncoming danger. Each time that he did this, he reported the same: neither human nor werewolf were tracking them, and he still hoped to reach Claw Haven by nightfall.

In spite of their time in the cave, neither of them had quite overcome the strangeness of their traveling together. So other than his constant reports, the two spoke very little to one another. The time passed in near monotony; the forest was unchanging in its snowy landscape and the repetitive crunching of porous snow beneath their feet was a constant heralding of another step into the unknown.

Only the gradual darkening of the sky and the dimming of the sun marked the passing hours. Kaima's eyelids began to droop involuntarily as the early night tricked her brain into wanting unneeded sleep. She had nearly drifted off in the saddle when she saw the white cones between the trees. They flitted in and out of view as more trees came before them, and she squinted at them now, instantly awake. They seemed to shine slightly in the darkness, but Kaima knew it was only their light color in the darkness that gave her that impression.

We have reached Claw Haven, Kaima.

She raised her head, sweeping her eyes back and forth to take it all in. They were nearing the cone shaped things, and now they became empty teepees, spaced along clearings in the woods. Some of them had been embellished with painted scenes of deer and crows while others sported sprigs of pine and dried flowers that wilted over the dwellings.

"Voren, this place is amazing!" Kaima exclaimed.

Before we were invaded, no human had set foot here in over a century. It is strange seeing it so empty. The teepees were deserted; no smoke trailed from their tops, and the entire camp was eerily quiet, devoid of all life and movement. The werewolf sniffed the air, but the scent of his kind had been long buried by the snow. None of the werewolves had returned since the siege. He turned his head back longingly in the direction of Valwood and Kaima felt a strange pity for the creature.

She realized she knew almost nothing of the werewolf, not what he looked like when he was in human form, not any of his favorite things or even his age. And even more strange was the knowledge that she *wanted* to know. *Did he ever romp in the snow like a wild wolf or throw his head back to the sky and howl for the sheer joy of it? Or did he loathe his wolf form like she had always been led to believe of their kind? Did he fear the moon and all of its terrifying changes or did he bask under her glow, a devil in animal disguise? What was he like as a human man? And how old had he been when he had been turned and became forever frozen in time?*

The nearly black wolf began walking again, and Kaima's thoughts were banished without answers. She squeezed her legs against Methea's sides, and the horse obediently followed. All fears of the werewolf had already been vanquished, for just as Kaima had grown to trust Voren inexplicably and almost wholly, so had Methea. A growl or snarl from the werewolf elicited no more response from the gentle mare than a touch from Kaima or a rub from Natalya had.

Ahead of them Voren barked excitedly, his tail waving, and Kaima nudged Methea into a trot. They caught up to the werewolf and he circled almost doglike in the snow.

I have picked up Natalya's scent. We can make camp here and follow her trail again at dawn.

Kaima nodded and smiled despite herself. The fervent hope that she had been forcing downward welled up again, and this time she did not push it down. She thought of Natalya, wielding her stake and coming up triumphant against a vampire. How strong her friend had been when Anesa had died, and how bravely she had sought out the werewolves. She stood at the edge of the trees, but she could see nothing hiding among them. *Where was Natalya now?*

Her hunger brought her back to the camp and dinner that night was a quick affair. They selected one of the teepees, and Kaima ignited a fire inside once more. Voren remained outside of the dwelling, sitting like a wolfish statue while she ate within. She invited him in, but he declined.

It was only after he was satisfied that no one was near, that he padded into the teepee and lay by the fire. He would spend the night's hours listening, as he always did, for danger while she thought of life and death and where this strange journey would take the two of them as she drifted into unawareness. Kaima had already fallen into a deep sleep, when she awakened with a start to the howling that was filling the sky.

It was a chorus of rising and falling song that came easily to even her human ears. Kaima pulled the bearskin blanket close to her chin, and Voren was instantly up, his ears pricked towards Valwood.

Vekoroh has called a meeting, he said, tilting his head slightly as he listened.

"What for?" Kaima asked, and worry for her people nudged away the last of her tiredness. She sat up, listening, but she could decipher nothing from the howls.

I am not sure. But we had better keep moving, he growled, and they stood up. *It is unusual for anyone other than Anraq to request something like this. I fear there may be turmoil in the pack. Who knows what has occurred since we left Valwood.*

Kaima doused the blazing fire with snow from outside and saddled Methea, while Voren explored the deserted village, his nose quivering in the snow. All the while he listened, but the howling had ceased, and his pack's voices did not reach his waiting ears or his open mind. The war must have reached a turbulent peak, and it crossed her mind that perhaps Voren no longer knew which side he was truly on.

With Natalya's scent strong in his nose, he followed it, sometimes in a linear path and other times doubling back as she had returned to a certain point. Still, other times, he circled almost indefinitely as she had often lingered in one area. In some places he lost her scent altogether, as it was interlaid by others of his kind.

All the while, Kaima followed on Methea, her hands fidgeting at the reins and her eyes casting furtive glances to the sides. She felt powerless to help; the falling snow had hidden all footprints, and her human nose could only detect the subtle smell of pine.

Voren seemed assured though, trailing the invisible path that only he could see with his sensitive nose. When they had reached the farthest teepee, his tail waved again, and Kaima knew he had regained the scent. For the remainder of the day he followed it, and they travelled in this fashion until the curtain of night was drawn around the forest once more.

As the werewolf did not need to eat, and Kaima had only packed a week's worth of food, she ate meagerly on horseback, and her stomach now ached with constant hunger pangs. She had grown used to the cold that attacked the little skin that she was forced to leave exposed to the elements, and her chest ached with the chill that seemed to clasp her heart in its iron grip. She kept Methea at a comfortable walk, not wishing to exhaust Natalya's mare again, and they trailed quite a distance behind the loping wolf.

When Voren's bark sounded in the far distance, it took a few moments for her and Methea to catch up. But as she cantered towards him, her face fell when she saw the werewolf.

His nose wrinkled in anger, and his lips were pulled back into a snarl. He pawed at the snow, his ears laid flat. He looked to her, and now she could see dread growing in his eyes as he looked to the distant castle on the mountain.

Natalya has been captured by Arkadith! He growled, and Kaima's hands went to her mouth as she gasped in horror.

~ Chapter Twenty-Three ~
Treason

     The previous day, Anraq, Latuk and Naktor found themselves running through the thick of the blizzard, neither affected by the piercing flakes in their eyes, nor the bitter cold. The chill that would have settled into a mortal's bones passed harmlessly over their coarse fur and did not slow their relentless pace.

     With their ears filled with the screeching gale and their eyes blinded by glittering snow, the three werewolves relied on their noses to guide them. The individual scents of the humans had fused into one as they had evacuated from the storm and from the very creatures that sought them out now. The werewolves latched onto it, following it through large banks and along the freezing river that meandered through the heart of Valwood. Soon, the scent strengthened in their nostrils, and they hastened their stride. The humans were close.

Most of the city's fighting men and those that had not fled to Dark Cliff Bay had barricaded themselves within the city hall building. It was the pride of Valwood's architecture, an enormous stone building lined with intricate street lamps and a gated iron fence that separated it from the rest of the city. A grand clock ticked from a recess in its front, and brilliant stained glass windows depicted birds, flowers and leafy vines.

The werewolves stood outside its front, feasting on the scent of terrified humans within. Anraq exhaled, and words began to form in his mind. His nose filtered through every scent, and he separated one from the others. He focused all of his energy on projecting the words into the mind of his chosen human.

Surviving Elder Vicktor Throm clenched his fists as the invasion into his head began, and his entire body tensed as Anraq's voice shattered his defenses.

Greetings, human. I am Anraq, leader of Claw Haven and of the greater pack. For centuries our kind has existed alongside one another, fighting, struggling, and never truly coexisting.

The power of Anraq's telepathy began to swell until every man, woman and child within the city hall now heard him speak. Each one of them stopped in their places to listen in awed silence, entranced by every word that rang through them.

We have killed bitterly on both sides, and you see now where the path of war has brought us. You have created your projectile weapons to destroy us, and until now we have met you with unflinching violence. Your men die with our claws in their hearts, and our kind fall, paralyzed with devastating silver. Our communal dead cry to us from the grave, and I ask you now if we may end this and look to a future together. Accept my offer of peace, and may you drop your silver as we will retract our fangs. I await your word, Elder.

The people within the building had listened without speaking, and now their voices carried to the waiting werewolves just outside it. Some were accusing, immediately contemptuous. Others hopeful and believing. But most were of simple incredulity, and a refusal to believe what they were hearing.

"We mustn't listen to him," said one woman, and a man agreed, nodding his head.

"We will die if we oppose them. We should accept the offer," said another and soon the conversation grew to involve nearly every person. The talk was a continuous clamor of disorderly speech, and the werewolves could no longer pick a sentence from the din. They prowled the outside, waiting. Finally Elder Vicktor called for silence and rose to a podium that was stationed at the head of the room.

"As the lowest ranking elder in Valwood, I never expected to take on the burden of being Chief Elder, but here I am, and I intend to lead us to prosperity and peace. We have fought the werewolves, and at the cost of destroying many of them, we have lost too many of our own. If we rebel now, we almost surely face death. If we accept Anraq's offer of peace, we invite in the possibility of hope. The wrong decision can cost us precious human lives, and even one loss is too many even if victory is assured. I cannot pay that price if the alternative is there." Elder Vicktor raised his voice until it carried easily to the Alpha's ears.

"Here me now Alpha of the werewolves. We accept your offering of peace and extend ours as well. But know this and heed my words; if your offer proves false our men down to the last generation will hunt you. Our pursuit will drive you from your forest until every last one of you lies dead. That is our word," and now an audible cheer rose from the building.

Your words are brave and true, Elder, and I would expect nothing less from you, Anraq replied into each of their heads. *And let your silver bullets be swift and accurate if you find any falsehood in our claim.*

The Alpha turned his head to the werewolf that stood at his right. He dipped his head before speaking, and when he was finished, he began walking towards the forest, motioning for Naktor to follow.

Latuk, I trust you to handle our relations to the humans. I have much to rebuild in Claw Haven now, and it is time to reunite the Pack.

The wise healer dipped his head as well, lowering it nearly to the ground in his respect. When he rose the two werewolves had been swallowed by the frosty mist, and he turned back towards City Hall. An owl skimmed along the buildings, nearly touching them with its darkly feathered body and glided over the trees. The werewolves were below, at times unseen as they passed under the thick canopy of snowy trees, but the bird never lost them. Nor did it seem uncomfortable under the raging light of day; it was a black ghost against sky blue and blazing sun.

The werewolves ran through the woods, easy in their lope but not in their minds. Although Naktor's eyes gleamed with thoughts that only he knew, they were troubled and did not leave his mind easily. Anraq ran with the preoccupation of one distracted, for he more than any of the others, had much work to do. And so when he had flashed his side at Naktor to alter their course, and the bird had screeched loudly enough to wake the forest, he did not know he had been thrown from his feet until he had careened into a snow drift. Naktor stood over him, growling savagely, but he was not predisposed to monologue. He had no words for his Alpha or his betrayal, and his mind was finally clear.

Without warning he had buried his muzzle in Anraq's throat. Using his own body as leverage, he managed to flip the

Alpha over again in the snow, and in the struggle Anraq had clamped down onto one of Naktor's forelegs. The pain was immense and Naktor gasped raggedly, but he bit deeper, until the hot river of blood bubbled from his Alpha's ruined neck, and it ran down his own throat. He closed his eyes against the crimson spray, and so he did not see the radiant white light that was already dimming from his leader's eyes.

The fallen Alpha scrabbled uselessly in the snow, floundering under the weight of the other werewolf. Neither immortal would release the vice-like grips they held onto one another's flesh.

In a desperate attempt to free his neck, Anraq sank his teeth in farther, until the femur beneath his fangs had snapped in two. Naktor howled terribly into Anraq's torn throat, his voice frayed with primal agony.

Naktor faltered, falling heavily forward onto the broken leg, and it seemed as if he might let go. But although cowardice had been his legacy, he had also inherited the unswerving perseverance of the victor.

The two immortals struggled for several excruciating minutes, but Naktor's youth and quick attack had given him the edge over the older and less agile werewolf. Anraq's throat could not close under Naktor's relentless attack, and his blood began to empty in the snow, flecking it with pink and red foam. Naktor could taste bone, tendons and flesh, and all were sliced through with his canines.

His injured leg mended nearly as fast as Anraq could break it again. His grip was loosening though, as Anraq lost more and more blood. His jaws finally slackened on Naktor's leg, and the younger werewolf wrenched it free. He slumped forward in the snow, still limping. A moment later the bone had resealed itself, knitting together beneath his flesh, and he renewed his assault on Anraq. The Alpha snarled feebly through his broken larynx and sank lifelessly to the ground, nearly buried in white. The pearly glow of his eyes had been extinguished completely, and his side was unmoving without breath. Anraq was dead.

Naktor stood triumphant over his kill, the Alpha's blood still dripping from his jaws. He raised his tail in defiance, and his stiff legged stance dared any creature to defy him. The next moment the true weight of what he had done had fallen over him, and his earlier pride now seemed foolish. The strength left his body; his legs nearly buckled beneath him, and his tail lowered until it came to rest between his hind legs. He looked down at the mighty Alpha that had led his pack for three quarters of a century. He was at least fifty pounds heavier than Naktor and death had not diminished his size.

He circled the kill, sniffing at the air, but the thick copper smell of Anraq's blood blocked all other scents from his nostrils. He shook his head to and fro, but as far as he could see the forest was empty of werewolves. He slunk through the woods, stealing amongst the trees to conceal his presence. As he went he swiped his muzzle through the snow in a vain attempt to clean the damning blood from his mouth. But when he reached the rapids, he followed them to a nearly frozen lake.

The current that struggled to break through the thin layer of ice had failed to veil Naktor's reflection, and when he studied himself he was dismayed to see that it was still stained red. He had lost patches of fur in the fight, and he bled from numerous scratches that were beginning to heal before his eyes. When he met his own glowing eyes, he found he could no longer look at himself, and he sprang away from the river.

There could be no hiding what he had done, and he realized as he followed the river's bank that he had no *desire* to hide it. As killer of Anraq by werewolf law, he would become the

223

new Alpha. But he knew he would be met with much opposition. Many of the werewolves still believed in a futile treaty with the humans and that they could eventually live alongside them peacefully. His face wrinkled into a snarl. *Had they forgotten Celestial Hold so easily? Or the recent invasion that had them fleeing from the forest that they had lived in for centuries?* Humans had always feared them like they had feared their brethren, the wild wolf. The skies had once been alive with the wild songs of the wolves. But now only the howls of his own kind echoed forlornly into the night for Valwood's citizens had long driven the wolf to extinction from these lands. *That is our future if I cannot change it,* he thought bitterly as he ran.

The night fell all around him, shrouding him in her deceptive darkness, but the slick blood still shone around his muzzle. He swiped his tongue across his lips, and he could feel the strength of the Alpha coursing within him as he headed towards Valwood's center. He would meet up with the pack, *his pack now,* and show them the path of freedom. Some of them would not believe him at first, but they would eventually see reason. With the humans removed their kind would flourish unmolested under Zulae's reign, and they would never again be driven from their homes.

~ Chapter Twenty-Four ~
The Shifting Tides

The lights of the city glimmered warm amber in the wake of death. As Naktor approached the lucent streets, he became a thing of shadows, a black wraith that melded into the dark buildings, or a swiftly fleeing creature that was no more wolf than stray dog. His eyes became another pair of lights, albeit a whiter pair, which took in all of the city's dangers and its hiding places. His scent however, he could do nothing for, save for a grisly swim in the frigid rapids that had left him sodden and chilled to the bone.

He shook off the excess water, showering the nearby buildings and snow with freezing droplets. His body was like ice, but the river could not rival the terrible coldness of death, and so he was not uncomfortable. The moisture that he had not been able to shake away had frozen to his guard hairs, stiffening and edging them in white frost and further roughening his appearance.

He had bought himself precious little time before meeting the rest of the pack, and he chose his steps with care. He walked as lightly as he could, leaving hardly a trace of his passage, his ears alert and his nose constantly quivering with the bombardment of city scents.

He could smell some of his pack mates, and he detected no signs of suspicion in the air. They walked easily, their minds unfettered. Naktor slipped downwind into the darkness as they passed, unaware of him. When they had disappeared from his view, and their movements had slid from his sensitive ears, he continued his path through the singed buildings. He could smell Kivah ahead of him, and he could tell the werewolf was alone. He jumped into the wreckage of one of the burned buildings (the *General Apothecary* as he read on its broken sign), and projected his voice from inside.

Kivah, he growled and waited, his heart beating wildly in his chest. If he could not garner the support of the werewolves, he would face exile or possibly even death.

What is it, Naktor? Came the reply, and Naktor worded his message carefully.

Anraq has taken us down the path of destruction with the humans as its weapon, and now he has met his demise. I am here to take over leadership of the pack.

Forceful shock reverberated from the werewolf into his mind, and then the creeping of grief. He could hear Kivah approaching.

Are you sure? If your words are true, then the future of the pack and the humans is uncertain.

Dead sure. I've seen it myself.

Now Kivah stood at the ruined entrance. Naktor did not have time to prepare himself before the other werewolf sprang through the door. The glow from Kiva's eyes illuminated

Naktor's face even as he attempted to back into the gloom. Aside from cleansing him of his scent, the river had also washed away much of the blood that had stained Naktor's muzzle, but some red still gleamed around his nose. Kivah's eyes widened, than narrowed as he began to snarl. His legs seemed undecided in approaching Naktor or frozen a moment before flight, and he merely stood there, utterly at a loss for movement.

The blood of our Alpha is on your lips, and it betrays you. What have you done, Naktor? Kivah was snarling now, and he raised his head, but he stood only an inch taller than Naktor. Even without the hindrance of the bullet wound, he had never been the fighting type.

I have merely delayed our extinction. When the humans perfect their projectile weapons of silver, do you think they will heed our pleas for peace? No, they will burn Claw Haven to the ground just as they did Celestial Hold, and they will never cease to hunt us from our woods. I have come to take my rightful place as the new Alpha, and I will make sure that every man falls for what they have done, Naktor projected.

I am sympathetic to your cause, and I know many of the werewolves agree, but I do not believe things will go as smoothly as you believe. Anraq was as beloved a leader as he was wise, and we will not forget this crime easily. I offer you my support, as that is a pack mate's duty, but I pray the ramifications of your actions will not be as dire for you as I fear, Kivah growled in Naktor's head.

I am in need of your support, and I am grateful for it. The others will come to believe in my vision as I lead us on a brighter path and more secure future. My actions were for the good of the pack, and someday they will reap the benefits of today's work, Naktor replied.

Kivah lifted his head. *Then let us run under Zulae's moon,* he declared. *As Anraq's absence is felt more deeply, the werewolves will formulate their own theories as to how he died. If you are to lead us then allay our fears and serve us through this difficult time just as Anraq had for seventy nine years.*

Kivah ensured that the knowledge of Anraq's death spread faster than the burning fires that had devoured Valwood. Soon every werewolf had gotten wind of the change in leadership, and now they gathered again at their meeting place, atop the ruined buildings that lay in Valwood's center.

Naktor stood on the uppermost perch, trying to flatten his involuntarily raising hackles. He looked down at the assembled werewolves, but his small size seemed insufficient in the minds of the pack members who remembered Anraq's stature.

He drew his head up proudly and once more felt the exhilaration of heading the pack. He growled louder until all of the werewolves could hear him.

Clan, let us now unite as we did under Anraq's reign. The humans have polluted this city with their hate and prejudice, and we stand in excellent position to rid Valwood of their dirty kind. Who among you will stand with me now?

Some of them snarled defiantly at him, mocking him and daring him to prove his leadership. Others stood frozen in their grief, staring numbly at the new Alpha in quiet bewilderment. Still, others nodded approvingly at him, gnashing their teeth in anticipation of bringing his plans of violence towards the humans to fruition. One voice rose louder than the others in his head, and Naktor was forced to meet its owner's eye. Vekoroh was growling steadily at him, his one eye staring daggers at him in the moonlight.

The murderer of Anraq dares to stand in his place and even invoke his name under Zulae's moon!

Anraq has lead this pack to their inevitable deaths! All should thank me for ensuring our survival, Naktor snarled back. He glanced at Kivah and at the sickening wound that still covered much of his flank. Kivah returned his gaze hesitatingly, and Naktor knew in that moment that he was losing the support of the pack. He looked into Vekoroh's challenging eyes, and Naktor foresaw his own destiny in those pale orbs. He whined slightly, though in the chaos the sound did not carry to the werewolves' ears below. He backed up, but there was nothing behind to save him from what he must do. His own eyes closed in a wince as Vekoroh's words sounded in the heads of every single werewolf in the pack.

I challenge you for the title of Alpha, Naktor. As the snarling howls grew to ring throughout all of Valwood, even the hidden humans far below could hear them.

Naktor could think of no way out. Confronted by Vekoroh's challenge, only two choices presented themselves: either fight to the death for his claim for leadership all over again, or flee the fangs of the pack. He thought back to his last fight with another werewolf. He remembered one-eyed Lehova in the human's house. He remembered his own throat being torn open and the strangled cries he had struggled to make under the smothering of death. He remembered his returning strength too, the adrenaline that was cascading through his veins and the vivacity of his renewed life even in the face of his curse. He had looked into Lehova's face, his one eye glinting and the other socket gaping widely blank at him, a faint glow still cast from somewhere deep. He had lost once, but he would not lose to this new foe.

229

The title can only be ripped from my claws, Vekoroh, he found himself snarling, and lowering his face until it was nearly even with the other werewolf's. He dropped lightly from the fallen rooftop.

The two werewolves circled one another, eying each other for the perfect place to strike first. Vekoroh's advantage in height was even more pronounced in the limited space, and fear clouded Naktor's mind with useless urges to flee. He stifled his own voice in his mind with his audible growling.

The rest of the clan stood in a ring around them, unwaveringly silent. Not a breadth of movement rustled the staring pack, and Vekoroh and Naktor knew that at the victory of one of them, they would spring into vicious chaos to finish off whichever werewolf fell. This was the vying for leadership as it should have been, in the clear view of all of the werewolves, and Naktor knew not a single member would fully support him until he defeated Vekoroh in this honest battle.

Their minds cleared, uncluttered with invasive thoughts. Instead they diverted their coursing energy to their paws, down to each extended claw, and to their waiting fangs. They rushed at each other, testing for weaknesses and resuming their endless circling just as swiftly. Like the wolf, they flashed in and out, clipping with their fangs before whirling back into their defensive positions. Occasionally, their teeth were met with hide and flesh and a roar of rage marked the bitten adversary. A moment later their wounds had both mended, and they stood facing each other, hackles raised to their full height.

Naktor tightened his body into a defensive crouch as Vekoroh circled him. He swung his muzzle to each side, and his eyes twisted in their sockets with his attempts to keep the other werewolf in view. Like a spring, his muscles uncoiled, and he leaped at Vekoroh. His teeth closed on the larger werewolf's ear, and he wrenched away with his jaws, flaying it into tattered shreds. Vekoroh's torn howl was swallowed by the wind, and he pinned Naktor to the ground. He planted his paws onto his chest while Naktor squirmed below, his fangs snapping at empty air.

Vekoroh glowered down at him, his eyes glinting. Naktor could see steely hate reflected in them, and he realized it was his own terrible hate. It ran through every part of him, to the paws that longed to run down a deer, to his fangs that wanted to taste the succulent flesh it could not eat. Or the human hand that rested beneath and grasped at a ploy of normalcy within Valwood society. For the life that had been ripped from him and now denied him, for every aspect of his horrible curse. The toxic self-loathing that had driven him to murder their revered Alpha in cold blood. That hate grew between him and Vekoroh now until it was a palpable thing, and Naktor knew as Vekoroh bit down into his throat once again, that none of them had ever truly escaped from that hate. It lived in all of them, whether they were human or werewolf, and it had finally come to destroy him in the form of dripping fangs.

Now his own ravaged howl had come to rent the air, and Vekoroh did not stop until his blood had emptied and the white glow had ebbed from his cloudy eyes. Naktor did not feel the onslaught of the clan that had turned on him, no longer in a neat circle, but in a frenzied horde of claws and teeth that had brought him to his bloody end.

The werewolves were silent, each dipping their heads towards the new Alpha. If they had any thoughts of dissension they did not voice them now, and the violence visibly fled from their weary bodies. Under the light of the three quarter moon, they howled as one feral savage beast, declaring their hate, their grief and their loyalty to the pack as they stood united once more. Tucked away in the city hall, the human citizens covered their

231

ears of the horrible sounds that came to them, unaware of Anraq's death and that their peaceful truce now hung on the whims of this mysterious new Alpha.

"What do you mean, captured by Arkadith? Natalya was the vampire huntress. None have defeated her!" Kaima paced back and forth, wringing her hands. She slumped down in the snow, nearly succumbing to the tears that were brimming in her eyes. *It couldn't be.*

I know his scent well. I have not forgotten it not even after a hundred years, Voren growled in her head. Kaima looked up at him, her face shining with tear tracks.

"What chance does she stand against him, Voren? Please tell me that she still may live!"

Their scents grow faint here and mix with the smell of ash. It is difficult to discern what has happened. But I do not scent blood, neither Natalya's nor Arkadith's. Take comfort in that at least.

"But where could he have taken her?" Kaima asked, wiping her eyes with her sleeve. When he did not reply right away, she looked at the werewolf. He had stopped sniffing the ground and stood perfectly still, facing away from her. He seemed to be thinking intently as he looked into the woods, his head cocked slightly to the side. Only his one ear acknowledged that he had heard her; it was rotated in her direction and pricked upwards when she spoke. She stood up from the snow and slowly made her way to stand beside him.

The scent of ash is stronger here. Arkadith must have transformed them both into moving shadow...., he growled, still a

232

living statue. His words were faded in her mind as if he spoken to her from quite a distance, but he had not moved.

"Voren," Kaima murmured, interrupting his pensiveness. His gaze snapped back to her, and finally, she had his full attention.

"*Who is* Arkadith exactly? And what has he done with Natalya? I need to know that we can still find her."

Alright, I will tell you everything that I know if you wish it, but it may not soothe your fears to know. Arkadith is the oldest living vampire that we, that is to say humans and werewolves, know of. If there are others that are as old as him, they are not as powerful, and your friend Natalya has managed to keep them from Valwood permanently. Until now. Arkadith is a master of mind control. He has superior strength even to mine and speed to match. If he has indeed captured her, I fear that she is almost certainly already dead. And if she has died, so too are my hopes of ending my curse, for it was I that allowed him to rise. I am sorry, Kaima.

Voren watched the hopeful expression on Kaima's face deflate into silent despair. Her tears pooled behind her lids, and this time she did not wipe them away.

"But if there is a chance…we must continue. She has managed to kill every other vampire she has ever dueled, perhaps she could do it again," she said but the words fell flat upon both of them.

Arkadith is not a fledgling vampire to be defeated by a mere human girl and a common werewolf! Even Natalya stands little chance against him. He will be aware of our presence long before we reach him, and it will be no large feat for him to kill us if we do make it. That is the path we face if we continue now.

Kaima squared her chin, her hair waving in the wind and in that moment she looked more woman than adolescent. She

233

seemed to take wisdom from a source that was older than her seventeen years when she spoke now.

"If there is a chance, however small that Natalya is still alive, then I have no choice but to take it. This isn't just about rescuing my friend anymore. This is bigger than all of us. Your chance to lift your curse rests on this journey as well as our peoples' last chance for *peace*. Besides, only death waits for us in Valwood now." Voren dipped his muzzle to the red haired girl in a respectful bow.

For a hundred years I have dreamed of righting the wrong I had committed for resurrecting that monster and ending the curse that has been wrought upon me. Let us go now, and whether our quest ends in victory or our deaths, may we find Natalya and bring her home.

With Voren leading the way, and Kaima galloping behind on Methea, they reached the end of the great forest.

Nightfall found them at the base of the mountain crag that housed the legendary castle. The breeze that blew from above raked Kaima's face raw with frigid cold, and she shivered terribly. Cast in shadow that darkened the night further, they looked up at the fabled castle. They took in the scowling gargoyles that glowered at them from its corners and the beautifully colored stained glass that glowed from the windows of its towering spires.

Kaima's nose had gone pink and numb with cold, but Voren's nose twitched quite uninhibitedly. It was here that Natalya's scent had changed, though Kaima remained unaware; having not been blessed with Voren's senses. She was still giddy with anxiousness, but as they traversed up the mountain, she heard the werewolf's voice in her head again.

Natalya was here; only a few hours ago. It seems we've just missed her, Voren growled.

"We are close then!" Kaima exclaimed, turning towards the giant stone steps that led to the castle, but still the werewolf had not moved. He was still staring at the castle, his body rigid, and the beginnings of a snarl lifting his lips.

"Voren?" Kaima asked timidly, following his line of sight towards the fortress. Finally he turned and began heading north, only stopping when Kaima had not moved.

Come, there will be no more need to enter Arkadith's lair, he growled. With that foreboding thought still ringing in her head, Kaima followed the werewolf into the darkened forest once more.

~ Part IV ~

~ Chapter Twenty-Five ~
Awakening

All was black. She was dead, cold, and heavy. She had eyes but no sight, skin but no feeling or touch. A heart that lay still, with no will to pump blood into her body, and no air to expand her lungs and breathe. She was nothing and nothing was what she felt.

For an eternity or perhaps only a moment, Natalya lay in this state. She merely existed, as vague waves of thought or maybe just broken dreams flitted through her mind. They were her fondest memories or they were nothing, fragments of a past that might have had meaning to someone once, but now they were gone, forgotten.

Something had woken her, and her eyes opened. The blackness was unchanging though, and her pupils did not expand to let in light that was not there.

Did she really even have eyes? She wondered, but the thought had left almost before it had been conceived.

A strange pulsing filled the air and heavy warmth flooded through Natalya. She could hear a coursing, like a river inside her but around her at the same time, but she could make no sense of the sensation. One sound thudded louder above all others, and she realized it was her woken heart, fluttering feebly against her ribs like a trapped bird.

She had a body then. The heaviness spread to her extremities, and she moved a single finger with huge effort, but felt no pain. Sucking in stagnant air, she moved another. This time it was easier, and she merely felt stiff now. Her back was against smooth wood, and her hair was spread all around her as if it had been arranged there. She tried to think, to remember, but her thoughts were sluggish and confused.

Get up. The thought had burst through her swirling half-thoughts with an urging force. And then panic. *Arkadith! Had he done this to her? She was gone and now she was back? How? And where was she now?* Her thoughts had jumbled again, and she couldn't summon the energy to put them back together again.

Make words. She opened her mouth to speak, but her throat was raw, her lips cracked and flaking. *Why wouldn't the words come?*

Dripping blues and reds filled her head and seemed to run down the walls in her disorientation. She was so thirsty, but *first she must get out of here.*

She tentatively put out her hands and felt something like a roof just inches above her head. She rose as much as she could and pushed onto it with a growing sense of claustrophobia. But she was so weak it took all her strength to escape her black prison. She was breathing heavily, and it took her a moment to recover from the strenuous movement.

Sunlight was streaming through a picture window in such brightness that she was forced to shield her eyes from it. She moaned and gasped weakly as her skin began to hiss and burn, and she stumbled away from the light and into the shadows of the room. Almost immediately, her skin cooled, but Natalya had barely noticed.

From the shadows, her eyes grew accustomed to the sudden light, and she was able to take in her surroundings. She was in Arkadith's home, that much was clear from the décor, but she had never been in this room before. She surveyed its belongings with faint interest until something on the floor caught her eye. Something long and black and her eyes widened in horror. She backed away, steadying herself against the wall, shaking with silent fits of fear. Arkadith had trapped her in a coffin.

Her thoughts flashed back to the darkness and the emptiness. The truth came to her calmly and without emotion, but she could not say it aloud. *She had died.* And now she was back.

Thirst. There it was again, a frantic need to drink, so strong she could barely think of anything else. She fled the room and ran down the stairs to the kitchen. It was empty of staff in the morning hour, and she was glad to not run into anyone. She quickly located the sink and began searching for a glass, but the kitchen had been meticulously cleaned since last night. She opened cabinet after cabinet until she found a crystal wine glass and reached for it with shaking hands. The glass fell from her grasp to the floor where it shattered, and she could only stare at the wreckage stupidly.

Ignoring the broken glass, she turned to the water reservoir and thrust her head into it to drink. She felt the cool liquid pass over her tongue and swallowed as much as she could. She stood up and turned off the water, unable to drink anymore.

She felt uncomfortably full but her body still screamed with thirst.

Natalya was dizzy, and she leaned onto the counter for support. She was now overcome with exhaustion. *What had Arkadith done to her?*

Her heart had been frantically beating only moments before, but something now seemed to be weighing it down. The beats grew more sluggish and more time began to elapse between each desperate pump of blood. A painful weight seemed to have settled over her chest, and she held a hand to her breast to ease the pressure.

Then it stopped beating. Natalya gasped and slumped forward, the oven in front of her swaying in her vision. She began to fall, and she threw out her arms to catch herself, but instead she fell painfully onto them. Her eyes struggled to bring everything back into focus, but her sight was beginning to darken. She remembered white arms, her own bright white arms like a ghost, before she blacked out completely.

She did not know how long she remained there before she felt herself being lifted back up. Through her blurred version, she could see Arkadith supporting her, and she instinctively leaned into him. He smelled comforting somehow, like refreshing rain after a hot day, and she nestled her head into his collarbone. Her eyes were closing now beyond her control, and she felt herself slipping in and out of consciousness.

Arkadith produced a glass of startling red liquid and held it to her lips, and she cupped it in both hands while he poured it gently down her throat. The second it had touched her tongue, her body had leapt towards the drink, and her eyes flew open. She was now acutely aware of everything: *that Arkadith was not sleeping during the light of day as he should have been; he was here, and she was in his arms.* She pulled away from him and lifted the glass higher as she drained it. She swilled it until not a single drop remained, and still she licked the rim for just one more taste.

Her heartbeat had returned in full, and she felt living energy pulsate through every vein. The coursing sound was back, the river of red delivering sweet nourishing blood to each part of her body.

She felt more alive than she ever had in life. The pressure had been lifted from her chest, and Arkadith released her from his grip. She took one tiny step forward, then another and another, exploring the room as she never had before. It was breathtaking, the detail she could now see in perfect clarity. She was mesmerized; she studied the mortar between each stone that made up the kitchen wall and she could make out every crack, every wrinkle and every flaw. The wall was not merely grey, it was red, clay, brown, earthy and silver all at the same time. The rug in the kitchen was a mishmash of competing fibers that held every color of the rainbow in their threads. Her eyes went to the flames that lit the kitchen, and she was amazed by the blues, reds, oranges and yellows that gave life to the blaze.

And with her newfound clarity came perfect memory, and the events of the night before came crashing into her mind. She remembered Arkadith drinking, draining her, *killing* her and the endless blackness that had marked her death. She felt repulsed by the vampire in the room, and she backed into the kitchen wall, all the inebriation she had felt from the drink gone.

"What have you done to me?" she shrieked in a voice that was not her own. "You, you *killed* me! Valwood needs me! My *father* needs me! The werewolves…" Natalya sputtered off, no longer able to find the words to voice her emotions. The Vampire only watched, unfazed until she broke off sobbing on the floor.

"Natalya the great Vampire huntress…now a vampire." Arkadith moved to stand over her, smiling coldly at her suffering. "I could have left you dead, and instead I have given you eternal life! You should be grateful."

Her arms were splayed out against the wall behind her, her fingertips clenched, and she slowly relaxed them. They were so white against the stone even through her blurred tears. She brought them to her face to examine them. They were as pale as she had seen Arkadith at his lightest, and her stark blue veins were jutting out of her arms as if trying to escape her body.

"*Grateful?* I felt myself weaken…and *die,* Arkadith."

"I *saved* you," Arkadith growled, injecting venomous emphasis into every word.

"Saved me? *Saved* me? You should have…you should have left me dead! What has happened to me?"

"You wish to know the mechanics of what I did?"

She hesitated. Could she bear to know the answer? She was quiet for a bit before she nodded.

"Creating a vampire is a very complicated matter, Natalya. And a delicate one at that. It will not be easy for you to hear, and I do not know what you remember." When she did not seem dissuaded, he nodded, resigned.

At once Arkadith's demeanor became distant. He began talking, yes, but it seemed as if he had removed himself from the picture. He spoke as if someone other than he had done it, his tone lifeless and monotone.

"A victim must be drained completely for the process to happen," he began, gauging her expression. Natalya tried not to wince. "I fed off of your blood completely until there was no more left to quench my thirst. I drank until it led to your death, and you collapsed. Perhaps you do not remember that," he added.

Natalya closed her eyes. In her mind she was traveling back to the previous night, the night that had marked her end as a mortal. She inwardly probed at the memories that she had been fiercely guarding in order to save herself the pain of facing them. She felt ready now, but she was unprepared for the vision that had been brought forth.

She remembered the pain of his fangs on her neck. Those pointed teeth had literally sucked the life from within her, and so distinctly did she recall that she felt she was reliving the pain this very moment. She remembered struggling to cry out as the life within her was fading into nothingness. She was remembering her own death so acutely that she felt as if she was dying even now. She had lost all traces of life and thought had lost all meaning. She did not know how long she had stayed in that state before she had awakened, as such a feeble life form. She had cried out desperately for blood until Arkadith had opened one of his own veins.

He had then guided her mouth to the dripping blood from his wrist and like a newborn infant she had latched onto the only sustenance her screaming body had recognized. She drank deeply from his blood, slowly and hesitatingly at first. Then as she felt her dead body rising into liveliness, she began to laugh wickedly as she drank more ravenously.

The thirst that had been burning in her throat was finally sated and he did not make her stop until he had weakened himself to the point of near starvation. Then they had both collapsed, exhausted and full, to rest on his floor.

She had fallen asleep, and he had gone, but it was not long before he had returned with more blood for her. She did not ask how it had been procured, she only drank from it greedily. And as the days passed and she took more blood in, she had rapidly began regaining the strength that would far surpass any level she could achieved in her previous life. She remembered her first tentative steps as a predator, a *vampire.* The ease of a leopard in a human's body. The snakelike fangs that slid naturally down her lips as she fed and the comfort she took in their sharpness. The details her eyes could never have taken in as a human and the ease of which she could hear every sound in the castle. If she stopped to listen, the sounds from the outside forest came easily to her ears: the steady songs of the insects, the throaty croaks of the bullfrogs and the guttural call of the nighthawk on the wing. She gasped as the full realization of what Arkadith had done in one night came to her.

"And then…I awoke in the coffin," she murmured, opening her eyes.

"Yes," Arkadith answered.

"In the midst of day sleep. As if I were dead."

"Yes. You will grow used to the feeling, in time."

"I am a vampire now," she said.

"Yes."

"No longer human."

"Superior to a human."

Natalya turned to look at him strangely.

"*Superior,* Arkadith?" She turned away from him again and walked to the dining room window. The curtain was still drawn, a black barrier before the sun. She lifted her hand and ran it slowly down the fabric, hesitating. Then with a flourish, she drew open the curtain.

At once she closed her eyes as the searing heat began to raise steam from her arms. She did not move, not even when her skin began to blister painfully. Arkadith ran to the window, and slammed the curtain shut. Her skin immediately began to cool and mend.

"Is this what you call superiority, Arkadith?" she asked.

"You cannot allow yourself to be touched by the sun."

"This is not an *enhancement*. This is an affliction! How can you call it anything but that? I am a monster now!"

"You are a vampire, Natalya, neither good nor evil! You will do what you need to do to *survive!*" Arkadith snarled.

"I must feast on the blood of humans!" Natalya covered her face in her hands and ran. She turned the corner to the stairs and climbed them as quickly as she could, checking over her shoulder to see if Arkadith had followed but the vampire had not.

She found her room and heaved open the door. She flung herself against it, barricading it from the inside. Her chest heaving, she turned her head to look from side to side for something she could use. She noticed her curtains had been drawn while she had been downstairs, probably by Anna. Her eyes focused on the vanity, and she went to it. She grabbed a wooden end and pushed it onto its side. Everything inside shifted noisily and a few of the drawers slid open. She lifted it by two of its legs and dragged it across the room. The vanity was relatively easy to move, and she did not find herself straining from the effort. She wedged it against the door, just under the handle and sat on her bed, surveying her work.

She did not really expect it to hold against Arkadith, but she had no other plan. It did not matter for she was alive.

Alive, she thought dragging the word out long in her mind. Last night she had died, but today she lived. She was not sure of Arkadith's motive for turning her, but some part of her still reveled in her newfound life. Death, even a valiant one was a frightening prospect, and her body still fought to keep its hold on this life, even if it was a cursed half existence.

Well not entirely alive then, she revised bitterly. Her heart beat now with the blood that Arkadith had given her, but she knew that it would eventually stop beating until she drank blood again. Her pale and dead body could only mimic life, she could not truly have it. She could borrow it from others, but their blood could never sustain her for too long.

She wondered how long before she would need to feed again. Arkadith never went longer than a day in between if he could help it, but Natalya knew that was due to preference rather than necessity. She did not know the answer, and she pushed the thoughts of blood from her mind, grateful that they did not rouse her thirst.

She drew her legs onto the bed and crossed them, resting her elbows on her thighs. Although she could not imagine Arkadith's plans for her now, she did know that she could not remain in this castle with the creature that had transformed her into a monster. But the sunlight still lightened her curtains from the outside as it struggled to permeate throughout the room, and she knew that while it lingered she could nothing.

And so she waited. She had not yet acquired the endless patience of an immortal so she filled her head with thought.

She thought of Kaima and wondered if Methea had once again sought refuge in her barn. She imagined the mare following the sweet tempered girl, her mane and tail swishing gracefully in the wind as she eagerly reached for a carrot, her hooves crunching in the soft snow. Natalya smiled slightly at the thought. But worry pulled down the corners of her mouth when her thoughts drifted to Valwood. She wondered if her dear home had yet been ravaged by her father's war. Even worse was the uncertainty if he himself still lived, or if his bloody ambitions had already cost him his life.

Natalya wiped a tear from her eyes and was surprised to see that it was tinged red. She flung it from her hand and watched as the single drop dissipated into thin air. The blood that had been so prominent a moment before had all but dissolved in the room, and even her eyes could not pick it up anymore. She wondered if it were that easy for Arkadith to kill, knowing that his victims' lives would be eventually forgotten, turned to dust and lost to time. She shook her head, unknowing.

She would go to her father and try to stop the war if it was not too late. Perhaps she could blend in with the humans as Arkadith once had. The plan blossomed in her mind, and as it swelled as she gained hope. Could it be that not all was lost?

She climbed out of the bed, pacing and thinking and returning to the bed again when she finally tired of walking. Neither Arkadith nor Anna rapped on her door, and she stayed in silence until the curtains were solid black once more.

When dusk had fallen, she went to her window. It was no longer locked for Arkadith had trusted his human charge to not leap to her death, but she had no such qualms now. She pushed it open and climbed onto the sill, hunched in the window. Her chocolate colored hair waved in the cold wind, but it felt only pleasantly cool to her skin. She took one last look at the room, and she whispered aloud, "One day I will return here and I *will* kill you Arkadith."

With that she turned to the forest and jumped. Time seemed to slow as she fell, and she positioned her legs underneath her to take the impact. It was not a perfect landing, her Vampiric grace had melded painfully into human capriciousness, and she fell heavily onto her ankle. She cried out, hissing, and her fangs involuntarily elongated in response to the injury.

The twisted bone began rotating back into its proper place with sickening crunches, and she winced as her flesh rippled over it. She had seen the werewolves heal instantly from injuries, but it was unnerving watching her own body do it.

She tentatively put some of her weight on the twisted ankle, then stood up when the pain became bearable. She walked

247

barefoot through the snow, limping slightly at first then running to the trees as her ankle mended fully. With no destination in mind, and unaware that her friends were only hours behind her, she fled, trying only to put as much distance as she could between herself and Arkadith's castle.

~ Chapter Twenty-Six ~
Bloodlust

And so Natalya found herself alone for the first time in over two months. She leaped from each snowy precipice, and by the time she reached the whitely frosted trees, she learned to trust in her Vampiric grace. It blessed her body with limberness and balance that was unhindered by her long dress and only seemed to grow as the night wore on.

Here she moved slowly through in this unfamiliar wood. She was unused to the way her skin did not flex or stretch with her movements and the unnaturally cold barrier that it was, impervious against the seeping chill of the winter winds. It was as if her senses too had finally arisen after a seventeen-year hibernation. The snow did not merely feel cold; it was porous, crisp and easily squeezed into pure water under her grip.

Dripping tree sap that had been frozen in their travels formed amber striped icicles that gleamed from the trees even under the moonlight. She passed by snow tipped fronds that had burst their ways through the snow, the bubbles of moisture clinging to their tips dirtied by tiny clumps of dirt. She could smell the dormant crinkled flowers beneath, frozen potpourri that wafted upwards into the air like perfume.

The quiet forest was layer upon layer of delicate sound. Somewhere close a cricket shifted its gossamer wings, a bird rustled its feathers within its perch and a vole turned in its burrow. She learned to ignore the sounds that did not indicate danger as she still listened for Arkadith, wondering if he had followed her here. There was no sign of the vampire though, no scent of ash to overcome the smell of crisp pines and no sound to betray a predator's movement.

Even at her cautious pace, the miles disappeared beneath her feet faster than they would if she were still human. Soon she even began to entertain the notion that perhaps the vampire was not coming for her at all.

Well why would he, for he had fulfilled his plan, she thought ruefully. In his castle, most of her thoughts had been devoted to survival and little else. But now, in this serene forest at night, she realized she had all the time in the world to plan, to live and to simply *think*.

Watching her broken ankle heal itself had been one thing, but the thought of being forever undying still eluded her. *Immortal.* The word felt foreign even as it flashed through her mind. *Unless she was staked through the heart.*

As if anyone could, she countered not without some amusement, and she smiled despite herself. She felt giddy with fear; of her newfound powers and of Arkadith, and she fought it with humor. She knew how fear could creep its way around her and settle into her chest and squeeze her heart until she could only succumb to it.

The vampire within her laughed fiendishly, and she felt instantly sickened. She swallowed anxiously, but the ravaging thirst that she had felt in the castle was not upon her. *Not yet.*

She paused when she reached an oak tree and leaned into it. The vampire was not tired; she felt like a machine that could travel the earth's length if she had the time. No, it was mental exhaustion that had taken over as she had feared it would.

She followed the tree's trunk with her eyes, up to its spreading limbs that stretched their ends to the stars. Although weighed down by snow and earthly limits, the tree continued its growth into the sky, not knowing it would pass from this life before ever fulfilling its quest.

Natalya's fingernails found grooves within the tree's bark, and she raked them downwards. Her nails had grown into sharp ended claws, and they gouged into the protective layer of the tree. The bark that she had peeled away fell amongst the snow to be buried as if it never were.

Was life as meaningless as those little pieces of fallen bark? The tree lived on, passive to her attack. It simply continued its futile upward journey, unaware of her or anyone else that told it otherwise.

Even the vampires had been easily snuffed out as she staked the life from their undead hearts in her former life. Their immortal strength had not protected them in the end, and they too had come to be swallowed by the earth to give nourishment to nature's creatures.

She released her grip on the tree and began walking once more. She was nearing Valwood and with every step her dread grew.

Fear had driven her to this point, and she had been foolish to think she had kept it at bay. *Fear of Anna, the woman that had gone mad living in the castle, fear of the vampire Arkadith and*

251

fear of the monster that was growing inside her. And fear was driving her towards Valwood and away from it at the same time.

The city was her home and part of her would take comfort there, close to her people. But now that she had been turned, she knew she could never live among them. She remembered the frenzied, agonizing thirst, and it sent a chill through her. The blood she had taken with Arkadith had subsisted her for now, but how long would it be before she felt the terrible thirst again?

She imagined herself in Valwood, trying to blend in with the humans and the futility of her own journey was harrowing.

Could she fool the humans just as Arkadith did? Would her own father point his gun at his only daughter and fire a bullet into her heart? If he even still lived, and she realized she might be returning to a home without him.

Had the war raged on in her absence? Perhaps some of the werewolves had been able to make contact with the humans and make peace? Natalya sighed sadly, unable to conjure enough belief in the hope. Guilt added its crushing weight to the fear in her heart. She had not made it in time to warn the elders and stop the war before it began.

How many deaths would come to lay on her conscious? And how many more would join them? The vampire was laughing again inside her head, and Natalya dropped to her knees mid stride. A scream tore itself from her throat, and her hands clawed at her hair, pulling it out in small clumps. For a time, she wallowed there on the snowy ground, allowing the waves of self-pity to overtake her. When her screaming had ceased to remedy her grief, she stood up. She felt slightly better but her problems could not be fixed by crying in the snow.

A new problem presented itself. Her screaming had scratched her throat slightly raw, and now she felt *it*. The tiny inkling of soreness with the urge to drink. It was not all consuming yet; she could fight it for now.

And when it becomes too unbearable to fight? She asked herself. She merely shook her head but to whom she did not know in this deserted forest. She concentrated on placing one foot in front of the other. When she made it to Valwood…*well then she would see.*

She consulted the sky for the position of the moon and was relieved to see she had a few hours of solid nighttime left. She had not yet grown used to fearing the sun, and the act of doing it now was disconcerting.

Her skin was flawless, uniform in its bruised pallor, showing no hint of the blisters that had seared it open with steaming welts just yesterday. And yet she winced at the memory, remembering vividly the damage the sun had inflicted through the picture window in Arkadith's castle.

Natalya worked her tongue inside her mouth as she walked but she could draw no saliva from her glands. Her teeth felt brittle and dry, and she swallowed reflexively, but it did not soothe the pain in her throat.

She ignored the sensation, occupying her mind with as many questions as she could muster. But with no one to answer any of the dozen of them that were floating around her head, her thoughts quickly turned to the thirst that she could no longer ignore.

The scent in the woods had changed. A crisper iciness had arrived, and she knew she was close to the river. She ran to it and within minutes she had reached the frozen expanse.

It was no effort for her new body to break through the thick barrier of ice to the life giving water below. She struck at it with her closed fist, and her bloodied hand began to mend even as she had lowered her head to drink. The water that which sustained and nourished all life apart from her, was as inedible as she had expected. Just as the water in the kitchen's reservoir had failed to satisfy her, so did this water, and she choked it up, sputtering incoherently. She sat by the river, her hands over her knees feeling more hopeless against the beast that raged inside her.

The thirst had come on stronger than she had prepared for, and the shrieking devil within her urged her to drink. She craved the sweet metallic taste of freshly spilled blood, and now she could think of nothing else. Her body began to divert its energy toward her predatory senses, and her sight, hearing, and smell awakened again as they never had before.

At every new sound, her head would swivel towards the source. She would freeze, a tigress before her prey, only her eyes scanning the trees for movement. These changes were not apparent to her, and she did not marvel at the arousal of her instincts. Here she was queen, and her mind emptied of all thought. Only the acquiring of fresh blood was pertinent, and human processes were only a hindrance to nature's finest killer.

A small flurry of disturbed snow betrayed her prey's presence. Her eyes locked onto it and she crouched, creeping closer. Her nose drew in the scent and her ears seemed to expand as she neared.

The rabbit that had been excavating its warren froze. Its ears were upright, sensing the danger, and like her, only its one visible eye blinked at the vampiress. Natalya could not look away, for the rabbit had drawn her predatory keenness for movement, and so they became locked in a delicate balance.

Not even the rabbit's nose twitched, for its instincts had likewise been roused, and they commanded from it only the statuesque qualities of prey unseen.

Its ruse was ineffective, and Natalya inched closer. She dared not to run, to startle it into a desperate bid for its burrow. *Not yet. Closer.*

In the presence of prey, her thoughts had been reduced to pure instinctive carnivorousness. And like the werewolves that drew strength from their brethren the wolves, here she drew strength from the lone tigress who must bring down her prey without the aid of the pack.

The rabbit shot through the snow for the balance had shifted towards flight. Its legs kicked up a spray of falling snow, and Natalya had momentarily lost track of it. Her eyes reacted with a speed that her human eyes had never achieved though, and within a second, she had caught her prey in her sights once more.

She ran at the rabbit. Not as a clumsy human that long struggled after foregoing its two extra legs, but as a vampire, long stridden and graceful, on two perfectly sculpted limbs. She overtook her prey, and she tore into its neck with her elongated fangs. Her actions were without thought, emotion or hesitancy, and after killing it, she tasted its blood. She drank eagerly, already savoring her renewed vigor.

But the blood was just like the water, and she instantly began to gag, forcing the useless liquid from her mouth while her inner vampire hissed indignantly. She flung the rabbit away from herself in disgust, leaving its body to feed the crows.

She was growing desperate. It was clear to her now that she could not escape her lust for blood. Her body thirsted for it, pure and unpolluted straight from a freshly opened human throat, and the vampire within would not settle for less.

She could feel the tears again, blurring her eyesight, and she ran. Not towards Valwood this time, for the fear that had been driving her towards her home now drove her away from it. She thought of Kaima and her father and scenes of their delicious spilling blood flashed in her conscience. With a cry, she flung her hands at her face trying to claw the images from her mind, but they only grew darker as her physical body weakened. Her pace began to slow as the hours wore on, and still she had not drunk.

She smelled them before she could see them. A small group of men, perhaps four or five judging by the individual scents that had melded to mix with ale and cigars, were walking a ways ahead of her.

She could smell death and a recently fired gun, but no metallic smell of silver lingered in the air. This was a hunting party, and they had outfitted their muskets with balls that were not made of that deadly material. She could scent the lifeless deer they had taken, and after their successful hunt they would be heading back towards one of the lodges that were scattered amongst these woods for the remainder of the night. Though they were clearly from Valwood, Natalya did not recognize any of the men, and for that she was grateful.

They were quickly approaching, and Natalya flattened herself against a tree, her claws digging into the bark. She shuddered as she scented their blood again, running eagerly towards her in their veins, and her eyes slipped into utter darkness. When her vision returned her eyes had blackened over their irises, but she was unaware of the change. She felt her conscience mind forced down by the vampire's will, and she could only submit to it. It was just as it was with the rabbit, but this time the vampire's strength coursed over hers, masking Natalya with a devilish smile that split her face monstrously and revealed her waiting canines. She did not think as she had with the rabbit; all traces of her humanity were buried beneath savagery. She only moved with the refined nimbleness of the predator, her thoughts hidden under layers of instinctive drive.

She was not conscious of moving from behind the tree. She did not bother to try and conceal herself amongst the shadows or brush, and it did not matter. The predator's eye ruled here, and the men's feeble senses did not alert their masters of Natalya's presence until it was too late.

The first man bled easily. His skin tore under Natalya's claws, and her fangs pierced deeply into his flesh, finding his jugular. The first time she had ever drunk blood at Arkadith's castle, she hadn't truly tasted the liquid life that was pouring down her eager throat. Now she savored it, relishing the metal taste and the way it slid over her tongue. It was intoxicating, the essence of life that was fading in her mouth, and she was dimly aware of her own laughing.

She heard the gunshot a split second before she felt it, and it sent searing pain that jolted through her human psyche. Her eyes flickered. Her fangs retracted then elongated again. The pain was immobilizing, and she released the man from her grip. He slumped to her side, struggling to speak through the wound in his throat. A moment later all of his blood had emptied around him, dying the snow a nearly blackened ruby. The scent roused the vampire within again and Natalya slipped into unknowing once more.

The remaining men fired at her but the vampiress was not to be killed so easily. Her body forced the bullet from her shoulder and the hole closed, hissing slightly as steam plumed from the wound. The other men were dispatched easily, half blind, slow and clumsy in the night with muskets that were slower still. Only the bullets could match her speed, and the sound of them betrayed their movements long before they could find her vulnerable head and heart.

She drank deeply from the men, and when her uncontrollable thirst had finally been sated, her eyes opened and her vision returned. They were brown once again, and she watched her skin flush pink with fresh blood. The sensation felt pleasantly warm as the stolen blood strengthened her own body, and she stood up slowly, rejoicing in her newfound power. Her shriveled lungs expanded, and she inhaled for the first time since she had left the castle. Her power swelled with the drawing of breath, and she closed her eyes, letting the tides of it cascade and build through her veins and her beating heart.

When they opened again, she gazed down at the carnage. The sated vampire faded from within her, leaving room only for human sorrow.

Her body had betrayed her. Blood stained tears welled in her eyes, and she did not fight them. She lowered her head, and her body was wracked with sobs.

None of the humans had been drained; instead, she had only tasted one's blood before moving onto the next. Their bodies mirrored Anesa's. There was no neat puncture wounds in their necks where her breath had stroked her victim's neck. Instead, the five men had been literally torn apart, their limbs bent in awkward, impossible positions, some with blood still oozing from their many wounds.

She didn't have it in her to do this, *did she?* The memories came in fragmented shards, and she gasped when glimpses of the slaughter returned to her. With the blood, her mind was clearer than ever, and she tried to block off the memories as they came, but she was powerless to stop it. Her mind played the grotesque scene over and over again, with no way to shut it off.

She was running again. She was faster than ever, a pale ghost that sailed over the snow with every leap, but she hardly noticed. As the dawn approached, she sought refuge in a musty cave she had scented earlier.

It was there that she would spend the daylight hours, asleep and far away from her people. She had no materials for a fire, and her body did not require the warmth, so she merely lay on the cave's floor and waited. Not even the dawn could chase away her dark thoughts, and as the sun's light brightened the cave, she sighed bitterly.

"*Monster*," she murmured out loud to herself. She had no other word for that which she had become. Natalya coiled a lock of her hair around her finger as she thought on her predicament. Here in the cave, her people were safe from her for at least a few days, and she breathed more deeply. She began to plan, but the words echoed hollowly in her head, only lies that brought false comfort. She would hold out for as long as she could, but even now the thought starving and dying without blood brought her more fear than the savage demon inside her.

"I will never drink another human's blood again," she vowed, forsaking her own need for blood and giving into the urge that called for a nearly deadened state of day sleep. There had been no sign that Arkadith had followed her that night, except for a strange white faced bird with a gray body and coal black eyes that had flown over the cave unseen, and was now heading back towards the mountainous peaks.

~ Chapter Twenty-Seven ~
Reconciliation

Natalya's scent lingered in the air, beckoning Kaima and Voren into the quiescent woods. Voren had circled the black gate that guarded Arkadith's castle, sniffing all around it in a meandering pattern. He had confirmed that although she had spent a long time with Arkadith, she had recently escaped. Voren was hesitant, but Kaima's exuberance seemed to bolster him, and they were quick to follow.

Kaima had been ecstatic, and she had charged through the forest, convinced the two of them were about to find her long lost friend. Voren seemed cautiously optimistic, and he tracked her at a slower pace, at times sniffing the air several times with an oddly glassy stare as he looked into far off places. Kaima brushed off her sense of unease every time he did this, and with her close behind the swift footed werewolf on horseback, they had gained a considerable distance on her trail.

When they reached the river, they lingered at its side and Kaima wondered what strange thing had punctured the ice so fiercely. There was no sign of a fallen tree limb or fleeing creature to explain the large cracks. Voren appeared to lock on to Natalya's scent once more, and his posture became rigid with obvious anxiety. It was as if something he was smelling had disturbed him greatly.

"Is something wrong?" Kaima asked.

It's nothing. He trekked slightly west before crossing the river into the shadows of the trees on the far bank, and although Kaima worried he was growing despondent, she followed.

A few hours later, Voren's nose twitched excitedly. Kaima sensed the change in him, and they quickened their pace. They approached a cave, and Voren formed a barrier with his body to halt Kaima's path just before they had reached it.

"*What are you doing?* Natalya might be in there!" She tried walking around the werewolf but he blocked her path.

We'll wait here until dusk, he growled firmly.

"Why are you stopping me? My friend is in that cave and we did not come this far for nothing!" The werewolf's ears flattened against his head, and he dipped his head as he turned back towards a clearing, his tail motioning for the girl to follow. Voren sat on his hindquarters, and Kaima settled onto a small boulder that had not yet been fully buried under the snow.

Before we enter that cave there is something you should know.

"What?"

Natalya has spent a lot of time with Arkadith.

"I know! And that is why we should be in there, helping her! She's probably terrified after everything she's been through and—"

Kaima, Natalya is no longer... human.

261

A silence hung in the air. Kaima's eyes widened slowly as the forlorn despair creeped into them. Her hands rose to her cheeks, clutching them so hard that small grooves were etched into her skin.

"Are you sure?" she asked in a whisper.

Her scent has mixed with the deathly smell of ash. I did not wish for it to be true, but I have suspected it ever since we left Arkadith's castle. He turned her, he snarled savagely.

"We were too late…" Kaima stood up, walking methodically in a circle through the snow, not bothering to lift her feet with each mechanic step she took. She did not cry; her tears for her friend, her people and her own fate had already been spilled. Her expression turned from one of someone who had given up all hope, to of reckless conviction.

"We must still try to talk to her."

No! She is an undying vampire now, a feeder of human blood. She will no longer know love, friendship or mercy. I'm afraid this is where our quest ends, Voren growled, defeated.

Although fear now clouded Kaima's eyes, her voice did not shake when she spoke. Her hands had lowered from her face and now balled into fists.

"It does not matter what has happened to her. From the time we both could walk, we have been friends, and her heart is a pure one. Whatever Arkadith has done to her, she will not harm me."

I forbid it. We leave now, Voren replied, his body already turned towards Valwood while Kaima's eyes glittered with anger.

"Forbid it?" she snickered. "I am not your wayward child, Voren."

I will not have another death on my consciousness.

"Your conscience!" she shrieked suddenly, and Voren reeled back at the cruelty in her voice. "Is that all you care for, beast? Natalya can die as long as your conscience doesn't trouble you in the night!" Voren recoiled as if she had struck him, and he turned his head, a seething growl rumbling in his throat. All of the werewolf's teeth were bared, his lips pulled back and his face wrinkled in rage. Kaima backed up at the sight of Voren's anger.

You dare…you know nothing of me, human girl. Not me or my kind. In Celestial Hold, I risked my own hide and saved Natalya when I could have left her to be killed by rogues!

"I know. I shouldn't have said that, I'm sorry." Kaima's anger left her and she seemed to deflate into a fearful maiden.

Its ok, replied Voren and his face had lost all of its prior ferocity. His tongue rasped along Kaima's fingers gently. It was the first time he had ever touched her and Kaima was moved. She smiled slightly.

"Thank you, Voren," she said, placing her hand tentatively on his back. The fur leveled under her hand and she dragged her fingers through it slowly as she spoke.

"I know you do not want me to talk to her, but I would die for her. And even if it is likely that she will try and kill me, I will do this with or without your protection. But it would be a whole lot easier if you accompanied me."

I see now that I could not stop you, and I do not really wish to.

"You would have to kill me first." She allowed a slight smile to grace her lips.

Then let us wait until nightfall. I do not relish the thought of waking a sleeping vampire. I will do my best to protect you, but I ask that you prepare yourself for the worst. I'll stand guard while you get some sleep. You are going to need it.

When the day's warmth had faded and the forest glowed under silver moonlight, Voren roused Kaima awake with his nose. Despite their exposure to the elements, Kaima had been quite warm with the heat of the werewolf's body and the bearskin blanket she had taken from Claw Haven. She groaned, rubbing her eyes, but she was alert within seconds, her fierce resoluteness also awakened. Voren looked at her as if he wished to speak.

"Don't try and talk me out of it again, please. I must do this."

I would do no such thing. I only hope the depth of your friendship is as powerful as you say it is…for your sake. Let's go. She will be rising soon as well.

Kaima saddled Methea and stuffed the blanket into the bag that hung from her side. She mounted the horse and they set off for the cave.

It was not a far ride, and as the cave came into view once more, Methea would go no farther. She planted her hooves into the snow and snorted fearfully.

What is wrong? Voren asked when they had not followed.

"I'm not sure…her horse won't move. She's terrified all of a sudden," Kaima answered, trying to kick Methea into action. The horse's eyes were rolling and she reared up, nearly throwing her rider. Kaima could not suppress her cry as she struggled to stay on the mare.

"This isn't working! I'll have to walk with her." She dismounted and walked to the horse's front, holding the mare's head in her hands. Her hands rubbed the stricken animal's nose, trying to calm her.

"Shhh, shhh," Kaima whispered, and Methea calmed at her touch. She took the reins in her hand and led the trusting horse on foot to the mouth of the cave.

An animalistic hiss greeted them from inside. Voren began to growl warningly, and Kaima backed away slightly, though she did not run.

"Natalya?" she asked fearfully into the darkness. From within, Natalya had backed into the farthest corner of the cave, still hissing. Rather than coherent voice, all that emanated from the cave were terrible, guttural shrieks and growls.

"Natalya, it's me, Kaima." At her words the vampire had finally found her voice.

"I could smell you. Your blood calls to me. You have brought Voren too. *Why*?"

"I wish to talk to you." Natalya cackled manically, and when her laughter had subsided, she screamed.

"No! Get away from here before—", the shrieking laughter had started up again, and her voice faded into into the deliriousness of the vampire within.

"I won't leave you, friend."

"You must. I am *so thirsty*…I do not want to kill you!"

Kaima, you heard her. We must leave now, Voren growled.

"No!" Kaima screamed into the cave. "Kill me if you must, but I have come to help you."

"Help me? You cannot help me unless you wish to have all your lovely blood spilled!" Her words dissolved into madness once more, and they could hear a strange mixture of crying and demonic laughter.

"What of your people Natalya? We have lost this war without you!"

"Everyone comes into this world to die. This is nothing new. Leave me before you join them!"

"So that is it then. Your people, Seth and me. We mean nothing to you anymore?"

"Seth? Kaima?" Recognition seemed to flare in Natalya's voice and Kaima's voice strengthened.

"Yes Natalya. And we *love* you. Your people love you. Talk with us, please."

"Alright... I will speak with you. But Voren must stand between us and stop me if...no matter *what*, he must stop me."

I will, Voren growled into both of their heads. He placed himself between Kaima and the mouth of the cave, ready to attack if the vampire did.

You may come out now, Natalya.

Slowly, agonizingly, Natalya peeled herself away from the shadows and approached them. Kaima was trembling, and when she saw her, she jumped with a slightly audible gasp.

The transformation had ravaged Natalya's body. Not a mole or wrinkle marred her; even the tiny birthmark on her neck had disappeared. But her skin was far from clear. Like tiny blue spider webs, her veins scrawled across every part of her body. The once honey brown irises of her eyes were now unfathomably black, and her pallor was sickeningly pale. Blood that had been dripping from her mouth had dried and congealed over her neck and stained her dress. It was worse than Kaima could have even imagined.

"Oh Natalya, my dear friend, what has Arkadith *done* to you?" Natalya's eyes were locked on Kaima's throat, and she shook with the visible effort of raising her gaze to meet hers. Kaima lifted her hand as if to breach the gap between them and the bristling werewolf, but she did not step closer. She could see Natalya fighting the Vampiric rage that had taken over her body, and she allowed that small thing to bring her some comfort.

"*No other human should ever be plagued with this curse.* I *fear* it, the vampire within me, and I *fear* Arkadith," Natalya whispered in a ragged voice.

"Then come with us to Valwood. Hide among your people, and let that vampire never find you again!" said Kaima. Natalya's eyes began to mist again with tears that were tinged red and she shook her head.

"You do not understand. I've done things, horrible things already, and there can be no life for me in Valwood now. And there can never be peace in our city while Arkadith lives. I must go to him now, for he and I are the same. I will learn of him and his ways, but I will never become like him. Perhaps I can find something in the castle that will aid me in destroying him. As a human, I stood no chance against him, but as a vampire I might. And only when he lies dead do I have a chance of returning to the life I once lived," Natalya answered.

This is not a fight you can win by yourself, Voren growled. *For now we shall go our separate ways. Kaima and I will return to Valwood and talk to Anraq. She and I are living proof that werewolf and man may find peace. Together, it may be possible for us to convince some of the werewolves to fight Arkadith. Return to the castle and feed Natalya. Replenish your strength and when you are strong again I will come for you. There is still time to save Valwood.*

Natalya nodded, but she began shaking and her gaze locked on to Kaima's throat. She was losing control, and she stepped towards Kaima, her mouth frothing. Voren snarled menacingly, and he rose to draw her attack.

"Go now then, before I am unable to stop myself," Natalya managed to say before she descended into delirium once again. But Kaima and Voren were already striding towards Valwood. When the cave was just out of sight, Kaima pulled up on the reins and whispered in a voice that she knew would carry to the vampire's ears.

267

"Goodbye, my friend." She kicked Methea into a gallop and then she was gone, leaving Natalya to her sweltering thirst.

Natalya too left immediately. The searing in her throat had lessened now that she was no longer in the presence of her prey, but she still needed blood and soon. She travelled as swiftly as she could on foot, heading towards the mountains again. Even with her superior strength, each movement was a struggle; every vein scored a blue path across her skin, jutting outwards in a desperate bid to fill themselves with blood. Her sunken eyes were losing their ability to focus, and when she pulled herself onto the final cliff face where Arkadith's castle lay, she could feel them closing involuntarily and her vision giving way to darkness. Sightlessly, she pulled herself through the gate, relying on her other fading senses to guide her. When she reached the great door, she faltered, the castle swaying before her half closed eyes. She could not gather the strength to reach the knocker. Close to starvation, Natalya collapsed at its entrance, waiting for either Arkadith or the deadly sun's rays to find her.

~ Chapter Twenty-Eight ~
The Vampire's Will

Dusk found Natalya within the confines of her black coffin again. Her eyes opened, and for a time, she merely lay within, almost daring to believe that everything she had experienced had been one long and terrible nightmare. But the memories came with a wave of nausea, and she pushed upwards on the lid. When she had freed herself, her heart sank.

She was not in her room at Arkadith's manor. She stood up slowly, her eyes falling over everything she could see by flickering torchlight, to the shackles that hung loosely from the walls, the pillars that rose to its ceiling and the light layer of straw that littered the dusty floor, and she realized.

She was in a dungeon. The scent of long spilled blood that had seeped into the crevices percolated throughout the room and inspired revulsion, not her thirst. A dank chill had settled into the castle's floor, and now it rose to dampen the air, but Natalya was unaffected. She put her hands on the stony walls and listened. Only faint sounds came to her sensitive ears from upstairs.

She tried the door to the upper levels, but of course it was locked. She could hear nothing of Arkadith or Anna, and she slammed her body weight against the door. Even with her enhanced strength the door did not budge.

"Arkadith!" she screamed at the top of her lungs while the vampire within stirred. She put a hand to her head, momentarily dizzy. When her outburst elicited no response she began to pace wrathfully, a caged tigress. For the next hour she did not let up, her energy undiminished until she heard a crash from upstairs. She froze midstride, senses alert while she listened.

The vampire had returned and from the sound of it he was dragging something heavy. Natalya backed away from the door when she realized he was coming downstairs. The door was thrust open and Arkadith, grunting with the effort of pulling his charge, heaved a man down the stairs and into the dungeon with Natalya.

"What is— what are you doing?" Natalya cried, but Arkadith had already slammed the door closed. "No!" she shouted again, beating on the door. "You will release us, Arkadith!" She heard his muffled voice, easily from upstairs as if he were at her neck, whispering in her ear.

"You must learn to enjoy the kill and feed as you are meant to. You will slay this man and drink."

"I won't do it! I'll starve first!"

"I'm afraid you have no choice. The vampire's will is stronger than your human will. Surely you know this by now, Natalya." She could hear his receding footsteps into the refuge of the castle's spires. He was out of earshot now, and Natalya resumed her pounding. She only stopped when the feeble sound of the man's groaning interrupted her. She turned around.

270

The first thing she noticed was the trickle of blood that was gently flowing from his scalp where Arkadith's fingernails had presumably dug into the man's skin. She swiped her tongue over her lips, drawing in the iron scent of the crimson river. She could feel her fangs extending and her eyesight flickering, before an inhuman snarl sounded from her throat.

"No," she growled and the changes stopped as abruptly as they had started. *She was not that thirsty yet.* The words slid from her mind, heavy with lies she was telling herself. In truth, her vision still faltered, and now her head swayed with the intoxicating scent of blood and her efforts to hold it upright. *She needed his blood.*

Still she fought the change and sat down on her coffin, her elbows resting on her knees as she thought. The man had come to and now he slid himself to the farthest recess of the dungeon, as far away as he could get from Natalya.

"It'll do you no good," she muttered to the man and sighed bitterly. He could only moan again, and now Natalya turned to really look at him. He was handsome, probably in his late twenties with tousled dark hair and the creeping of a mustache that shadowed his face. His wide eyes, staring fixedly at her, were a striking shade of hazel, and when Natalya looked into them she could see shards of emerald, amber and gold topaz. She could hear the blood within him, and it was a rushing in her ears. She fought the urge to be nearer.

In the presence of the vampire the man seemed to be losing consciousness again, but he stubbornly clung to lucidity. Natalya turned away again, trying to busy her mind. Somewhere near a rat scuttled across the dirty floor, and she swallowed, repressing a shiver. Rats were bad omens, present only where decay and disease reigned in her city. *Valwood.*

271

She thought of Kaima and Voren, and the edge was lifted from her thirst. She was gladdened that Kaima still cared for her despite her burden, and hope for their blooming plan surged within her. But as the night wore on, and it became harder and harder to block out her thirst, her thoughts grew darker. The reality of maintaining friendships as a vampire began to settle on her chest almost like a physical weight.

Her eyes had momentarily gone sightless again, and she jerked her head up. Her throat began to burn, and she blinked several times in rapid succession, trying to bring the man into focus once more. The seconds blurred into minutes and Natalya wavered, hovering between awareness and blissful witlessness. When her vision blackened again, she nearly slipped completely. The tigress roared, clawing for control. How easy it would be to give in to her, to let her take control and sate her debilitating thirst.

Human. I will never drink from a human again. At once Natalya's eyes flew open. She had remembered her oath. She looked down at her skin, painfully aware of how thoroughly starved for blood she truly looked. She had lightened to an impossible whiteness and each vein protruded from her skin until they looked like they would tear away from her flesh. And all the while her thirst grew.

She chanced another look at the man, but he did not stir. *Fainted again.* She was not surprised but this made everything harder. Now she was left to fight her inner vampire alone, without his voice to bring her mind back into sharp clarity. She was not old enough to resist blood like Arkadith could.

But he never resisted a drink if he could help it, she thought. She laughed darkly, but the noise that had come out of her was an inhuman shriek, and it frightened her. The sound had roused the man too, and he attempted to back away even further, but his back was against the wall.

His movement had drawn her predatory eye again, and she felt herself slipping into the unknowing trance of the vampire caught under the bloodlust.

Oh not now please, she thought desperately. But she could not stop the inevitable. Her eyes dimmed again, and this time her irises did not revert back to their liquid light mahogany.

She held out for one more hour before the tigress had risen, and the vampire had taken over completely. She rose from atop the coffin and stalked towards the man. He shrank away, sensing the change that had come over her. As she approached, she felt her dying strength grow in the presence of fresh blood, while he seemed to be losing his.

But was she truly strong? What was strength when you couldn't control your own burning impulses? Rapidly her thoughts changed. When she had been human, every emotion had been distinct, tied to the mood a situation commanded or the unique phenomena her senses brought to her. Now everything had changed. Thirst, hunger and need had blended into one amplified sensation. Anger became directly tied to sorrow, and one could not be invoked without arousing the other, if she dared to remember the life she had lived before this one.

She had reached the man. He thrashed in his efforts to rise from the floor and escape, but in the locked dungeon there was nowhere he could go. In his terror, he had tripped over his own legs and he fell into a tangle of struggling limbs while the vampire stood over him, already relishing her kill.

"Away, creature of darkness!" he yelled, his fingers forming a shaking cross. From somewhere far away the words had stirred pity in Natalya's mind, and she wished she could do just that and leave, to go far away from this place. But here was where she was, and when she reached for his throat there was not a human thought in her mind.

The man was cornered. He tried vainly to defend himself, but Natalya evaded his feeble strikes easily and pinned him against the dungeon wall. She looked into his terrified eyes, but she was only a predator locked with her helpless prey, and she no longer knew mercy. Her fangs lowered to his neck, and she hesitated just long to exhale on his neck. Her warm breath was like a gentle fog against his skin, and he shuddered beneath her, just as she had once done under Arkadith. She knew the feeling, the knowledge that death was about to close icy fingers over her body. But for him there would be no unending curse to follow, and somewhere deep in Natalya's psyche she nearly envied him.

All of the control she had fought so hard to keep, as she felt herself slipping and giving into the vampire's will, had fled and her fangs came down hard on his neck. She heard a ragged intake of breath as he gasped, and then he was shouting in her ear as he doubled his assailment of strikes and blows. They fell harmlessly against her body, rousing no more of her interest than the straw that was strewn across the stony floors.

She continued to drink until his blood ran from her chin, and his strikes grew weaker until they ceased altogether. She meant to pull back and stop, and as her mental clarity grew she found it easier to grapple with the vampire and regain dominion of her own mind.

But it was too late. The man's vivid hazel eyes were staring sightlessly at her, glazed over in death, his hand still closed in a gradually relaxing fist. Natalya lowered him carefully onto the floor, her tears mixing with the blood on her face. She looked down at him for what seemed like hours until she heard footsteps coming down the stairs.

The door opened, and she looked up to see Arkadith standing in the dungeon, his hand outstretched for her to take it.

"So you finished him off then. Good girl," and as she rose, he invited her into the light up the stairs, and out of her dreary prison.

A few hours later, Natalya had gone out to the courtyard within the perimeter of Arkadith's castle. The dead man lay in a heap next to her. She had gone back for him and carefully dragged him outside.

She had chosen a beautiful spot to be his resting place. The many beginnings of wildflowers were starting to make their way upwards through the light dustings of snow, all the way to the iron fence.

She began to dig into the earth with only the strength of her own body. She scooped handful after handful of frozen dirt, glistening with sweat. She did not pause in her toil even as the end of the night approached. Instead, the work brought her a melancholy joy, and soon she had dug a sizeable hole into the ground.

"You're burying the man?" Arkadith asked sharply in her ear. His sudden appearance did not take her by surprise; her ears had caught his every movement. She did not answer. She did not wish to hear his objections or even hope to make him understand.

"Natalya, it is almost dawn." The news brought no enlightenment. She could hear the warming of the coming sun's rays already and the steady lightening of the sky. Still, she ignored him, and she began to dig faster, until the grave was nearly large enough. Arkadith moved to stand by her side, and she feared he would take her hand and drag her back into the castle before she could complete her work. Instead, he too knelt by the ground, and began to work as well. Natalya paused to look at him, uncomprehending, before she returned to the digging with renewed energy. Although the dirt clung to Arkadith's black coat and breeches he made no move to rub it away with his hands.

They dug in silence, not stopping until Arkadith could stand easily in the hole. It hadn't taken them long to complete with their improved strength and speed. Natalya moved to drag the man into the hole and Arkadith moved quickly to help, supporting his head so that it did not snap backwards as they lowered him within.

Together they covered the man in dirt, and gradually he began to fade from their view, one with the earth. When only a mound that was streaked with dirt marked his presence, Natalya walked through the snowy grass, searching. When she came across a large rock, she grabbed it and placed it at the mound's head. The headstone seemed insufficient, but it would weather the elements and stand unchanging over the years to mark the man's grave, and that was enough.

The sun began to peek over the horizon. Arkadith stood up and began to walk back towards the castle without a word. When Natalya did not move, he turned towards her, curling his hand in a subtle gesture for her to follow.

She could now see the rising sun glowing through the gaps in the trees, but she remained next to the grave. She wished to say something meaningful, but nothing she could think of seemed adequate.

Her skin began to warm. It was merely uncomfortably at first, and then it gradually began to heat until her skin burned, and she gasped in pain. Smoke began to curl rapidly from the open sores that were beginning to develop on her exposed arms. Only then did Natalya finally rise to follow Arkadith.

When she had reached the shadow of his castle, she turned back, giving the grave one long final look. Her sores were already beginning to close in the absence of the sun's light.

"I'm sorry," she whispered simply, knowing the words could never be enough. She stepped back into the safety of Arkadith's castle, leaving the man in the grave to an eternity of peace that she knew would elude her for as long as she remained a vampire.

~ Chapter Twenty-Nine ~
Her Wavering Resolve

Caught in the grip of day sleep, Natalya's rest was punctuated with terrible dreams of blood and fire. When the all-consuming flames had scorched her into wakefulness for the third time, she pushed on the lid of her coffin and stepped into her room. The daylight was fading behind the black curtains, but there were still a few hours of dangerous sunlight left outside. The conflagration was still burning red against her eyelids as she stood up, and she shook her head slightly, blinking it away.

The dreams had only gotten worse since she had been turned. Valwood was a living inferno, rife with the screams of her bleeding people. Oh how they had bled, the red rivers running down from their necks and seeping into the ground. Not even the near comatose state of day sleep could chase her nightmares away or banish her thirst for good.

Silent as a ghost, she slipped from the room. Her bare feet padded catlike on the carpeted stone as she slid the door closed behind her as quietly as she could. She walked down the hall, alone for a mere few minutes.

Anna was walking down the hall, pushing her tray. It was devoid of food and drink, only a goblet of blood balanced in its center. Now that Natalya was a vampire, there was no longer a need for the lavish doting of the cooks, and the ruse had been quickly abandoned.

Anna glared at her, her eyes never leaving Natalya as they passed one another, but her spell had been broken. Her twisted reverence for Arkadith had once chilled Natalya, but no more. Now the woman was beneath her, prey to be ignored for Arkadith had claimed her, and Anna clearly reveled in it. Furthermore, she disgusted Natalya as well as arousing from her a strange perversion of pity. The feelings unnerved Natalya as much as she suppressed them, and she was relieved when the woman disappeared around a corner.

She could never bite the neck of this willing victim, this human that defied life and rejected what Natalya had lost. Her blood only repulsed Natalya even as it leapt from Anna's veins, waiting to be devoured.

Nor could she taste the blood from her tray. It had called to her, tempted her, and yet she had denied her body what it desired above all else. The strength the now buried man's blood had given her was fading, but Natalya did not waver in her decision. Anna had merely chuckled, enviously it had seemed, and Natalya was sickened at the woman's reaction at her steadfast refusal to take the blood in passing. So this woman had wished for what Natalya now had, strength threefold what she possessed in life, and greatly enhanced senses in exchange for a never ending ravenous thirst.

Well she could have it, Natalya thought bitterly, and her hate for the old hag doubled. She crept down the stairs, not wishing to draw any additional attention to herself. Her feet took her absent mind to the library, and she was greeted by walls upon walls of books on every subject.

She began to peruse Arkadith's collection, starting from one end of the room to the other. She skimmed through every book on vampire folklore that she could get her hands on, but none of them alluded to anything that she did not already know. Stakes through the heart, decapitation and burning were all echoed in the legends, and they revealed nothing that she could use against Arkadith.

Apparently the authors had never come across an ancient vampire of his caliber. There was nothing described about how to evade his elevated mental prowess nor how to defeat a man that could turn into living dust. When her last book proved to be only drivel about garlic and devoid of anything useful, Natalya replaced it back onto the shelf. She skimmed through the rest of the titles, gradually moving towards the end of the case as she did so.

At the end of the bookshelf, a nondescript book that was shorter and more slender than the rest had caught her eye, and she took it from its place.

It was a journal. The cover was blank, but when she turned to the inside page, she could see *I, Arkadith: A Memoir* written in ink on its front page.

Intrigued, she took it to the armchair and thumbed to a random page. She lowered herself into the armchair, her nose buried in the journal. In Arkadith's neat hand written scrawl, she read:

August 11th, 1309

I feel it every day that I am alive. Despite what I have read, my heart beats with vibrant life after I have drunk fresh blood. Does this not make me alive as much as any man? I should think so.

The thirst lives in every fibre of my being, but it does not consume me, for I am its Master, and it serves me.

She flipped several pages ahead where the entries grew farther and farther apart and continued to read:

March 18th, 1348

It is a new sensation, this love that I feel for her, my Elizabeth. It burns almost as hard as my thirst, and I intend to explore this new sensation as fully as possible.

She has not yet guessed that I am more than I appear to her: a man of grandeur and high stature. I must never allow her to.

April 10th, 1348

Our love grows stronger day by day. I have been introduced to her circle, but she has not yet questioned me as to mine. I have told her that my mother is ill of health, and she seems to accept that explanation. I have thus far managed to keep the thirst from rising.

June 12th, 1348

It is with the greatest joy that I write this entry. Elizabeth has accepted my proposal to marry. We shall wed as soon as I receive her father's blessing. But in my current state, this shall be a terrible feat, my thirsty torment be damned. I am confident that he should think nothing of my pale appearance, and I shall not dwell on it, for soon the wedding bells shall sound!

July 1st, 1348

This madness, this thirst, it is nudging me, threatening me to do unspeakable things to my love. I want her blood more fiercely than I have ever wanted anything, even the splendor of her lovemaking. Now I yearn for her neck more than the clasp of her bosom, but I am still its Master. I will not lose control.

As Natalya's eyes slid to the next page the writing became more scrambled as if Arkadith had rushed to get everything down with a shaking hand:

August 5th, 1348

I am distraught. I have done it. The thing I have feared above all else. My bride to be, my beautiful Elizabeth grows cold in death.

This thirst, this beast that I had once thought I had tamed, has deceived me. How did I do it you ask? Like all of the others. I drank from her trusting throat…

Natalya slammed the journal shut, not wanting to finish. She remembered Arkadith's recollection, and her imagination filled in the rest. Nauseas, she returned the journal and returned to the armchair, lost in thought.

The werewolves had been wrong. Somewhere deep within Arkadith there was a man buried beneath the forever thirsting vampire. Man enough to help her bury the man in the courtyard and enough to have loved this Elizabeth.

His love had not won out in the end.

When she finally looked up, the curtains were black with the night's darkness behind them. She exited the library and wandered to the stairs, hardly knowing where her feet led her. The flickering light from the sconces were dim, but she did not need a lantern; her own eyes were sufficient in the darkness. She ascended the grand staircase, pondering on everything that she had seen and read. Her mind was conflicted, and as she traveled upwards to the northernmost spire, it was a moment before she realized she was not alone.

Arkadith had his back to her, and he was staring wordlessly at the moon through the tall open window. His clothes and hair ruffled slightly in the wind, though his form was perfectly still. He too seemed consumed with his thoughts, and Natalya was surprised. She would have thought he would be hunting at this hour, and she swallowed her revulsion at the thought. She paused in the doorway, caught between the need to seek undisturbed refuge elsewhere in the castle and her need to satisfy her hunger for answers. He spoke before she could make a decision, and she knew she never could have come upon him undetected.

"What is it that troubles you tonight, Natalya?" he asked without turning around.

"It's..." she started to say nothing, but she remembered the strange compassion he had shown to the man they had buried together. In reading his writing she had felt an odd sense of closeness to this creature as she had learned of his struggle with the horrible thirst as well. She realized she had no desire to lie to the vampire.

"I just wanted to thank you for allowing me to stay here," she said finally, crossing the room to stand beside him. "Even after I ran away."

"A Master always cares for his creations," he said simply, still staring at the moon. She followed his gaze to it as well.

"It's beautiful tonight," she breathed, taking it in. It did not seem to her to be a smooth, flawless orb anymore. Now she was looking at it with fresh eyes, ones that could pick out the many craters that roughened its surface and the many different shadows that colored it into nearly every shade of black and gray. And yet it was still breathtaking, the single benign presence in their lives, always reliably there, gently lighting the nights for them. The two of them could only stand in awe of its presence.

"It is always beautiful," he agreed. "But tonight, it does seem particularly serene." He turned to her for the first time, his eyes searching hers.

"You have changed much. You have grown wiser and more discerning." She smiled without humor. Her smiles these days were always heavier, always pulled down at the corners by lingering sadness. She had noticed it too. She was more thoughtful, and less impulsive. More restrained and less shortsighted. Yes, she had indeed changed much.

"You were a newborn," he continued. "You had to test your own way in the world before you could open your eyes and truly see. I did not worry for you. I knew you would return."

This she could think of no response to, so she redirected her attention to the open window again. She walked up to it and the breeze gently pulled at her hair. She laid a finger on the black curtain that had served as her faithful shield from the sun's deadly rays ever since she had been turned. She trailed the rippling pattern of the fabric, staring intently at the place where only hours ago the sun had brightened and heated it with is blinding light. Arkadith seemed to understand.

"It is so…interesting, is it not?" he asked, and Natalya turned her gaze away from the night, and into the vampire's face. He seemed more man than monster tonight.

"That something so simple, so *uneventful* to mortals could be so devastating to one such as us?"

Natalya stood for a while without speaking, and Arkadith did not take offense to her silence. She stared into the curtain's folds, thinking intently. She did not see it as mere decoration, but as a barrier to the world that she had once been a part of and was now so separate from. Seeing Kaima and Voren had not bridged that gap. The memory of seeing them had only served to remind her of the life in Valwood that would forever be denied her, and it only brought her more sadness. Now, as she studied each individual thread and fiber of that barrier, she realized that the world had never before held such a forbidden wonder. She turned towards Arkadith again, bewildered now by his simple dismissal of all that she had lost. Of what they had *both* lost.

"I'd always loved the night," she finally answered. "The moon's gentle silver glow, the beauty held in the stars and the darkness that cloaked my senses and made me truly feel alive. I am a child of darkness now," she said softly, her voice hardly above a whisper. But her tone quickly hardened as she raised her voice.

"But I loved the daytime too. I loved the warmth, the full spectrum of brilliant color on the flowers and the birds. And I miss the sun. I can no longer watch it rise, spreading blazing yellow and orange across the sky. I can only lie in wait for it to fall below the horizon so that I may not die under its rays. What a horrible curse that you have brought upon me! You may have chosen to forget, all of those years ago, but I do not wish to forget what a fine thing the sun is, Arkadith."

"You cannot spend an eternity reflecting on the past, Natalya. You have years and years of immortal life that were bestowed upon you. Do not *waste* that gift."

"A gift that I cannot share with my people is not a gift at all," Natalya answered, gazing into the forest that lay on the border of Valwood in the distance, beyond even the scope of her vision.

"You really miss them, don't you?"

"More than words can say," she said sadly. The vampire swept his cape in a wide arc, nearly enveloping the girl in the swirl of his floor length cape.

"Then come with me. I have something I would like to show you." Natalya nodded, no longer in fear of the vampire. She had already experienced the true horrors of death; nothing in this earth could compare.

She stepped closer to him, and she could hear his heart beating. As she nearly lost herself in his embrace, she could almost forget that it beat only in steady determination to cling to a life it did not truly have.

His cape billowed around them, and they were swept away into darkness. Travelling in this way was thrilling, and Natalya was aware of each new sensation as it passed through her. She was lighter than the wind, feeling within each molecule the speed and coldness through which they travelled in the night. She was only dust, and in mere minutes, she found herself solid once more atop a rooftop. They were perched like human gargoyles on the tallest spire of Valwood's great church, the edge of the forest at their backs. They could see all of Natalya's city under the star studded sky, to the dusty signs that marked each building to the shadows and orange firelight that flickered within each street.

Even after being ravaged by the flames, the sight was still beautiful in its reluctance to fall to the fire. Her people's land sprawled further than even their eyesight could see; even the distant lights of the farms were nearly invisible to them.

"This is wonderful," Natalya gasped and some of the brightness came back into her eyes. "But lonely as well, for I am no longer among them."

"Lonely," Arkadith scoffed, his voice dipped in scorn. "Humans are the loneliest ones on this earth. Among all of nature's creatures, only they are graced with enough intelligence to mourn and question the meaning of their confusing existences. But they were not graced with enough to find the answers to the great questions of the universe. They spend all of their time looking up into the sky, wondering how they came to be instead of seeing and knowing what is right in front of them. We vampires are the lucky ones, for we possess all of their intelligence but none of their questions. We answer only to our natures, and in that, we find peace."

"You once compared a vampire to a lion, saying that they did not feel guilt when they hunted. And yet I feel guilt. And you must as well, for you helped me bury the man. *Why*, Arkadith?"

"A lion does not feel guilt when he hunts, it is true," Arkadith answered thoughtfully. "But nor does he feel hate. It is possible to kill with neither, Natalya."

She looked away, not altogether convinced, content for the time being to merely look out onto the world.

This life that she had left behind, it seemed so near to her that she could reach out and touch it, but her hand caught only the passing breeze.

Arkadith followed her gaze and together they waited in the night for the moon to fade into lightness once more. The two vampires had found peace in their own ways, for they had figured out their places in the order of things.

But as they shifted into scattered dust once more and flew under the full moon's dimming light, Natalya knew she did not like it. And when the daylight had finally spread its light over the receding moon, and she pulled closed the lid of her coffin to sleep, she fought against the knowledge that she and Arkadith were almost the same.

"Almost," she whispered in the enclosed darkness of her holding. And it was with less conviction that she thought of her vow to return to the castle and slay the vampire Arkadith.

~ Chapter Thirty ~
Freeing the Tiger

An abhorrent blight upon this earth, that is what we are, thought Natalya as she stepped out of her coffin, unravelling herself from the tangle of her nightmares once again. She thought of Arkadith, and when she pictured the vampire, she did not know who lived under the distantly wise and almost *fatherly* façade. Was he the man who had spoken to her gently of the moon's beauty only the previous night? Or the the monster that had killed her mother so horrifically all those nights ago?

She closed her eyes as her mother's scream, still so prevalent in her ears after reliving Arkadith's memory, echoed in her mind. She thought of the others. Anesa, her wonderful mentor and brave Elder Tomas, brutally killed by the fledglings Arkadith had brought from the dead. *It was always the vampires,* she realized that had been responsible for the adversities that her beloved city had faced, including the war that they now found themselves in. She knew now that she could never be free from her maker's will while he still lived.

A nudging in her mind jerked her from her contemplation. Her head rose as she heard his familiar voice. *He had returned.*

Natalya... her name was nearly a whisper in her head but unquestionably Voren. His voice rose and fell in volume as if he were very far away and the mental connection between them was fading in strength. She raised her head, listing intently as she strained to catch every word, but he spoke to a place where ears were not needed.

...to help defeat Arkadith...I have brought others... With no way to communicate to him that she had heard, she went to the window and opened it, scanning the entrance and surrounding trees for a sign of the werewolf. Even with eyes comparable to an eagle's, it was a while before she could see him making his way to the entrance of the castle. He was a creature of shadow as he moved cautiously, aware that his scent would be wafting towards the castle. He began speaking again, and as they made eye contact, they both knew their pact had been renewed.

The time has come for Arkadith's reign to fall. The words were clear in her head as the distance between them had been closed. *Lehova, Kivah and Tovu have agreed to fight with us. Once we have defeated him, a new era of peace with humans can finally be established. Meet us here at midnight tonight, and we will end this barbaric tyranny.*

Natalya nodded and the werewolf returned to the shadows. Every day of her training and every trial in her seventeen years had been leading her to this moment, and her resolve hardened against the vampire. She had searched nearly every part of the vast castle. Every hall, every floor and every spire except for that which contained Arkadith's coffin had come up empty of her weapons and of her amulet. If she were to hope to defeat him, she would need them now.

The two guards outside his door were very solid barriers to her possessions, and she turned her thoughts toward them. She did not try to delude herself into thinking that evasive action would be enough to get past them.

She had once thought nothing of staking an undead vampire through his still beating heart, but she had never considered the killing of two humans in cold blood that she did now. The notion sent a wave of white-hot dread to the pit of her stomach, and she shuddered. To kill, even to right the wrongs that had been wrought upon her and her city was nearly too high a price to pay. She did not fear them or their weapons, only for her own black soul that was about to darken one more shade.

She held out a hand to push open her door, but she hesitated, her hand still poised to twist it open. The familiar sensations of the vampire returned and her body responded with a thrill of anticipation. She began to resist, to fight as her canines dropped to her bottom lip, and her eyes darkened, but she paused, shaking slightly as the Vampire gradually took over. Far beneath the many layers of her subconscious she could feel the raging tigress, clawing at the bars she had been locked behind somewhere deep within Natalya's mind.

She felt the fear again, the chilling dread she had felt before she had killed the men in the forest. Then, her emotions had been wholly different; the hunters had been innocent, and she had slain them to sate a thirst that could never be satiated. She had not known herself under the control of the vampire's will. This was different, outright murder planned while her human nature still reigned.

The tigress whispered in her ear, promising many things as she prowled the confines of her cage. She graced Natalya's lips

291

with a purr of everlasting beauty and power if she would only reach out and take it. Even for Natalya, the nudge of the beautiful tigress was hard to resist. How tempting her lies were, and she nearly unlocked her and unleashed the full power of the vampire.

No. She could feel it again, the slipping out of control as she had in the dungeon, but this time she would not surrender. She was engaged in a battle of wills, the outcome for which would rule her, vampire or human, and Natalya was determined that the vampire never conquer again.

In the invisible struggle within her own mind, Natalya eventually prevailed, and she felt her teeth retract and her pupils lighten. She emerged, her humanity intact, and it was with a clear head that she pulled open the door to her room and exited into the hallway.

This mastering of her own thoughts drained much of her energy though, and as she made her way up to the staircase she began to feel the first burnings of her thirst again.

As slowly as she could she reached the top of the stairs, her clawed fingers trailing the banister in an effort to prolong the moment where she would face the two guards.

The men did not appear to have noticed her outright as she reached them. Only a subtle twinge in their expressions betrayed them to the vampiress. They stood, their shoulders squared to the door, rooted to their places by fear of displeasing their Master. Their eyes stared stonily ahead, their limbs rigid against their bodies, for they had recovered their air of of stiff indifference quite swiftly.

Though their eyes had not flickered once, Natalya knew they were aware of her. She could feel their eyes on her, on her body in the red dress with the corseted bust that she wore. She was uncomfortably aware of the expanse of her breasts, threatening to spill out on top, but she was at the same time grateful for the distraction she knew it caused. Arkadith had provided her many expensive dresses, but she had chosen this one tonight for both its provocative neckline and that it laced up in the front. Thus it rendered Anna's assistance wholly unnecessary, a fact for which Natalya was very thankful.

She stood at the threshold of the hall, gathering herself. She touched upon the hypnotic power that throbbed just below her consciousness and felt the tigress leap. She had never been instructed in the ways of her power, but the instinct needed no direction, and she concentrated on her message.

Open the doooor, her voice commanded in a hiss. No audible sound came from her lips. The voice wended its way through the air and slithered into their minds. When Arkadith had spoken into her head, his voice had been authoritative, and she had known no option but to obey. And although his power rested in her veins, her voice had been gentler and more suggestive as it came to rest in the forefront of their minds. From here, it was up to them. She could only plant the idea in their heads; she possessed no power to bend the men's actions to her will.

It took only a moment before one of the men began fumbling in his robes, until the other had grabbed his wrist.

"What are you doing?" he growled and the other shook his head, abandoning his quest for the key. His mental fortitude had returned and Natalya felt it like a solid barrier against her attack. Her features began to soften until she appeared to them more human than vampire.

Please open the door for me, and this time her voice was lilting, more feminine than snakelike and pleading. But the men did not heed her ploy.

The tigress roared, and this time Natalya released her, knowing she would not be able to defeat both men without the vampire's full power. As the tigress was freed from her mental bars, Natalya felt their energies join, and her eyes darkened, her sight vanishing for a second. Her fangs began to grow and this time she did not try to stop the conversion.

She slipped into a blissful paradise of a far off reality, her desires one with the vampire's. When she met their gaze again, it was with the cold purpose of the predator who had locked sights with its prey, and Natalya was no more.

The men reached for their weapons, prepared to guard the door's contents at any cost, but she was not where she had been a moment before. She drew upon her abilities and rising into a cloud of ash, she reappeared between them, her canines fully extended.

She grabbed the neck of the closest man and tilted his head back by his hair, revealing the angular grooves of his throat. She did not hesitate before sinking her fangs into his flesh. Her bite had not been aimed at just any small vein for feeding, but instead his jugular, and blood was already pouring from his body.

She inhaled deeply, momentarily intoxicated by the scent of blood that flooded the hallway. The other man had crept behind her, his arms above her head, about to plunge his sword down onto her back as she eagerly fed. But as the energy in his muscles released and he thrust the sword downwards, she disappeared and his weapon scythed only empty air.

His companion was on the floor now, his hands pressed to the gaping tear in his neck. The blood flowed freely between his fingers and he rocked in his place, desperately trying to stave off his blood loss.

Natalya materialized behind him, leaving the dying man to the floor. He whirled to find the vampiress at his ear, and she gripped his shoulders from behind.

"Now get your key, and open the damn door," she commanded in his ear, abandoning her attempts at hypnotism. She threw him from herself with strength enhanced by the blood that was now running through her body. Dazed, and knocked against the opposite wall, he nodded and frantically dug in his robes for the key.

He produced it, and tried to insert it into the padlock with a shaking fist. Instead, he promptly dropped it.

"Get it now," Natalya hissed, opening her ashen mouth, a black mamba smiling wickedly. He dropped to the floor, grabbing wildly for the key before trying it into the lock again. This time it opened, and Natalya pushed the man aside, wasting no time entering the room. The man ran down the hall, over his dead other in a pile of bloody robes and out of the castle, leaving Natalya to wonder how far he would get before meeting Arkadith's wrath.

The room was lit by the cool sapphire glow of her amulet. Suspended inside a glass bell jar, it hung, dormant and waiting, on a pedestal in the center of the room. In only seconds Natalya had crossed to the room's center and come to stand over the necklace, her face caught in its blue shine.

She hesitated, her hand on the lid before she lifted the jar. Although the necklace had been bound to her, loyal in its magic, she did not know how it would react now that she had been turned. Would her own amulet come to sear her flesh as it would another of the undead?

In one abrupt motion, she pulled the jar from its stand. The amulet began to fall from its hangings and Natalya reflexively caught it. She winced, waiting for the burning pain, but it never came. The power in its ancient stone awakened, and instantly the room was swathed in violet light. She felt an energy pulse through her body as the amulet's magic began to bind itself to her own Vampiric power again.

She clasped it around her neck, and she instantly felt more protected. But she still needed her weapons. Her eyes swept through the newly darkened room, her vision guided by the direction of her amulet's glow.

Arkadith's chamber was absent of a bed; instead, a long mahogany coffin took its place against the wall. The only other source of light was a dimly lit candelabra atop a desk that illuminated the elaborate portrait of a man above. Natalya came to stand below the enormous painting, and she realized; it was of *him*. His fangs were missing and his eyes were a warm shade of deep brown, but it was unmistakably a portrayal of a younger Arkadith.

Before he had been turned, she thought. She studied the painting and all of her questions about him came rushing back. But the vampire was out hunting now, and Natalya did not know when he would return. When her thoughts turned to whatever hapless victim he had chosen that would never again see the morning sun rise, she returned her attention to her search.

She was lucky that the grand room was free of clutter. Whatever else Arkadith may be, he was not disorganized. She came to the desk and eagerly began opening each drawer. When she reached the bottom handle, she wrenched it open to find her stakes and the holsters she had used to bind them to herself beneath her clothing. She eagerly strapped the two of them to her thighs, but in the dress's flowing train she felt oddly exposed despite their invisibility.

She hurried from the room, not bothering to hide the signs of her rummaging. When Arkadith returned to the castle, fresh from the power of young blood pulsing throughout his veins, he would find his dead guard and then she would have little time. On the way to her room, Natalya stooped to take her fill of the dead guard's blood. When her own strength was fully restored, she exited the castle to wait. When the vampire returned, she knew the battle that would determine which of the two immortals would join the dead in their earthly graves would finally commence. When the next night came, she would see to it that Arkadith would be the one to rise no more.

~ Chapter Thirty-One ~
The Final Battle

Incited by the heavy scent of ash, the savage desire to kill
was enlivened in each of the werewolves in the presence of their
most hateful enemy. It was only Natalya, but they still fought to
suppress their instincts as she neared them, too quickly for her
languid pace.

It is good to see you again, Natalya. Natalya smiled when
she recognized Tovu's friendly voice. Her eyes turned to the
others. Lehova nodded at her, one eyed and imposing, and Kivah
flicked his ears in acknowledgement.

"I am grateful for your help, Kivah," she murmured.

This old wound has not killed me yet, he growled with fire
in his white eyes. Natalya smiled grimly, and her eyes fell over
Voren. Their faces seemed to share the same sentiment. Though
they were very different, they were now very much the same as
well. No words could soothe them, but for Voren at least, the day
brought some small promise. She nodded at him before she saw
them emerge from the shadows.

"Kaima!" she exclaimed, resisting the urge to pull the girl from Methea and embrace her friend. Although she had drained the fallen guard dry, she could still feel the call of Kaima's blood, and she loathed stepping closer. She could not help but notice that Voren was still standing protectively in front of horse and rider. She read in the werewolf's eyes that he would stop at nothing to destroy her if she attacked Kaima.

"What are you doing here?" Natalya asked, looking from her to Voren.

"I know I will not be of much use in the fight against Arkadith, but my father wanted you to have this." She twisted in her saddle and held out the musket that had been strapped to her back. "It doesn't have much ammunition, but one bullet should be enough."

"Thank you," Natalya said as she took it. The weapon was uncomfortably heavy in her arms, and she instantly missed the light grace of her bow or the precision of a stake in her dominant hand. Her discomfort must have been obvious because Kaima dropped a bundle at Voren's paws. At a nod from her, he began to transform.

Kaima's mouth fell open in shock; she had never seen Voren change forms. Nor could Natalya look away as he rose, his bones crunching and shifting. He grimaced as his muzzle shortened, and his eyes dimmed and shined yellow amber. The dark fur rolled from his body to be replaced by sandy blonde hair that fell to his shoulders in easy waves. The tattoos on his body shined more intricately than Natalya remembered. He reached for the bundle which turned out to be clothes, and bent to put them on.

"I will wield the gun," he said to Natalya, offering his hand out to take it. His eyes narrowed at the castle. "For so many years,

I have longed for this moment." He turned to look at Kaima and his gaze softened. "Perhaps this is the day that my curse will end."

"I hope that it is," Natalya answered.

"Do you think that he can be defeated?" Voren asked sharply.

"I am not sure…" Natalya said. "But I do know some of his blood lives in my veins. I was created from him and some of his strength runs through my body. As for now, all we can do is wait." She turned to look at the sky. To her eyes, the stars seemed near enough to touch, and the last vestiges of clouds faded before the slightly waning moon. She could see a speck, flying towards them from the forest. It grew larger as it neared, into a silent winged bird, and Natalya locked eyes with the owl that had followed her since discovering Anesa's body.

Its long lashed black depths seemed to swallow her, and a picture was arranging itself before her eyes. She could see Arkadith, sneering as his eyes directed the owl's sight, but her unwelcomed invasion into the owl's mind nearly severed his mental connection completely. She could not tell where he was and it did not matter; she knew he could appear in a matter of minutes in a pillar of air if he so wished. The werewolves at her back snarled as they stood on their hind legs. They clawed the air with their fronts but the owl sailed above them, just out of reach of their deadly paws.

Natalya drew an arrow and loaded her bow. She could see each individual barb of each of the bird's feathers, and she took careful aim. She pulled back the tension and released the deadly energy of her bow. The arrow flew towards the owl, the feathered end slicing through the air. It dipped from its arc and began its descent, plunging towards the earth where it came to rest harmlessly in the grass. Natalya hissed angrily. She had missed.

The owl flew into the ranks of the werewolves, still worrying them with its talons. It dipped and retreated into the skies, ever repeating its mocking attack, with the werewolves unable to join it in flight.

Natalya loaded the bow with another arrow, following the owl's movements with its silver tipped point. She kept her bow trained on the owl and let go once more. Her eyes easily traced the arrow's flight as it shrieked and wobbled on its intended course. This time, it pierced the owl's belly, and the bird careened wildly. A death cry ripped from its beak as it dropped like a stone, landing in a lifeless mound. The bird's body had broken from the fall, and its eyes were already beginning to gloss over in death.

Several miles away, at a remote inn where he had met his luckless prey, Arkadith gasped as he felt the impact of an invisible arrow. He uttered a curse as he tore open his black waistcoat to the ruffled shirt beneath. His eyes were met with blood that was dripping from a slit in his abdomen. He was no longer in the owl's mind, and from this distant building, he was blind to the fiends that he would face at his own castle.

As his wound sealed and his flesh began to repair itself, he closed his eyes, concentrating. He seemed to fall into the floor of the inn, though he did not reach to steady himself with his arms. He was merely gone one second, and then the next a column of rapidly spinning dust and dirt had risen from the worn carpet. He willed himself away, leaving his fallen victim, a fruitless harlot with bright red lipstick and an open mouth, drained by the bed as he spirited himself to his castle.

Kaima, you need to get out of here. Take Methea and flee to the trees. Wait for us there, and we will return for you, Tovu growled. The girl wasted no time in spurring the mare into a run, and soon they had disappeared into the surrounding forest. It was only moments before they could hear Arkadith's laughter in the wind, echoing darkly around them. Their heads turned in every direction, trying to locate where the vampire would appear.

They could see the dusty wind rising at the castle's door, and Arkadith slowly materialized in the mountainous fog. He began to approach, his expression one of disdainful amusement.

"A fledging that has turned on her Master," he said, shaking his head before turning to the werewolves. "And you fools. To be squandering your immortal lives by refusing the luxury of the kill and denying your very instincts!"

Tovu met the vampire's eye levelly.

A life without savagery is not a life squandered, Arkadith. With that the three werewolves attacked, and Natalya and Voren stood amongst the commotion. They did not fire the gun or release an arrow from the bow, lest they hit one of the werewolves with a misplaced shot.

Arkadith's fangs were bared as his inhuman powers were pitted against the werewolves' strength. Even against them all, he was a commanding threat. They circled him warily, Kivah with a pronounced limp, as they waited for the right moment to strike with their fangs.

Tovu leapt at Arkadith's back, and the vampire whirled to face him. With one strike the werewolf was thrown backwards, and with a yelp he landed heavily on his side. Arkadith was upon him in an instant, and when he lifted his head again it was shining with freshly spilled blood.

Lehova ran to Arkadith, his jaws open for the killing bite. But it was as if a magnetic shock had surged between him and the vampire, and he was also thrown to the ground. Arkadith ripped into Tovu's side with his fangs, and more of the werewolf's blood came to soak the ground. Natalya screamed, but it was a moment before she heard her own voice, and she scarcely remembered firing an arrow at the vampire's heart.

But he had vanished again in a dusty cloud and her arrow struck the ground, quivering where it stood. Lehova had gotten to his feet and the four of them ran to Tovu's aid.

He was frantically panting, his side shaking with deathly spasms. He was on the verge of losing control of his transformations while his body desperately tried to heal itself. Natalya could hear his exhausted heart beating erratically, but there was not enough blood to surge through his veins.

"He has lost too much," she choked out, her black eyes swimming with red tears, and the werewolves did not have to ask what she had meant.

K-kill him, Voren, Tovu managed to gasp in their heads as his eyes began to close. *Escape this horrible curse, as I could not.* His body relaxed, and he seemed to sink deeper into the grassy soil as if his spirit were already trying to find rest in his earthy grave.

Natalya was sobbing now as she stroked his stiffening fur. *Not Tovu,* she thought, the only coherent mantra she could voice in her head. *Tovu,* the first werewolf that had openly and without question, accepted her wholly into Claw Haven.

"You will be missed, my dear friend," she whispered, and she graced his closed eyes with a kiss so delicate that her fangs did not brush along the fine furs of his face.

303

As Natalya slowly stood up, shaking with pain and grief, she was reminded of Anesa, and her hate towards Arkadith only intensified. This vampire that killed without remorse, had taken so much from her and now Tovu had come to join them.

"He will pay dearly for what he has done," she managed to say, her hate clenching her teeth together.

"I know," Voren agreed softly, his hand on her shoulder. His yellow tinged eyes met hers, and they shined. Not with the sheen of the wolf lurking just beneath them as they usually did, but with tears that mirrored her own at having lost another of his pack mates. Lehova and Kivah raised their heads in a mournful howl that carried down the mountain. Its quaking voice questioned everything they knew about their dark fates, and sought a goddess that did not answer them.

The four stood united, ready for Arkadith to reappear. They listened for his laughter or a mocking of their sorrow, but only the wind heeded them as it blew from the neighboring bluffs.

Then they heard it, a gut wrenching scream so full of pain and terror that came from the woods.

"No!" Natalya shouted, running to its source and wrenching her stake from its place at her thigh. "He's got Kaima!"

The others sprang into action and Kaima, torn from the mare's back, was struggling in Arkadith's grip as he strode out of the woods with her. One hand was clasped around her throat, and she gasped as she struggled to breathe. The vampire had no words for his enemies; instead, he bit deeply into Kaima's neck, and the air was rent with a fresh torrent of her screaming.

Even with her Vampiric speed, Natalya had no hope of reaching her friend in time. Still, she tried, and as she ran towards them with Lehova and Kivah close behind her, time seemed to slow. But although he had not moved, he did not seem to get any closer, and Kaima seemed to be fading as the vampire strengthened on her blood.

A deafening shot rang through the air, and a gaping wound appeared in Arkadith's front. Natalya turned to look behind her, and she could see Voren, obscured behind a pall of smoke that rose from the musket he had just shot. The silver musket ball had shredded its way towards Arkadith's lung, and he staggered backwards, throwing Kaima away from himself and clutching the bloody hole in his chest.

Voren was immediately at Kaima's side, helping her to her feet and wrapping her in a sobering hug. The bite to her neck had not been serious, she was only white faced and shaken while Voren held her tightly in relief.

As Arkadith had stumbled backward, it had seemed as if his death was imminent, but the musket ball was already loosening from his torso. He smiled a horrible smile that was tainted with uncertainty, but Natalya was already upon him.

As he slowly recovered, Kivah and Lehova made moves to rush in and help, but Natalya sent them off with a shake of her head.

"This is my battle," she said and in that moment she knew she would fight him to the bitter end, even if it resulted in her death. The two werewolves shrank back into the woods to guard Voren and Kaima as she recovered, and to watch anxiously as Natalya sparred with Arkadith.

Her amulet glowed, casting both of their faces in ruby light, and it was impossible to say whose was wrinkled in greater hatred.

In human life, her speed had been no match for his, but now she rivaled him with a strength that was all her own. She had given herself completely to the tigress, and she reveled in the vampire's power, speed and deadly cunning. She laughed, a sinfully cruel sound as she dueled Arkadith at close range. As always, he relied only on the strength that rested in his own wiry body, while Natalya gripped both stakes, one in each closed fist, as she sought to drive each of them through the vampire's undead heart.

He did not try to sway her mind through hypnotic power this night. Nor did he try to close his hands around her throat and feed, as he once had. Her amulet was an enchanting shade of crimson, and it burned between them, threatening to sear his skin with deadly poison at the slightest touch.

And so it was that Natalya had gained a slight edge upon the vampire Arkadith. Her power only swelled as she cleaved to the law of the vampiress inside her. All of her savage brutality and hellish prowess she embraced, as she grappled against his raw and monstrous might. And when she surfaced, she had truly metamorphosed into a creature so terrible that it seemed her undying hatred could be bound by no impediment.

While Natalya's powers only heightened, Arkadith's weakened. The damage to his lung was nearly irreparable. He needed to rest in order to regenerate, but under the stress of battle his ability to heal himself had been severely compromised.

Still worse, the blood from his victim ran from his wound, and he could not draw upon the reserves of strength that normally ran through his veins. And so when he only slightly lost his footing, he could not recover in time. Weakened by the loss of blood and the terrible tear in his chest, Natalya held her stake over his heart, and it was clear he could do nothing to stop his fate.

She drove the point through his wound, and as it reopened, Arkadith screamed in agony, an animalistic lament that hung in the air long after his throat had ceased to produce sound.

Natalya twisted her weapon until it found his heart, and Arkadith dropped to his knees, and still she did not stop. As he had once taken her to her grisly death, she now took him to his as well. Only the next night would bring no chance at life for him.

And as his broken heart released the remainder of his stolen blood into the pure white of the snow, the beginnings of dawn began to arrive.

Natalya released her grip on the fallen vampire and ran to the castle's door while the werewolves could only watch aghast as he reached for her, his hand desperately clawing, but only getting handfuls of snow. She exhaled deeply, and the tigress faded as her powers diminished. Her eyes lost their blackness, and her fangs receded.

Aren't you going to finish him? Kivah asked, his voice touching upon the edges of scorn as he and the others followed her into the castle.

"I will let the morning daylight overtake him," Natalya answered and from within the castle she drew a curtain just open enough for them to watch the vampire's demise. Her expression was echoed in all of their faces, one of grim resolution.

The view was sickening. As the sun rose above the mountain, the snow glinted lustrous yellow, and Arkadith resumed his futile trek for the castle's entrance. But he had already been caught in the sun's rays, and smoking large welts began appearing on his exposed skin. In a voice raw from hoarse screaming he tried to give voice to his anguish, but his parched throat could not as his body was being boiled. A tiny flame erupted from his arm and it flared, growing, as the sun breathed life into the fire. It danced and spread to the rest of his body. As the sun glowed benignly above, Arkadith was only a mass of burning flame, betrayed by one of the few creatures he had dared to care for.

When Arkadith's body had been burned beyond recognition and his corpse dissolved into the golden sunbeams, Voren's lips began to move. They all turned to watch him, their horror of what they had witnessed, replaced with cautious eagerness. He seemed to be chanting a prayerful mantra, but the words were soundless from his mouth. And when he tested his curse, his body seemed to shift more sadly than painfully. When the transformation was complete he looked up at them with mournful glowing eyes. And as Zulae's moon lost her silver pallor to the rising of dawn, the werewolf was unchanged.

~ Chapter Thirty-Two ~
Their Uncertain Future

When dusk fell upon the world again and Natalya stepped out from her coffin, she knew it was for the last time. Clasping it tightly in her hands, she dragged it across the room and laid it out of sight within the closet. She took a deep breath as she gazed at the coffin where she had rested safely from the sun, but when she closed the door she knew her mind was made.

No breath rises from a vampire's chest unless he has just fed. Their existence is an illusion, for they pretend to live when they are deader than we.

"I cannot undo the past, but I can remember your words, Tovu," she murmured aloud.

Leave it behind, a voice encouraged, and she turned to see Voren behind her. In her preoccupation, she had not heard him. She nodded sadly at him. Coffins were for the dead, and she knew she would never be able to join them in their restful slumber.

"I am sorry your curse was not lifted," she said, raising her head to meet his eyes. The werewolf exhaled sharply as if he were sighing.

It is what I expected, he answered simply. But he looked out her window and to the stars. *But I cannot pretend that I did not hope.* There was nothing she could say to absolve the werewolf of his curse, so she simply shared in his grief. For them, the dawn had not brought redemption for either of their plights.

She left the room to wander the halls and he followed, each absorbed in their thoughts.

The castle was a hollow shell without Arkadith. In the absence of its evil master, it had been stripped of everything that had cast it into fabled legends, and its fearful aura was lifted.

She did not know what she was searching for, and the castle provided no answers. But in a way that she could not explain, this place had become her home. Even now, after everything that had transpired within its gloomy walls, part of her was unwilling to leave. Voren seemed to understand, and he stayed close beside her.

She found herself climbing the great staircase toward the upper spires. When she reached the top, she turned down one of the many winding halls. She could hear a voice, hoarse and crying, and she froze when she realized it was coming from Arkadith's room. The rest of this floor was empty; there were no guards to stand at his door, and the dungeon was silent without prisoners.

She felt her fangs sliding to her lower lip where they came to rest, digging slightly into her flesh. Her body's response to the possible threat was only a mindless reaction, for after killing Arkadith, what was left to fear? She went to the door and opened it. Voren hung back, his eyes lighting the dim hallway.

She could see Anna, bent over with her back to Natalya. She was next to the desk, looking up at the image of Arkadith, and crying horribly. She was clawing at the painting between her wracking sobs as if she could bring that still and impassive depiction of him to life. When he did not leap from the painting and into life, she turned to Natalya.

Her face was streaked with grime and fresh tears. She crawled along the floor, tugging madly at the skirt of Natalya's dress when she reached her. She jutted her bloodstained neck up at the vampire, and as their eyes met she dissolved into a fresh set of convulsing moans.

"Kill me now, vampiress so that I may rejoin him in death!" she begged. Natalya wrenched her hem from Anna's brittle grip and turned towards the door. Although she felt the slight nudging of her thirst, it was easily banished, and she resisted the urge to sate it with the mad woman's blood. And when she turned to give Anna one final look, disgust was evident in every line of her furrowed brow.

"Now that Arkadith is dead, there will be no one to feed from your veins. You will begin to age again and eventually die, with no one to even bless your grave. A fitting fate for one who has longed for cursed immortality. Take your things and flee from this castle, Anna. Go and never return."

Natalya strode from the room. She did not care whether or not the woman heeded her wishes. She and Voren descended the staircase and found the others in rooms on the lower floors. They met under the moon's light, in the fields outside the castle's gate.

Voren resumed his protective stance before Kaima, and Natalya smiled at her sadly. She knew that things would never again be the same between them, and her mind was burdened with yet another layer of sorrow. Her gaze rested on each of them while she addressed the three werewolves and her lifelong friend.

"Now that Arkadith is dead, there can be hope for peace between Valwood and Claw Haven."

We will return before there is any more bloodshed, Lehova growled and he looked over to Kaima and Voren. *If ever there was proof that it can be done, I think they are it,* and Natalya swore the werewolf smiled. She looked at Kaima and smiled too, wanting to say something but words were never enough.

She pondered on every event, every change that had led her to this very moment. She thought longingly of her human life, and of her change into a vampire. *Surprisingly, the transformation had not been purely a negative one,* she reflected. She had delighted in her newly heightened senses and the strength that coursed effortlessly through her body. She was resistant to all diseases, impervious to nearly any injury. *But the horror of the bloodlust, of all of the lives she had taken…*she looked at her friend, and was thankful that she was not thirsty.

"It's ok," Kaima said as if she had read the vampire's mind. "You are my dearest friend, and you will be forever, no matter what this life has thrown us. I love you."

"I love you too, Kaima," Natalya said, and tears stung her eyes.

You have done so much for all of us, your people and werewolves, Lehova growled and Natalya smiled, needing to believe him.

"Tell me, what has become of my people in my absence?" Natalya asked and the werewolves averted their eyes. Kaima let out a tiny sob.

"Our people have fought bitterly to survive, and it is with less strength every day that they faced the werewolves. I am sorry, Natalya, but your father did not survive the war."

The vampiress nodded, and the tears that she had been holding back now fell unimpeded.

"Then there is no life waiting for me in Valwood," she said. "I am only glad that he never had to see me like this. When you go back to our city, please tell my people that I did not survive the struggle against Arkadith."

"But Natalya, why?"

"My only wish is that I am remembered as I once was, and not for what I have become."

"What will you do now then?" Kaima asked with misty eyes as well.

Natalya looked up at the starry sky in silent acceptance to all that she had gone through. For a few moments she was silent in her contemplation, ever patient as the immortal is before an unending sky. She fancied she could almost see Zulae's benign face in the veiled shadows that graced across the moon. She forced herself to tear her gaze away and she lowered her face to her friends.

"I am a predator now, and I will go feed in the night under the moon. I am her daughter now, and I will obey her. And although I must forsake the sun, I will never forget its beauty. But the world will never know peace while my kind exists. I will leave to follow the vampires wherever they may hide, until our bane is gone from this earth."

She could not risk even a friendly embrace, and so she stood up to leave, before meeting Kaima's eye once again. "Take good care of Methea." Her eyes fell onto each of the surviving werewolves: brave, one-eyed Lehova, to sharp-tongued, but loyal Kivah, and finally on Voren. Her gaze lingered on him; he that was more wolf than man. "Good bye, my truest friends," she whispered.

And as Natalya walked away, the four were left in a strange silence that none could bring themselves to break. They watched until she had disappeared into the trees, her head held high and her dress wrapped in unnatural fog.

~ Epilogue ~
Natalya's Legacy

All was not well in Valwood when the three werewolves and Kaima returned. They walked with Tovu's body straddled over Methea's saddle, while the girl led the mare on foot. As they crossed the border into the city, they hugged the tree line wherever possible, painfully aware as to how exposed they were to wandering eyes.

When they reached the inner buildings, Kaima stopped unexpectedly. The devastation of her war torn city was nearly more than she could bear.

"It is almost worse than I remember." She trailed a finger against the brick of the still standing blacksmith's shop. Her finger came up black, and she rubbed the soot away, sighing wistfully. Voren's eyes softened, but he had no words for her. They moved on at a slower pace, and when they made it to the fallen Apothecary, even Kaima's heart beat with brewing apprehension.

The air was pregnant with the scent of death, and Naktor's fatal struggle for leadership was written in the dried blood and the few scattered hairs that were dispersed across the fallen roof. Voren's head sank in despair.

Anraq held all of our hopes for peace. When he spoke, people and werewolves alike listened. Some Alpha's lusted for power, but he only quested for wisdom. And where others killed, he fought for justice. I only hope Vekoroh will follow in his ways.

"I am so sorry, Voren." Kaima whispered, running her fingers soothingly through his fur.

You have nothing to atone for, Kaima. Both of our people have suffered a great loss.

"Indeed we have. And now, it is time for it to end," Kaima declared. They hastened through the city, the werewolves trailing the scent of their pack. Soon they had reached them, in a secluded field just outside the city's edge. Voren heard his new Alpha's words in his head, but their way was barred by two large werewolves that leered down at them.

Why have you brought her here, Voren?

The time for war has ended, Vekoroh. She is a friend of Natalya's, and comes for the same reasons that she did.

The two werewolves backed away to allow them to pass. They dipped their heads in respect for the girl that had wandered through their village not so long ago. When they reached the Alpha, they recounted everything that had occurred since Voren's disappearance. How Natalya had forsaken her thirst in the name of her and Kaima's friendship, and how she had destroyed the true cause of the war. She had been the living catalyst for peace, first among her and Voren, and then between all of Valwood and the werewolves.

Vekoroh had listened to them speak without interruption. When they had finished, he had looked into Voren and Kaima's eyes, and the glowing glimmer from his own had softened.

You have both been through so much. We all have everything to thank you for. Anraq's treaty will reign here, and if the humans will it, the war will be no more. The path to peace will be a long and hard one, but I am willing to undertake it.

Voren bowed his head, and he and Kaima were allowed to speak on the alpha's behalf to the humans.

They were able to gain an audience with Chief Elder Vicktor Throm. He proved to be agreeable, and a new treaty was drawn, that all, werewolves and humans alike, were present for.

And so a tentative peace was restored that night by the looming wall. Elder Vicktor stood in its center, flanked by Vekoroh. A funeral was held and a prayer said over Natalya's spirit. It was believed to be lingering in Valwood still, and only Kivah, Lehova, Voren and Kaima knew differently. Natalya, the seventeen year old girl who had, against all odds, and facing almost certain death, ventured into Claw Haven to end the war and save both of their peoples. Everyone that was assembled bowed their heads in honor, and the wind carried roses from their hands to the grave that lay empty.

The forever staring skull of Sakarr was retrieved from the woods and also returned to the werewolves, so that it, along with Tovu's body, could be buried under Zulae's blessing. As his old friend was lowered carefully into the ground and the words said over him, Voren could see the contentment in his face. Although neither of their curses had been broken, he would take solace in knowing that Tovu had finally found peace.